KING OF THE HOLLY HOP

The Milan Jacovich mysteries
by Les Roberts:

Pepper Pike

Full Cleveland

Deep Shaker

The Cleveland Connection

The Lake Effect

The Duke of Cleveland

Collision Bend

The Cleveland Local

A Shoot in Cleveland

The Best-Kept Secret

The Indian Sign

The Dutch

The Irish Sports Pages

King of the Holly Hop

KING OF THE HOLLY HOP

A MILAN JACOVICH MYSTERY

LES ROBERTS

GRAY & COMPANY, PUBLISHERS
CLEVELAND

This book is a work of fiction. Names, characters, places, and incidents either are products of the author's imagination or are used fictitiously, and any resemblance to actual events or locales or persons, living or dead, is entirely coincidental.

Gray & Company, Publishers
www.grayco.com

Library of Congress Cataloging-in-Publication Data
Roberts, Les.
King of the Holly Hop : a Milan Jacovich mystery /
Les Roberts.
p. cm.
ISBN 978-1-59851-038-6
1. Jacovich, Milan (Fictitious character)—Fiction.
2. Private investigators—Ohio—Cleveland—Fiction.
3. Cleveland (Ohio)—Fiction. 4. Slovenian Americans—Fiction. 5. Reunions—Fiction. I. Title.
PS3568.O23894K56 2008
813'.54dc22 2008013949

Printed in the United States of America

10 9 8 7 6 5 4 3 2 1

To the memory of Shannon Lee McBride.
She couldn't stay with us quite long enough to
finish reading my last book.
I wish she could be here to enjoy this one.

KING OF THE HOLLY HOP

CHAPTER ONE

Three surprises make a high school reunion strongly resemble a visit to hell. First, you're surprised some of the people you were sure would be there are missing. They've either moved far away, or they have no desire to join the reunion. Second, you're surprised some of those you never dreamed would attend actually show up.

Third: you find yourself there too.

The weekend of my fortieth high school reunion—dear old St. Clair High School in the St. Clair–Superior corridor on the near East Side of Cleveland—was to begin on a Friday evening in February. February is a singularly lousy time to have a reunion, but I found later that the hotel had been booked way in advance during the more pleasant spring and summer months. I carefully chose my wardrobe for the evening, and had left it hanging in my office closet all day—the one just across the Cuyahoga River from downtown Cleveland in an old building I'd purchased several years earlier with a bequest from an elderly aunt. Checking myself out in my bathroom mirror, I thought my black wool blazer looked nifty, even on somebody as big as I am, and I donned it for the cocktail party with gray slacks, a darker gray shirt, and a muted red-and-gray necktie. Then finally I girded my loins and drove across the river to the Crowne Plaza Centre Hotel downtown.

I stepped off the elevator into an alternate universe in which everyone wore plastic-covered name badges. The men were consciously pulling in their tummies as the women strove equally hard to flaunt what remained of their girlish figures. Some faces rang distant bells for me, and in my mind I attempted to de-age them, imagining how they looked when they were seventeen.

A few people nodded at me as they strove mightily to remember my name. A few waved or smiled insincerely, and I'd bet they didn't recognize me, either. One man I didn't remember, now a heavyset bald guy wearing a checked sports jacket, looked at me and whispered something to his wife, covering his mouth with his hand like a wicked plotter in the court of the Venetian doge. I hadn't the vaguest idea what he was saying about me. Until I registered, I wasn't "official," and no one would speak to me.

The woman sitting sentry under a WELCOME banner with our class year emblazoned on it wore a short, perky haircut and what looked like a strapless 1954 prom frock made of gingham, with a huge matching bow over one of her generous breasts. I recalled neither the name nor the cleavage.

"Hi-i-i-i," she said with an upward inflection, and rose to shake my hand. "I'm Gerry Gabrosek. Remember?"

The name tag identified her as Geraldine Gabrosek Bokar. I recalled her then—an indefatigable girl who always served on the dance committee, the senior picnic committee, the prom committee—and she'd been president of the French club, and in the hostess club too. She'd always organized her own social life, and most of her girlfriends' lives, too.

"I'm Milan Jacovich," I told her.

"Everybody knows who you are—the private detective. You're famous." She leaned over the table to press her cheek to mine, and strong perfume wafted up from the valley between her bosoms like swamp gas. I didn't bother telling her that "detective" is a police rank, and that I'm actually a private investigator.

She fluttered on for a while and then gave me my name badge, a schedule for the weekend, info sheets I never got around to reading, a biography sheet with paragraphs about everyone attending, my Saturday night dinner ticket with table number affixed, and a complimentary drink coupon.

One complimentary drink. Subsequent drinks I'd have to pay for. It was boding to be a long damn night.

I pinned my badge to my jacket and made my way into the main room. There must have been two hundred classmates and spouses in there. Some, who'd stayed in the lower echelons of the labor force like their immigrant parents, looked stiff and awkward in their dress-up clothes. Others seemed at ease, smiling and aggressively sociable. Lots of hugs and handshakes and manly backslaps going on, and air kisses galore. The gathering was an emotional clusterfuck.

The attire of some seemed a part of their anatomy and the confident way they held themselves, as if they went to parties like this every week. They knew exactly what to do, how loud to talk, and just how to hold their drinks in one hand while trying to consume hors d'oeuvres. They'd come to the reunion to strut and preen; they claimed bragging rights.

Then there was Gary Mishlove, a microscope geek who had publicly vomited in junior year chemistry lab while performing an experiment with spoiled milk that had stunk up the whole second floor for a week. He'd always been a short, chunky guy and I recognized his face almost immediately, but his body had acquired an extra two hundred pounds and he was now dangerously obese.

Gary was talking to Maurice Paich, the school's favorite actor. How he ever survived in a tough neighborhood with an interest in acting and hauling around a moniker like Maurice, I'll never know—but he wound up as a radio announcer for a local station. At his side his wife, a pretty, brilliant blonde whose name, I learned from a quick peek at the bios, was Meredith, was casing the room and inspecting everyone except her husband, and seemed to have an early start on an evening's heavy drinking.

I was surprised Stupan Godic had bothered attending. From an immigrant family like mine, he'd returned from the draft after serving in Southeast Asia, damaged and embittered, and spent the next thirty-five years sunk in heavy drug use. He was medium height and still very skinny. In a wrinkled sports jacket over a blue denim shirt with collar and cuffs hopelessly frayed, he wore a half-angry and half-dreamy expression. He was lost in the traumatic events of the seventies and unready to step forward into the twenty-first century. We talked for a minute and then he shuffled away, carrying his war memories with him around his shoulders.

I made my way to the bar. The bartender, young enough to be the offspring of anyone in the room, poured me a Jack Daniels on the rocks and took away my complimentary drink ticket.

A big-eyed woman approached me, dragging her reluctant husband behind her like a kid accompanying his mom on a shopping spree. Her hair was pulled back into a severe bun, framing a Modigliani face. I recalled the smile but nothing more. Arlene, Eileen, Elaine—I couldn't quite pick out the right name.

"Milan Jacovich," she said, "how fantastic to see you again." She at least remembered how to pronounce my name; it's *My*-lan, accent on the first syllable—not *Mee*-lahn or Mi-*lahn*—and the surname is pronounced with a *Y*, not a *J*, as in *Yock*-o-vitch. She embraced me warmly, putting her soft cheek against mine, kicking in at least one memory. Somewhere, forty years ago, for some reason I didn't recall, I'd kissed her. "Ilene Silver. Remember?"

I confirmed the spelling on her name badge. Ilene. I'd been close, anyway.

"It's Ilene Seltzer now. This is my husband, Toby."

Ilene Silver to Ilene Seltzer—she didn't have to change monograms on the towels. Ilene told me they had two children, and that Toby was CEO of an engineering firm in Broadview Heights, in the western suburbs. Losing interest quickly, I flatlined after the third sentence, smiling and nodding and not listening to a thing.

Then something over her shoulder caught her attention. "Ooooh!" she squealed. "There's Tommy Wiggins." And without so much as a "See ya," she powered toward our school's real celebrity alumnus.

Tommy Wiggins had grown taller since I'd known him. He was now just under six feet, slimmed down a lot, his full head of hair generously sprinkled with silver. Fame had taught him to wear his charisma well—it hovered around his head like a nimbus. Classmates roared toward him like linebackers determined to sack the quarterback, clamoring to bask in a small sliver of his angel shine.

Clevelanders aren't impressed with celebrities, except for the ones who wear their jockstraps to work, like LeBron James. Local

TV personalities get nodded to, but are rarely bothered. However, all my former classmates seemed to feel a certain proprietary interest in Tommy Wiggins because he'd gone on to famous things. In high school, he'd been shy and slightly pudgy and very dreamy, interested in what were perceived to be arcane and not very manly subjects like art and theater. He'd gone to college in central Ohio, majoring in creative writing. When he moved to New York, seven of his plays were produced on Broadway—six of them smash-hit comedies. He'd won two Tony Awards and a Pulitzer Prize, and when they made his work into movies, he'd earned two Oscar nominations for the screenplays. He was a big shot in both New York, where he lived, and in Los Angeles, where he kept a condo, and he frequently made the tabloid press as he married and divorced twice. His second wife was a sexpot movie actress nearly thirty years his junior, and he had been linked to other women even more famous. He'd attained a success most Clevelanders only dream about, and that's why all his former school chums were fawning all over him.

I stopped to talk for a while with high school sweethearts who had made it permanent the year they both graduated from high school. August Turkman—we called him Augie—had gone to work in his father's dry cleaning store in Maple Heights and married Amalia Zelka six months later. Now Augie owns that dry-cleaning store and two others, and after forty years of marriage they both still looked happy. That was nice, I thought, even when Amalia told me they'd moved to a much bigger house in Maple Heights and now raise Welsh corgis.

"Bitsy" Steinberg—now Elizabeth Steinberg Miller—came over to greet me. She had the grace to admit we had never spoken in school, but she said she'd always enjoyed watching me play football, and introduced her husband, who owned a local chain of pool-and-patio stores and who frequently popped up on his company's commercials, talking too loudly.

I wandered the room, free drink in hand, encountering familiar faces. Men whose hands I'd never shaken hugged me like long-lost war buddies, and women were hell bent to kiss my cheek. Most were virtual strangers to me, but we shared a history of sorts. A snapped towel in the locker room, a copped feel under the bleachers, sweating out tests together, quietly hoping for the future—memories conveniently forgotten, but not diluted by time as it tumbles by.

Then Lila Coso Jacovich entered on the arm of her longtime consort, Joe Bradac, looking spectacular in a black cocktail dress that hugged the swell of her breasts. Her hemline ended two inches above her still-shapely knees. Joe, who owned a machine shop and virtually lived in service overalls, had actually shown up in a suit. It's the only suit I'd ever seen him wear that didn't make him look like a wholesale chicken salesman.

I found my way back to the bar and ordered another Black Jack. This time I had to pay for it.

I carry no torch for my ex-wife. Our split-up—all her idea, by the way—hit me hard at the time. By now, though, we'd been divorced longer than we'd been married, and had moved on. Whatever residual issues remained between Joe Bradac and me existed only in his head, not mine. I belted down half my drink and shouldered my way through the crowd to where they stood. Lila surveyed the room like a reigning queen, but Joe blinked uncertainly as he watched my approach the way a deer in shock regards an oncoming semi on the highway.

"Lila, you look beautiful," I said, bending to kiss her cheek. We never kissed anymore, not even cheeks, but everyone else at the reunion was doing so and it would have shouted tension had we not.

I didn't shake Joe's hand; I never did. He was always frightened that I'd crush it into jelly. It had eaten a hole in my liver that Lila secretly cheated with and then finally discarded me for someone like him, but Joe is exactly the kind of man Lila needs—one she can dominate and push around at will. Say what you will about me, then and now, nobody has ever pushed me around.

If they do, I push back.

So I was happy to be long gone from a home where major arguments occurred twice a week, at least one of them invariably on a Sunday. I still have feelings for Lila because she's the mother of my two sons, but each time I see her it reminds me why we aren't together anymore.

I disengaged myself from the happy couple and stood off to

one side, wishing I'd skipped the reunion altogether, when my attention was caught by a guy whose name I don't think I ever heard, even though I remembered him from St. Clair. In his youth his face was like a tomahawk, all sharp, brutal angles, and years hadn't softened it. Now he wore his black hair combed straight back and slicked down, sporting a mustache that drooped at the ends.

He'd tried out for high school football, I remembered, and during the scrimmage—he'd hoped to become a running back—he kicked one of the tacklers right in the stones at the moment of contact. About five minutes later, when he was taken down hard by one of the linebackers, he gouged the kid's eye with his thumb, causing some pretty scary bleeding. I never got his name and hardly ever saw him around after the coach told him to get lost. He was too far away for me to read his name badge so I could look up his bio. He might be a Baptist minister now, or a vacuum cleaner repairman, but he looked like a hired assassin.

The crowd had finally drifted away from Tommy Wiggins, and he headed straight to the bar for fortification. I came up beside him and reintroduced myself.

"I remember you, Milan," he said. "You played football, didn't you? As I recall, you were always very nice to me. I remember things like that." His smile seemed more genuine than the one pasted on when everyone swarmed around him, hoping to touch him. His hair was longer than that of most men his age who still had theirs, but he didn't need a haircut at all—the length had been cultivated for a more artistic look, and his golden skin proclaimed the gentle all-over tan of a New York tanning salon. He'd grown a lot more handsome in the forty years since senior class, but he didn't carry himself as though he knew it. He seemed more relaxed with me than with the reunioners who'd slobbered all over him, and I gathered he was always immensely comfortable in his own milieu.

"I guess I've changed some," he said, "but you haven't at all—except you had more hair when we were seventeen."

"You wear success well, Tom. Congratulations."

"Don't kid yourself." He accepted a martini on the rocks from the bartender, took a sip, and jiggled the glass a little so the ice cubes clinked. "Every writer I know—Oscars and Tonys and Pulitzers notwithstanding—is terrified that he's taken his last good shot, done his last good work, and his next effort is going to fall loudly on its ass in front of God and everybody else."

"Yours won't," I said. "You'll always have something interesting to write about because you lead such a fascinating life."

"Writers don't have adventures. We just observe them. Then we go sit all alone in a little room, type badly, and put it all down on paper."

I laughed. "Wasn't it Gore Vidal who said that writing comes from living a life intensely?"

"It's been intense—I'll give you that." He shook his head. "Some times were great, and some times were shitty. But thank God, it's never for a single moment been boring."

I leaned against the bar. "What brought you to the reunion, Tommy? You weren't really that close to any of us, at least not that I remember. And judging from your writing, you're hardly the sentimental type."

"I'm not sentimental at all; I'm cynical. But at least I'm funny cynical and not mean-as-a-snake cynical. This hoo-hah was just an excuse to come back to see my mother. She's in her eighties now." His face grew serious, and his smooth forehead wrinkled in a frown. "Besides, there's somebody here that I've wanted to tell off for forty years. I never bothered with it before, but this silly damn reunion is just begging for it." His grin was lupine. "Machiavelli said you must never wound a prince. Make sure you kill him." Then he smiled again. "Our classmate made that mistake."

It made me a little uncomfortable. "Who's your target?"

"Keep your eyes and ears open, Milan," Tommy said. "You'll find out."

He clapped me on the shoulder and wandered away. Like any good playwright, he knew how to end the second act in suspense.

I looked around again. Phil Kohn—Doctor Phil Kohn—was standing by the entrance, and his too-good-for-the-rest-of-you attitude reminded me that he'd always been the class snotnose. He'd bragged during senior year that he'd been accepted to Stanford, and he returned to Cleveland to become a cardiologist. His look confirmed he was one of those doctors who regarded himself as a deity, the same way he had been when he was seventeen. He saved most of his sarcasm and vitriol for jocks like me, and there had been several times I'd wanted to deck him, but then as now, he was only about five foot seven, and he was lucky that even back then I was six foot three. Now he was "portly," but he carried it well. No one set records rushing to greet him, because few classmates had liked him any better than I had.

Matt Baznik had come in with his pretty wife Rita Marie. I wondered if he'd speak to me, if we could rekindle the close friendship that had fallen apart so long ago when I'd saved his son from using and selling drugs. No good deed goes unpunished, I suppose, because he saw me for a second, his expression darkened, and he tore his eyes away quickly. Rita Marie saw me, too, and sent me a sad, quiet smile. I guessed there would be no resuscitation of that friendship this evening.

That's when I ran into Bernie Rothman, wandering all over the room with concern on his wide, homely face, looking as if he'd just been dropped on an alien planet. An odd duck, he was super-intellectual in school but sociable and well liked by everyone. Short, intense, and wildly philosophical, he'd been a double letter man in gymnastics and swimming, walking the tightrope between geek and jock. Now he was divorced, and taught English at a private Hebrew academy in Florida.

"Milan!" he said, his eyes lighting up. He threw his arms around me, at least as far as they could go—he was a small guy, the top of his head reaching just above my chin. I could smell the goop with which he'd slicked back his white hair.

"It's good to see you, Bernie," I said, disengaging. "I thought you lived in Florida."

"I do. I was here last year, of course, when my mother died." His eyes grew damp and red. "This is a woman who never smoked or drank, and ate healthy her whole life long, and then, BANG! The heart got her. A leaking valve, it was, that nobody found until it was too late." He looked away, gritting his teeth. Then: "Anyway, I wanted to see some of you people I haven't connected with in forty years. I wanted to touch base with you all again. Isn't it strange how you completely lose track of your classmates? I've been out of the loop."

His face was hangdog, looking as if he were in genuine pain. He moved closer to me. "I heard about Marko Meglich. I'm really sorry—I guess you don't want to talk about it."

I didn't. Marko Meglich was the only classmate I'd want to see again, and I knew I never would. We'd met over a schoolyard fistfight in the third grade, and remained close pals since then, through high school and college. For a time we were both uniformed police officers, although never partnered, and he used to refer to us as "Butch and Sundance." He thought of me as a clown like Paul Newman's Butch, while he was Robert Redford's Sundance Kid, coldly efficient and fast on the draw. I left the force after a few years to go private, but he learned copdom's political ins and outs, decided on rapid advancement, and wound up running the homicide division as a lieutenant. His captain's bars were never offered because several years ago he died, shot down in the street while off duty—and at risk trying to help me.

I've never gotten over Marko. Some grief never goes away.

Bernie Rothman's attitude changed—he seemed to have forgotten about Marko much more quickly than I ever have. All at once his eyes glittered, and his breathing became deep and rapid. "Anyone interesting here tonight? Um—you haven't run into Alenka by any chance."

Whenever anyone thought of Bernie during his St. Clair High days, they'd automatically think of Alenka Tavcar, too. She was amazingly pretty—and though we'd been good friends, living about eight houses apart on the same Slovenian street, there was no romantic spark between us. She and Bernie dated a few times, but he was a lot more serious about her than she was about him. When Bernie's Jewish parents discovered he was dating a Slovenian Catholic girl, they put their feet down hard and forbade him to see her again, and for the rest of our senior year he whined and moaned about it every chance he got until his friends grew sick of hearing him. Then Bernie went off to the University of Michigan and Alenka enrolled at Miami of Ohio, and as far as I knew nothing more ever came of it. Alenka's reunion bio said she'd married a man named Tom Clayburgh, lived in Olmsted Falls, and was currently selling expensive residential real estate.

"Alenka," Bernie whispered like a prayer. "Oh God, Milan, if she comes here I have to talk to her. There's been a big hole in my heart since the last time I saw her." Without another word he was off circling the ballroom, searching for the love of his youth. Alenka was married, and I didn't see the point.

The guy with the hatchet face and the Viva Zapata mustache stepped in front of me. Up close I could see his eyes were as hard as the rest of him, two black stones in the bottom of a creek bed. "You're Milan Jacovich," he observed.

I gawked at his name badge: Ted Lesnevich, it said. "Hello, Ted."

We shook hands. His were soft, almost feminine compared to his face. Whatever he did for a living, he used his head and not his hands. Nobody in Cleveland has a February tan, but his pallor was ghastly.

"You don't have to pretend you remember me," he said, "unless you remember I tried out for the football team three years running. I never made it." He didn't blink. "I always envied you."

"You envied me?"

"I see your name in the news sometimes—you're a fucking saint, aren't you? A Superman, fighting for truth, justice, and the American way." His tone was derisive, and I had the sudden urge to leap tall buildings at a single bound and land right on top of him.

"When I was twenty-two," he went on, "I applied to the Cleveland P.D. myself—just like you. But I flunked the exam. You got another chance to ignore me that time."

Being on the defensive was never comfortable for me, except in my old days of playing football. "I didn't ignore you. I didn't even know who you were, Ted."

He said softly, "But you know now, huh?"

I forced a smile to take away any sting of condescension. "What's your line of work?"

His face became a blank sheet of paper, and almost as white. "I'm in sales," he said, and didn't elaborate. He did a military about-face and marched off, leaving me with the impression I'd just been insulted. Lesnevich apparently hadn't changed much from when he gouged the eye of a tackler.

Out of the corner of my eye I saw that Alenka Tavcar had just walked through the door—and she was alone.

She'd grown from a pretty girl to a stunning woman. Her hair was lighter in color now, but she was still slim and wraithlike, dressed impeccably in a wine-colored cocktail dress with black roses on it. Everybody in the room looked at her—they couldn't ignore her if they chose to—but no one's mouth hung open the way Bernie Rothman's did. When he saw her he plowed directly toward her through the crowd like a heat-seeking missile. I had to look away.

Alex Cerne and Sonja Kokol came in, almost in tandem. Just as in school, they were friends—close enough that their respective spouses had bowed out of this cocktail party and sent them here together. The two of them, along with Matt Baznik and the late Marko Meglich, had formed my best-friends-forever group who'd never lost track of each other during the subsequent forty years.

Sonja had the original idea for this reunion and had put it together almost single-handedly, and when she called to implore me to come, I couldn't really say no. She needed all the classmate support she could rally. I hugged her. She'd been so busy I hadn't seen her for about two months. "You must be a masochist," I said, "for agreeing to organize this."

"Next time I look like I'll say yes," she said, "kick my ass, hard."

"It'll all work out. These people will loosen up after a few drinks until somebody punches somebody else for dancing too close to his wife."

She started to answer but a hotel employee in a dark suit rushed up and murmured something into her ear.

"Sorry," Sonja said to Alex and me, "but I'm wanted in the kitchen—some sort of emergency with the hors d'oeuvres."

We watched her bustle after the employee, and I said, "Maybe they ran out of Ritz crackers."

Alex shook his head. "Sonja's screwed herself into the ground putting this weekend together." There were so many people in the room now that they'd morphed into a single entity that buzzed, moved, and undulated in a comforting rhythm. "What a motley crew we are, huh Milan? Some of us blue-collar kids got educated and climbed the success ladder—and now we make more money than our parents ever dreamed of. But under the Brooks Brothers suits and the Donna Karan dresses, there's still something so lower middle class about us all."

"Even you? With your dental cottage industry now and your mansion in Rocky River?"

"It's not a mansion—it's a McMansion—a large and ridiculously expensive tract home. I'm the same as I always was. Slovenian blood is still thick and robust and ethnic—not thinned out by too many herbal body wraps and Botox and expensive Evian water."

"I don't drink Evian," I said. "I bet there are four guys in the back room filling Evian bottles with tap water and laughing their asses off."

The buzz of the collective animal crowd changed, became quieter and more intense, and I became aware of the shifting of mass as everyone moved toward the center of the ballroom, jostling for position to view a ritual execution.

Phil Kohn and Tommy Wiggins were in some sort of angry face-off, with an alarmed Sonja Kokol trying to get between them. Wiggins's face was almost purple, and veins stood out in bas-relief on his forehead. The martini he held shook so badly that the ice cubes were playing "Carol of the Bells." His eyes were bright with Jehovian rage. I've seen many people mad and out of control, but this was true fury.

In contrast, Phil Kohn was ashen, with a white line around his mouth, eyelids batting behind his glasses. One hand fluttered helplessly at the knot of his necktie, the other was raised in front of him as if to ward off an onrushing bus.

"I've been waiting forty years," Tommy Wiggins was saying, "to tell you, in front of as many people as possible, to go fuck yourself. I flew in from New York just for the pleasure."

"Tommy, Tommy," Sonja soothed, but no one paid any attention.

"You were a cruel, insensitive, arrogant little bastard who loved hurting other people," Tommy continued. "You haven't changed a goddamn bit."

Kohn's face twisted with embarrassment, and he tried not to meet the eyes of any of us surrounding him, as if we were waiting for a bull-baiting mastiff to attack.

"You think you're such hot shit," Tommy snarled. "Well, I'm richer than you'll ever hope to be. I'm famous all over the world—I get stopped in the street for my autograph. And I've fucked more beautiful women than you've ever jacked off thinking about. I was sick to death of you in high school—and not a damn thing has changed."

And with a flick of his wrist, he tossed the contents of his nearly full glass into Dr. Phil Kohn's face.

CHAPTER TWO

In a movie directed by Sam Peckinpah, the scene would have been filmed in slow motion like a gunfight. In real time, it was all a quick blur. I'm unsure what happened next. Nobody got the full picture. Wiggins threw his empty martini glass on the floor and stalked toward the exit, leaving Phil Kohn with gin running off his nose and chin onto the pristine expanse of his white shirt.

After a moment of shocked silence, everyone was babbling excitedly. To the teenagers we'd once been, the spectacle of a fight was as exciting as ever, but even more dramatic, because high school guys threw punches, not martinis.

No one approached Phil Kohn, not wanting to appear to take sides. Finally Kohn wiped his face with a napkin, trying to salvage what little dignity was left. Then he aimed for the door, finished for the night.

Sonja appeared at my elbow, flustered. "Jesus Christ on a crutch! There are always incidents, but I didn't dream it would happen this soon." She straightened her spine. "I should go see if Phil is all right." She moved away to smooth feathers, her duty as reunion chairperson. It had been a harmless, bizarre incident—only a blip on our personal radar screens.

On my way to the bar I caught Lila's eye, but she pointed her nose skyward and turned away, hooking her arm through Joe Bradac's. It didn't even bother me.

That's when I ran into Alenka Tavcar—literally. We crashed right into each other.

"Milan," she said, and the smile I so well remembered wreathed her face. She stood on tiptoe and kissed my cheek lightly. A wisp of blond hair had escaped from her barrette, waving provocatively. "I was hoping I'd see you. I wasn't sure you'd come. I didn't think this—zoo—was really your style."

"Why?"

"There was always a maturity about you, even in school. A gravity, I guess. And this little gathering is pretty silly."

"You caught the Phil and Tommy Show, then?" I said.

"I couldn't miss it. But I wasn't talking about them." She frowned and looked away.

"Bernie?"

She sighed. "He seems so shaky—it was embarrassing. I hope nobody else was close enough to hear him."

"He's still carrying a torch?"

"More like a forest fire. I couldn't believe it. I only talked to him for three minutes before he told me he'd never stopped loving me. Now that his parents are gone, he wants to marry me."

"You're already married."

"I reminded him of that. Actually, my husband and I are separated—for the last six months or so. But I didn't dare tell Bernie."

"First love is always the sweetest, Alenka," I said. "And sometimes the saddest. Bernie never got over you."

"It's time he did." A tremor shook her body. "There's something in the air tonight. Tommy Wiggins had issues with Phil Kohn he hasn't gotten over, either. Is lots of that going on in here? Is everyone nursing old wounds?"

"Teenagers all go through a baptism of fire," I said. "For some of us, the scars still show."

"Yours?"

"Maybe a few when I wore a football helmet. The real ones—the bad ones—came later."

"You live dangerously, don't you?" she said. "I read about you in the newspaper sometimes. Are you a stoic?"

I shook my head. "A realist."

"Why do I think that's a euphemism for 'cynic'?"

I laughed. "You accused me of being a cynic when I was seventeen. Remember? We were talking about religion or something, and I was trying to explain to you that I wouldn't go to church anymore. But now that I'm older and wiser, I'm the least cynical guy you'll ever meet."

She put her hand on my arm. Through my sleeve it felt warm and gentle. "Do me a favor, Milan. Tomorrow at the dinner, will you save me a dance?"

"If I can pry you away from Bernie."

She shook her head resolutely. "I'll kill you if you don't. I don't even want to talk to him again. We had a mutual crush at seventeen—but I had stuffed animals on my bed then too, and now I don't anymore. Bernie was deep and soulful and philosophical, and that appealed to the romantic teeny in me. Now we're close to sixty and he's just annoying."

I promised her more than one dance, and we parted to reconnect with the ghosts of childhood, pressing flesh and working the room like local pols at a rubber-chicken banquet, both trying gaily to appear as though we were having a good time and wondering how to make an inconspicuous exit—to go home and agonize over whether we should even come back for round two.

I talked for a while to Jack Siegel, a research scientist at NASA. That was no surprise. He had been St. Clair's resident science genius. He introduced me to his outgoing wife, Barbara, and I told her the story of how, in our junior year, when report cards were handed out, Jack had famously moaned, "Oh God! Five A's and two B's—my mother's going to kill me!"

Barbara nodded sagely. "Yep, that's my mother-in-law."

Jack laughed. "I was too dramatic back then. Mom just quietly told me how disappointed she was in me."

"We were all too dramatic," I said. "It came with the hormones. But you always had a sunny disposition."

"It was easier to be pleasant all the time than to be angry. I never had any fun. It pissed me off, but I kept quiet about it."

His wife squeezed his arm and rubbed herself against him. "Now Jack's making up for it. He has a *lot* of fun."

Jack blushed madly, grinning like a happy imbecile.

I moved on.

Byron Hoogwerf, walking with purpose the way he always had, came over and shook my hand earnestly, like we'd seen each other last week. He'd been president of both our sophomore and senior classes at St. Clair High, and even back then he shook hands with everyone he met in the hallways. His nickname back then, unbeknownst to him, was "Paws."

"Milan," he said, "that business with Phil Kohn and Tommy Wiggins was really shitty. It put a pall on things, don't you think?"

"I'm having a good time in spite of it," I said. The lie came easily.

"You have any idea what set Tommy off tonight?"

"Beats me," I said.

Perhaps he was taking any disturbance among his followers as a personal affront. "Okay. Well, thanks a lot, Milan," he said, pressing flesh again just as he used to, and scurried away from what was surely the longest conversation we'd ever had.

People were drifting off—about ninety minutes was all anyone could handle. I wondered how many had the fortitude to return for Saturday's formal dinner. I wanted to leave, too, but Sonja Kokol needed my moral support, so I decided to stick it out to the very end. Real friends don't ask much in a lifetime, and when they do, I have to respond.

It was painful some of the time, grindingly boring the rest of it. I was one of the few with no spouse on my arm, and I floated from one group to another, wasting time with small talk. I spoke to several of the ex-football players who had put on too much weight and were embarrassed about the change from their athletic days, and I was secretly proud I was only about five pounds heavier now than I'd been forty years ago—even though I'd lost a significant amount of what used to be light-brown hair. Hanging on their husbands' arms were a few women I'd dated—and kissed—before Lila and I got to that "serious" stage. I wondered what it might be like if I'd married one of them instead.

I groaned when I looked at my watch. It wasn't even nine o'clock.

About two more drinks and forty-five minutes later Sonja came running into the ballroom, her face ashen and her voice shaky. She picked up a microphone from a podium at one end of the room, clicked it on and waited for the screech of sound, and then said, "Everybody—please. Listen, please! There's been a terrible accident. I'm sorry, but we'll have to ask you all not to leave the hotel until the police can talk to you."

That started the buzz, with a decidedly worried tone. The crowd shifted again, moving slowly toward Sonja, like the red goo in *The Blob*.

Near the entrance three men in inexpensive suits and rumpled trench coats waited for Sonja to finish her announcement. I recognized one of them—Detective Sergeant Bob Matusen of the Cleveland P.D. Uneasiness scampered up my spine, and the hair on the back of my neck rose in a wave. Matusen doesn't show up to quiet too-loud music or write parking tickets. He's with the homicide division.

His head swiveled from side to side until he saw and headed for me, his hands shoved deep in his coat pockets. The coat was open to display the flipped-over badge in the breast pocket of his suit.

"You show up at the damnedest places, don't you?" he said. He didn't offer to shake hands.

"It's my high school reunion, Bob. What happened?"

He shook his head. "I'm not supposed to be talking to you, Milan. Everybody here needs to be questioned."

"Questioned?"

He raised his chin and his expression became an official one. "Do you know a guy named Phil Kohn?"

"Doctor Phil Kohn—sure. He was here earlier—an old classmate."

"He's not going to be getting any older," Matusen said. "He was sitting in his car in the parking garage, and someone capped him in the head."

CHAPTER THREE

Sergeant Matusen and his cohorts commanded three smaller rooms off the main ballroom to interview all who were left. Ten uniformed cops made sure nobody went anywhere. Detectives talked to the hotel employees on duty and to the garage attendant, who swore he'd never left his parking-fee cubicle. It was almost midnight, and most classmates were highly irritated they'd been kept downtown.

I was treated like everyone else, except that Matusen saved me for last, conducting the questioning himself. He looked tired—not sleepy, but as if the late hour had dulled his senses. Our many years of acquaintanceship allowed him to relate to me more like a professional than a suspect, even if I was one.

"So, Milan," he said, "what's all this about the pissing contest between Kohn and Tommy Wiggins earlier this evening?"

"I have no idea—something Wiggins's been dragging around all these years. He said his piece and left. That was the end of it."

"Why's that?"

"If Wiggins wanted to kill Kohn, he had forty years to do it before now."

"Or forty years to throw booze in his face and tell him to fuck off, too."

"He's too smart to make a public scene with Kohn and then kill him twenty minutes later," I said. "Why bring a gun to the reunion in the first place?"

"Maybe he always carries one. He's a good target. He lives in

New York, where the minute you step onto the sidewalk, you're in play. What about Kohn?"

"I haven't seen him since we graduated."

"Why's that?"

I shrugged. "We have nothing in common."

"Why didn't his wife come with him tonight?"

"How would I know? Ask her."

"I will," Matusen promised. He rubbed a spot on his temple to relieve what appeared to be a headache. "Who left the party before Kohn?"

"I wasn't paying attention."

"You're usually more observant than that."

"Only when I'm getting paid for it."

"Wiggins?"

"He stomped out of the room after the spat. What time he actually left the party, I have no idea."

He sighed and let his body relax a little. "Lieutenant McHargue won't be a happy camper when she sees your name on the guest list, Milan."

"McHargue isn't happy when she sees my name in the phone book."

Florence McHargue was the head of the Cleveland P.D. homicide division. She's never liked me. Maybe it's a racial thing—she's black and I'm white. Maybe it's a gender issue. Maybe she hates ex-cops who leave the department to become private investigators. My best guess is that she's never forgiven me because Marko Meglich, the man whose job she was promoted into, was my best friend who got himself killed covering my back.

Perhaps she just loathes my personality. I can't imagine why. When you get to know me I'm really cuddly.

"I'll point this out up front. This is an open homicide," Matusen said. "We don't need help, okay? You have no special privileges to hang around getting in our way."

"Message received."

"Another thing." He looked uncomfortable. "Nothing personal, Milan, but don't leave town for a while, okay?"

"I live here, Bob," I said. "Where am I going to go?"

He walked me to where I'd parked my car in the garage connected to the hotel, and we passed the yellow crime-scene tape encircling Phil Kohn's BMW. He'd been shot twice through the closed driver's-side window, the bullet holes at the center of two spider-web cracks. The windshield was spattered with blood and other things I didn't want to think about. The forensics team was taking pictures from every angle and making measurements. The coroner's wagon had already removed Kohn's body, and a tow truck stood by to haul his car into the impound lot.

"Your classmates feel shitty about their ruined reunion," Matusen said, his eyes on the forensics techs. "They got all dolled up and planned the entire weekend around this deal. I bet the rest of it gets canceled."

"Too bad. The rest of Phil Kohn's life has been canceled."

"Is it possible that Kohn wasn't the only victim? Maybe he was part of a special group—a clique or a club or something. Maybe somebody's got a hard-on for all of them."

"Improbable," I said. "But I don't remember him being in any club or group in high school."

"You don't? Jesus, you knew the guy, didn't you?"

"Barely. I really didn't like him, Bob."

He made a sour face. "I kind of wish you hadn't told me that, Milan."

I've seen more than my share of violent death, first in the army, fighting a war we didn't have the right to be in—not unlike the current war in Iraq. I saw accident victims and snuffed-out drug dealers in my years on the police force. In my current job, there have been even more ugly moments. But life takes strange turns no one really expects, and things happen.

At least they happen to me.

But with the exception of Marko getting killed, it had always been death once removed. Strangers—or people I'd known for mere days. The end of their lives didn't have a personal effect on me, because I didn't know them personally.

With Phil Kohn, it was different.

I couldn't stand him when we were kids, and I didn't know him as an adult. But the first day of school one September—I think it was the start of our sophomore year—he showed up with a dark shadow on his upper lip and chin that hadn't been there the spring before. It was a rite of puberty passage he seemed inordinately proud of, like the rest of us. I'd heard him laugh, seen him mourn over the rejection of some now-forgotten female classmate, and played several games of touch football with him in gym class. When we graduated, the alphabet placed him only two students behind me in the line filing up on stage for diplomas.

Now somebody had put two bullets through his brain in the same building where I was chatting up old acquaintances. It didn't seem right.

But it was none of my business. If I butted in, Florence McHargue would peel the skin off me in strips. Cleveland cops are good at what they do, McHargue better than most. They'd find the perpetrator soon.

Nevertheless, I had trouble falling asleep at home that night. I hadn't seen the body, but I'd seen the blood-and-brains spatter on the windshield—enough to keep me wide awake staring at the ceiling all night, at the crack in the plaster in the shape of Brazil.

Sonja Kokol called at about ten o'clock Saturday morning to tell me the rest of the reunion activities were canceled. She sounded exhausted.

"Do me a huge favor, Milan? I have all these people to call, or they'll show up tonight. Could you call and warn about twenty of them? I'm taking *A* through *G*, and if you could do *H* through *N*, maybe I can get Alex to round out the alphabet for me. Will you?"

It wasn't how I'd planned to spend my Saturday—but I'm sure Phil Kohn had made other plans, too. So I got out my list of attendees. The phone calls to those who had been there last night, still reeling from a once-in-a-lifetime occurrence, took nearly three hours.

My biggest surprise was Danielle Webber—now Danielle Magruder. When I told her my name she said, "Milan, how nice to talk to you. I saw you last night but it was so crowded I couldn't seem to get over to talk to you."

She remembered! I didn't think she'd ever been aware of my existence, and now she remembered. All at once, Bernie Rothman's long-simmering torch for Alenka Tavcar didn't seem quite so ridiculous.

I had to take a minute to compose myself before I told her why I'd called.

Danielle and her husband had left the party early, even before the Kohn–Wiggins incident began. When I told her about Kohn's death, she started to cry. I supposed it hit her the same way it had me—that someone she actually knew had died violently and senselessly. But her sobs were deep and wracking, and lasted for quite a while.

I wondered why.

She finally got herself under control, and eventually said we should get together for lunch very soon, and I agreed—knowing, of course, that we'd do no such thing. Another familiar, empty promise.

That blew the hell out of the rest of Saturday. Now I had only the prospect of a dull evening of reading. I mulled renting a good movie, but I wasn't feeling festive. A classmate had been murdered, and even if I'd never liked him, I couldn't shrug it off.

I spent all day Sunday with my son Stephen. Unlike his older brother, Milan Junior, whose growth stopped somewhere around five foot eleven, he had inherited some of my height. He was six foot three, which led him into basketball, and he was playing that afternoon with another pickup team over at Orange High School. I always enjoyed watching Stephen play basketball—I never got the hang of that sport when I was a kid. Afterwards we went for pizza, and threw a few snowballs at each other from the storm that had roared across the lake the day before and dumped its white booty all over Cleveland.

Sunday almost made me forget about Phil Kohn's death. I figured the police were on the case and I was safely out of it.

That lasted until early Monday morning when I got a surprising phone call from Danielle Webber's husband, Ben Magruder, who said he had a job for me and asked me to be in his downtown law office at two o'clock that afternoon.

I earn a fair portion of my income doing investigations for attorneys, but I'd never met Magruder. I'd noticed him with Danielle on Friday night, and I knew his reputation as one of the canniest defense lawyers in Ohio. Until I'd read the biographies I never knew he'd married the girl on whom I'd had such a hopeless crush in high school.

Now, across the desk, I saw he was a handsome man, in his late fifties, with dark curly hair and a tan earned on a winter vacation in the Bahamas. His capped teeth sparkled brighter than his buffed, manicured nails. The suit was pearl gray, and the flowing silk tie matched it perfectly. His appearance was chilly perfection.

His law firm was in one of the city's tallest buildings, the Erieview Tower, and the windows in his private office, looking north and east, provided a sweeping vista of the lake. It had snowed most of the weekend, so the lakefront was white and the water was frozen for half a mile out. We were too high to see where the plows had pushed the snow onto the curb in dirty piles that would only get dirtier as the winter wound down.

"My wife said you called on Saturday." He glanced at the framed, formal photograph of him and Danielle on a credenza behind his desk. Danielle's hairstyle dated the picture from at least fifteen years ago.

"I called several people," I answered, "to cancel the reunion."

"That's a dirty job. I'm sorry you got stuck with it. It's so ugly," Magruder clucked. "The police came by the house yesterday. I've been involved in many criminal cases, but I wasn't ever on the other end of things—being questioned by detectives."

"Are you a suspect?"

"Sure." He flashed perfect teeth. "So's Danielle. So are you—and everyone else who was there Friday night. That's what I want to talk to you about." He smiled wider. "After all their interviews and questions, the cops have a favorite suspect. Can you guess who?"

"I'd have to say it's Tommy Wiggins. Do I win anything?"

"Maybe a job. Wiggins has retained me as his counsel in this matter, and I want to retain you. We hope you can turn up a better suspect. The police told him not to leave town. He's from New York so that'll be inconvenient for him."

"It was inconvenient for Phil Kohn to get shot in the head, too." Magruder's smile dimmed—just a tad, but enough to put me off. "I don't think I'm interested, Mr. Magruder."

"Ben," he said. "Call me Ben. Wiggins asked for you especially."

"He did?"

"He'll be here in about ten minutes. Talk to him yourself—then you can decide. Fair enough?" Magruder smiled and coyly tilted his head to one side, delighted—the concept of fairness was brand new to him. "Of course it is."

He left me to think it over and enjoy the view, along with some coffee in a delicate porcelain cup. When he reappeared, Tommy Wiggins was with him.

Tommy looked haggard. If I'd just rescued him from a lifeboat in the middle of the Atlantic, he wouldn't have shaken my hand as gratefully, or as enthusiastically.

"Thanks for coming on board, Milan," he said. "I appreciate it."

"I'm not on board yet, Tommy. What happened with the police?"

"They came after me at my hotel and questioned me for hours."

"They questioned everybody."

"They said I had to stay in town."

The lawyer was leaning back in his chair, his hands folded into a steeple. "They have no right to demand Tommy stay in town," he said, "unless they hold him for questioning or arrest him. But I told him it'd be better for him to cooperate."

Wiggins said, "If it gets into the newspaper that I'm even suspected of killing anyone . . . "

"It'll make you more popular than ever," I finished for him. "In show business, there's no such thing as bad publicity."

"His publicity would improve," Magruder added, "if you can find us a nice, viable suspect or two to take the heat off him."

That irritated me. "You know as well as I do that private investigators aren't allowed to investigate open murders."

"But they're allowed to do damn near anything lawyers want them to—especially to clear our clients. If I hire you, you become an extension of me."

"Will you do it, Milan?" Tommy was pathetically eager.

I sighed, rubbing my hand over my face. I didn't want the best part of this case—but Tommy Wiggins looked as vulnerable as he did at seventeen. "You argued with Kohn and threw your martini in his face. Why?"

His ears got red. "This is very humiliating."

"I can't work with a bag over my head. I've got to know it all." I looked at Magruder. "That's the deal."

Wiggins sat down, hunched over, elbows on his thighs, and stared deep into some molten-lava pit of his own devising. "Mothers always tell kids to enjoy their childhood, because they'll look back at it as the most wonderful time of all. But that's bullshit. Childhood bites the big one. And adolescence—that's the keenest, cruelest hell of all."

He sat up straight and sipped his coffee. "I feel like a goddamn fool. I'm a pretty good student of human nature, and I know everyone has low points in their lives they never forget, no matter how hard they try—times of intense humiliation when people said things to them, maybe little offhand things that were bad jokes, that hurt so bad they never stop hurting. Offhand things that really *mark* them."

I had no idea where he was going, so I just nodded.

"I didn't have lots of school friends. Everybody thought I was kind of an oddball. Effete—they thought—because I liked theater and music and the arts."

"For the record," I said, "I never thought you were an oddball."

He waved a hand in dismissal and stole a worried look at Magruder, taking a deep breath to prepare himself for what was coming. When he spoke again, his voice was lower and more authoritative. "Milan, do you remember the Holly Hop?"

My mind was blank. "Was that a seventies dance like the Funky Chicken?"

"It was a school-sponsored Christmas sock hop during our senior year," Wiggins explained, "complete with cake and punch and recorded music and singing Christmas carols off key. Mr. Chernak, the biology teacher, even showed up as Santa Claus—and we all could smell booze on his breath."

I laughed. "I think he had a bottle stashed away somewhere and nipped at it when he could. He used to pop Sen-Sen all day long to mask his drinking."

Wiggins nodded. "Anyway, they held that dance in the boys' gym after the last class of the day."

I strained for the recollection, but the Holly Hop had no significance for me because I couldn't remember it at all.

"It doesn't matter," Tommy said. "Anyway, they named a king and queen of the Holly Hop. It wasn't a popularity contest—they just picked two names out of a hat. It was so stupid! Bitsy Steinberg was the queen. She might have won even if they'd voted. But now here's the irony—they drew my name for king. You remember it now?"

"No. Sorry."

"No reason you should," Tommy said, his ears turning red. "Just a goofy sock hop nobody took seriously. They even had silly crowns made out of cardboard and shiny paper they made us wear for picture taking. It was a pretty big deal to me, though, Milan, because I was quiet and didn't have any friends. It was the first time in three years at St. Clair that anyone paid any attention to me."

"It *was* a big deal, wasn't it?" Ben Magruder chimed in. His cool tone let us both know it wasn't a big deal at all—at least not to him.

"Anyway—Bitsy and I had to pose for yearbook pictures as King and Queen of the Holly Hop." Tommy chuckled coldly. "Why do I feel ridiculous saying that? They gave us scepters to go with our crowns and sat us on two big leather chairs they'd hoked up to look like thrones."

I was recalling an after-school Christmas dance, but it was still vague.

"And then," Tommy continued, his face even redder than his ears, "just when everything was quiet and the photographer was getting ready to snap the picture, fucking Phil Kohn yelled out, 'Hey, Tommy—somebody made a mistake. They should crown you the Queen!'"

The silence in the office was louder than a roll of thunder. I couldn't think of a thing to say.

Tommy set his jaw. "I wasn't smiling in that photo—check it out in the yearbook if you want to. I'm not gay, Milan—never was. Back then, for a straight guy in school, well that accusation's the worst thing that happens to you."

I had to agree. Even after all his adult success, getting humiliated in front of the entire class by a snotty, rich punk like Phil Kohn must have been one of Tommy Wiggins's darkest hours. "If it makes you feel better, Tommy," I said, "I don't even remember."

"I remember—vividly. Being King of the Holly Hop was a special moment in my life back then. But it was just a moment, because that arrogant prick ruined it."

"Kids can be brutal—and cruel. But most of us grow up. You couldn't have been pissed off about it for forty years."

He shook his head resolutely. "I've never forgotten it. And there were times, even when I was enjoying being famous, when it ate my heart out."

"So you came all the way home to this reunion just to tell him off?"

"Damn right," Wiggins said, "and to rub my fucking success in his face."

"Phil didn't seem to know what you were talking about."

"Maybe not. I was sure he'd think about it, though, and remember my humiliation at being called a queer in front of the whole class, even when I wasn't one. I don't know—maybe I'm still a middle-aged teen boy, but it's sort of haunted me all these years."

"The police will scrutinize you pretty hard for his murder."

"Would I be stupid enough to publicly tell him off, and then shoot him an hour later?"

I replayed the conversation with Bob Matusen in my head. "Maybe you didn't plan on killing him—but your temper got the better of you."

"Why would I bring a gun to a high school reunion?"

Ben Magruder leaned across the table toward Wiggins. "Don't ask the police's questions for them," he warned.

Tommy ignored him. "Do you believe me, Milan?"

"It doesn't matter if I do or not."

"A lawyer," Magruder said, like a pedantic professor lecturing first-year law students, "or the P.I. he hires doesn't have to believe in the client's innocence any more than he has to believe in Jesus or Muhammad or the designated hitter rule. He has to do the job to the best of his ability. I'm trying to do that, Tommy. Will Milan do his job, too?"

The last thing I wanted was to do this particular job. Stirring the ashes of a classmate's murder hit too close to home. Yet Tommy Wiggins was my classmate too, and his need for help overcame my distaste for poking around in something that was, in the end, too damn personal.

I sucked half the air in the room into my lungs and expelled it loudly. "You can count me in then, Mr. Magruder. At the usual rate."

Magruder's perfect teeth flashed bonhomie all over the place as he reached into his desk drawer for a contract—one the son of a bitch had prepared ahead of time. "Please, Milan," he said easily, "call me Ben."

Tommy Wiggins's relief and gratitude were palpable. He pumped my hand so hard it felt like he was trying to coax water out of a desert. He once again jumped on the chance to protest his innocence.

Dr. Phil Kohn was beyond my help, or anyone else's—but in the end, our first obligation is always to the living.

CHAPTER FOUR

I need a copy of Friday night's guest list," I said. I was back in my office after the meeting with Tommy Wiggins and Ben Magruder, and I'd called Sonja Kokol immediately to let her know what was happening to her crushed reunion.

"I can't believe they suspect Tommy Wiggins of murder," Sonja said. "He's a celebrity."

"So is O.J. Simpson."

Sonja was silent for a moment. Then: "I'm not thrilled Tommy's trying to get out of this by pinning it on one of us."

"It might not *be* one of us. Phil Kohn was aggressive and obnoxious. Maybe some stranger was mad at him, or somebody in his life who has nothing to do with St. Clair. But the guest list is someplace for me to start."

She sounded grudging. "When do you want to pick it up?"

"Tonight?"

"Sure. Come by the house. Have dinner with us while you're at it."

"I don't want to put you to any trouble, Sonja."

"No trouble. It's been ages since we've had you over. We might as well kill two birds . . . " She gasped. "Oh, shit—poor choice of words."

"You're entitled," I said.

I decided things would go easier for me if I let Bob Matusen know what I was doing for Tommy Wiggins.

"When she hears about this," he said, "we'll have to scrape McHargue off the ceiling."

"Can't be helped. I'm running a business."

"I'm in business too," Matusen said, "and I don't feel like getting shit-canned and learning a new trade when I'm this close to my twenty."

"Fine. So when I show up at the same time and place as you do, you'll understand where I'm coming from."

"You better understand where McHargue is coming from. There's nothing she'd like better than to see you working at a car wash."

I put the phone down and looked out my office window at the skyline across the river. The proud lines of Progressive Field were so close that I could almost reach out and touch it. Next to it is the hulking whale shape of the Quicken Loans Arena, now known to everyone as "The Q." For its first decade of existence it was the Gund Arena, which, if said fast, sounded too much like a sexually transmitted disease. The man who recently purchased the Cavaliers, who play basketball there, also owns the Quicken Loan company and named the arena after his business. If all big corporations continue to name sports arenas after themselves, we might be watching games in the Summer's Eve Douche Stadium.

I love Cleveland—but I wished just once that for a change I'd be chasing a case in the suburbs so I wouldn't go mano a mano with Florence McHargue.

I called Alex Cerne's dental office and offered to buy him a drink after work on my way to Sonja's. We met in a bar and both ordered a beer—a Stroh's, the beverage of choice for Slovenians in Cleveland, supporting Alex's theory that none of us is very far from our humble roots.

"Alex, you're in the medical community," I said. "You can tell me about Phil Kohn."

"I'm in the *dental* community," he said. "That's a different kettle of fish—or a kettle of teeth, as it happens."

"But you know more doctors than I do. Ever hear anything about Kohn?"

He rubbed his ear. "I recall a malpractice suit with him eight or nine years ago—but it's not inside information. I read about it in the paper."

"A malpractice for a cardiologist might mean somebody died. How did it turn out?"

"I think it was settled out of court. Look it up if you're interested."

"Did you see Kohn socially after high school?"

He shook his head. "He went to Stanford, I went to Ohio State. I ran into him playing golf once or twice, but we didn't spend five minutes talking. All I know is that he plays with very expensive clubs." He frowned. "Played."

"What's his marriage like, do you know?"

"How would I know? He didn't bring his wife golfing with him."

"He didn't bring her to the party Friday night, either."

"I didn't bring mine, either," Alex said. He didn't look happy. "Is this official questioning, Milan?"

"It's unofficial—I'm not a cop anymore."

"I have to tell you," he said, "I kind of resent it."

"That's why I'm paying for the beer."

"You'd have to buy me a brewery."

"I'm not grilling you, Alex. We're talking."

"And if I misspeak—if I use the wrong word or make a mistake—will you throw me to the wolves for killing Phil?"

"Did you? Kill Phil?"

Now his face turned angry. "Be real!" he snapped.

"I am. I'm hoping the killer is a stranger—someone we don't know."

"And if you find out Tommy actually did it?"

"I'll tell Magruder and he can do whatever he wants. Everyone is entitled to the best legal defense possible—even the guilty."

"If Magruder gets Tommy off, even if he's guilty, and he skates, how are you going to feel about yourself then, Milan?"

I didn't need that question, especially from a friend. I slugged down the rest of my beer and threw a crumpled ten-spot on the bar. "I look lousy in sackcloth and ashes, Alex. But maybe I'll drop by your office and you can drill on my teeth all day. How's that for penance?"

I'd like to believe I didn't stalk out in high dudgeon, but that's an apt description. Laws and ethics must be followed—otherwise we'd be living in anarchy. Alex Cerne touched an exposed nerve, and as I made my way to Sonja's place it throbbed and burned. How *would* I feel—how would I fall asleep at night—if I found Tommy Wiggins was guilty and I couldn't tell anyone?

Not very good.

I stopped off at Roza's Wine Shop on Detroit Road and bought a bottle of Zinfandel to take to Sonja's.

Her husband, Jerry Caruth, answered the door at their gray Cape Cod colonial in Lakewood. He was a financial analyst with the securities department of a major downtown bank, which meant he owned a huge wardrobe of elegant and conservative suits—but at home he looked casual in a long-sleeved black-and-white flannel shirt and battered jeans.

"Good to see you, Milan," he said, shaking my hand. "Make yourself comfortable. Sonja's cooking."

I liked Jerry—the perfect mate for Sonja, a steadfast island of calm amidst her whirling hyperactivity. He led me into the living room, dominated by a baby grand piano; he'd played jazz in his youth. A wood fire crackled invitingly, the scent of Sonja's pork roast wafted in from the kitchen, and Bill Evans's "Waltz for Debbie" hummed through the speakers of the CD player.

Jerry disappeared and came back with two opened beer bottles. He didn't have to ask what kind—he'd been married thirty years to a Slovenian.

"So, a murder at your high school reunion," he said, clicking his Stroh's bottle against mine. I've never drunk Stroh's out of a glass in my life. "What did we get ourselves into?"

"You're not into anything—you didn't show up Friday night."

He nodded. "There's nothing grimmer than a reunion—but I wasn't expecting anything as melodramatic as murder."

Sonja came in from the kitchen, wearing a red apron over jeans and a long-sleeved T-shirt. "Hey," she said. "Dinner's almost ready."

"Smells great."

She played with her apron hem. "I wish you were here just for pork roast, Milan. I feel funny turning those names over to you. The cops already have them . . ."

"I'm trying to help Tommy."

"I know—but the whole class might end up paying for it." She disappeared into the kitchen again. Jerry looked hard at me.

"It's a possibility," I admitted.

"Sonja worked so hard on this reunion," he said. "Now she blames herself."

"It wasn't her job to find out who didn't like who. She had to invite everybody. She did a great job."

Jerry stared into the fireplace. "That list, Milan . . . Just go easy. Okay?"

During dinner all of us kept the conversation light—until we were enjoying an after-dinner Amaretto and I brought up the subject we'd been avoiding all evening. I inadvertently let loose the elephant in the living room.

"Sonja, were you in contact with Phil Kohn over the last several years?"

Jerry answered for her. "Not really. One of my bank people had a coronary a few years ago and Phil took care of him. That was about it."

"Look," Sonja said, "he was from a fairly well-to-do Jewish family—he didn't hang out with us Slovenian peasants after high school."

"But we're all suspects, and Tommy is Number One."

Sonja's brows knitted. "Funny he'd go to Ben Magruder," she said thoughtfully. "Ben is Danielle Webber's husband—and Phil and Danielle dated for a short while during junior year."

That hit hard. "I didn't know that. I'm surprised. Phil was such a little toad. Hardly her type."

Sonja smiled sadly. "He had money, Milan—and that made him Danielle's type. She was always a materialistic little bitch, even as a kid."

"Oh?"

"She made us girls feel so worthless, with her designer clothes and the convertible her daddy bought her. I remember once I wore a new pink sweater to school, a really pretty one—and

Danielle came up and fingered the sweater, tossed her head and sniffed 'Polyester!' and walked away." Sonja reached for her Amaretto with a shaking hand. "I never wore that goddamn sweater again."

We were all quiet for a minute. Then I said, "How hot and heavy were Danielle and Phil anyway?"

"I had no idea. High school kids didn't always have sex like they do now."

"I wonder if Ben Magruder knows."

"So what?" Jerry put in. "This is the twenty-first century. Husbands don't make an issue out of their wives' virginity anymore. Or lack of it. Besides, it was years ago."

Sonja's face closed up, and she shook her head. "Jesus, Jerry," she said, and got up and left the room.

Jerry Caruth sighed. "I guess I put my foot in it again. I do that sometimes. Damn! High school was a bad soap opera, wasn't it? Flaring complexions and raging hormones and suddenly realizing there's another gender besides your own. Pressure from parents, pressure from teachers. And kids are angry because they aren't adults yet but want to be treated that way . . ."

Sonja came back in clutching a thin sheaf of papers, her eyebrows framing a scowl, and I couldn't tell whether she was mad at me, or at Jerry. I didn't know if she was a virgin or not when she married him, and I didn't want to know, one way or the other.

"Here," she said, thrusting the list at me. "There's an asterisk next to everyone who signed up to attend—and I put checks after those who were there Friday. I ran a few extra copies off on my printer—the police have the original."

"Thanks, Sonja." I slid the papers into my jacket pocket. Sonja watched them disappear as if something valuable had just been thrown into the ocean.

"Just one thing," she said. "I don't want to hear about any of this anymore. Whatever you find out, don't tell me. If I have to read about it in the papers, that's one thing—but just don't tell me. I don't want to know that somebody I went to high school with is a murderer."

• • •

At seven A.M. the temperature hovered at ten degrees, but the bright sunshine made everything look deceptive—a typical February tease on the North Coast. I didn't have to roll over and wake Jinny, who had spent the night with me—she was up, as usual, at 6:15 and had already showered and was half dressed when I opened my eyes.

"Hello, sleepyhead," she said, standing at my dresser, vigorously brushing her blond hair, well dressed from the waist down in a blue skirt, hose, and low heels. From the waist up she had on only a dark-blue bra. "You tossed and turned all night—did you know that?"

"Sorry if I disturbed you, Jinny. Yesterday wasn't such a good day."

"Was late last night not such a bad night?"

I got out of bed and padded over to her, putting my arms around her waist and kissing her bare shoulder. "If not for you—for late last night—I probably wouldn't have slept at all."

"It made me sleepy too," she said, and tapped me lightly on the nose with her hairbrush.

I made coffee for her and a cup of tea for me. That was a new thing, drinking tea. My doctor said it's healthier for me. I poured out two glasses of orange juice, and toasted two slices of whole wheat bread. I used to have a bagel or an English muffin with cream cheese for breakfast every morning, but whole wheat bread is better for the system, and without the cream cheese—or so my doctor tells me.

Jinny came out of the bedroom fully dressed and sat down across from me. "You're bummed out about old friends, aren't you?"

"Friends? Most of them disappeared from my life forty years ago. Now they're back." My hand moved automatically in search of a cigarette that wasn't there anymore. "Don't worry, it'll pass."

She sipped at her orange juice. "A friendship can go down like the *Titanic* over something nobody realized would be serious. Your friends—especially Alex and Sonja—would be just as happy if they never even heard of the doctor getting killed at the same party where they were circulating around being hosts. They want it all to go away without any noise or fuss." She took a delicate bite of toast. "Then you come around, Milan, picking at old sores, asking questions, and making them look at themselves in a way they never did before—so of course they got mad. Will they stop being mad at you after a while? I hope so. Either way, you pretty much have to go with it."

I worked on my tea. I like tea all right, especially Earl Grey, the kind I was drinking now—but it made me crazy to smell somebody else's coffee. "Do you think you'll get mad at me, too?"

"Probably," she said. "I've been mad at you before. You've been mad at me, too. It's different between lovers than it is with friends, even old ones like Alex and Sonja."

I tried not to smile. "Is that what we are, Jinny? Lovers?"

"Us? Hell, no. I just wanted to get laid last night, and I happened to be driving by and saw your light, so . . ."

"Go to work," I said. "If you're late, the entire city grinds to a halt."

She finished the last of her coffee. "Nobody knows I run this city," she said. "I never get any credit." She came around the table, bent down, and kissed me. It wasn't a passionate kiss, exactly, but her tongue flickered gently inside my mouth, and I tasted coffee—a little bit sweet because she always used a teaspoon of sugar. "I won't ask when I'll see you next, because you're totally involved in work—and I'm patient. But give me a jingle once in a while—just to fill me in and tell me who else is mad at you." She kissed me again and rumpled my hair, then headed for the front closet and her coat. Involuntarily I smoothed my hair back the way it was—there wasn't enough of it there to treat so cavalierly.

Then I started thinking of what had kept me awake half the night.

I'd left Sonja and Jerry Caruth with a sense of unease. Nevertheless, it was my job. I hoped Tommy Wiggins was as innocent as he'd claimed—but he'd acted like a damn fool Friday night, making a big fuss and throwing a drink. He's a successful playwright who sometimes turns into a drama queen. That wasn't a crime, of course—but killing Phil Kohn was.

I'd pored over the list of reunion attendees until after midnight. I didn't know where to start—so I bit the bullet and called Phil Kohn's widow, and arranged to talk with her later that morning. The Jewish custom of burying their dead quickly and efficiently had been followed on Monday afternoon. Now Adrienne Kohn was "at home" for condolence visits.

The house was in Moreland Hills, a very upscale eastern suburb that was home to more than one society doctor. The sweeping driveway was lined with hostas and rhododendrons. The Kohn home was a square red-brick Georgian—big, expensive, and ugly.

Adrienne Kohn, a short, small-boned woman with black hair and brown eyes, looked drawn and stressed. The tanned skin of her pretty face was pulled tight over pronounced cheekbones, partially from grief and partly, I suspected, from a radical face-lift. Her only makeup was dark lipstick, and she wore a gray sweater over black tights. Her hair was pulled into a high, thick ponytail at the top of her head—Pebbles Flintstone fighting off encroaching middle age.

"You and Phil were friends in high school?" she asked when we were seated in the cavernous living room. The furniture was all modern, blond wood and off-white upholstery, and the many paintings on the wall were nonrepresentational contemporary art, which I've never been able to understand. The house seemed less like a living space than a monument to affluence. On an end table was a large framed photograph of a young woman in the cap and gown of a graduate, standing between her parents in front of an academic building looming Gothic in the background.

"I knew him," I said. "We weren't really friends."

A bitter little smile lifted a corner of her mouth. "Then this isn't a condolence call."

"Not exactly. As I told you on the phone, I'm a private investigator."

She crossed her legs beneath her, yoga-style. "Who're you investigating?"

"An attorney has asked me to look into Phil's background."

"I see."

"I know you've been over this with the police already, Mrs. Kohn, but if you'd be kind enough to indulge me . . ."

"Make it Adrienne, will you? I don't like to be called 'Mrs.' by somebody older than I am. Okay—indulging is what I do best.

I've had thirty-three years of on-the-job experience, indulging. So fire away."

"Was Phil currently seeing any high school friends?"

"I have no idea who Phil saw. I've never met people from his high school—until you walked in here just now. I'm a northern Californian; Phil and I met at Stanford. When we moved back to Cleveland, almost all his friends were fellow doctors or scientific types." Adrienne Kohn swallowed audibly. "And their wives."

"How about his enemies?"

She looked off into deep space. "Who can say? No one is universally loved."

"Anyone in particular?"

She hesitated, chewing on the inside of her cheek. "I'm having second thoughts—talking to you. No law says I have to."

"There's no law."

"You're not a real police officer." Disdain crept into her tone and hardened her eyes. "Why should I spill my guts to you, give up family secrets? Phil's gone and nothing will bring him back, so what's the point?"

I chose my words carefully. "The point is that an innocent man could spend his life in jail for a crime he didn't commit. You wouldn't want that."

Her huge exhale could have blown out the candles on a kid's birthday cake. "Oh, hell." She wasn't looking at me. "You'll find out sometime. Everybody else knew it."

"Knew what?"

"That Phil is—was—a player." Now she met my eyes defiantly. "A skirt chaser. A pussy hound. He wasn't the best-looking guy in the world, but he had an oozy charm some women liked—along with that power doctors feel when they hold lives in their hands every day. He cheated on me more times than I have fingers to count on." Acid of self-disgust thickened her voice. "I yelled and screamed about it at the beginning, but eventually I learned to live with it. Isn't it amazing—the vast amounts of shit people swallow?"

"So you had marriage problems?"

She snorted unpleasantly. "Not so I'd kill him. I wouldn't do that to my daughter." She pointed to the photograph—her daughter had big, pretty brown eyes like her mother's, but otherwise she unfortunately resembled Phil. "Kristen. I know, it's a strange first name for a Jewish girl, but it's what Phil wanted. She's twenty-five, doing her internship right now in Pittsburgh—pediatrics. She knew Phil was a slut, too."

"You didn't love your husband, Mrs. Kohn?"

"At first I did—even though I loved money and status more. When I found him in bed with his best friend's wife, things changed—eleven years ago or so."

"Why didn't you leave him then?"

"Because I liked being a doctor's wife and all the money and prestige that comes with it. In your circles, you know all about it."

"In my circles," I said, "prestige means having a big TV set. But I know what you mean."

"Also—divorce means your so-called friends choosing sides. Mine always choose the one with the money and the power, so I wasn't going to kick his ass to the curb even if I wanted to."

"Ever cheat on him?"

She tossed her head, sending her ponytail whipping around. "That's a pretty rude question, isn't it?"

"The police will ask it eventually."

She sighed again. "They already have. Okay, yes—I did. Once."

"Is your lover jealous enough of your husband to do something radical?"

She shook her head. "No. It was a long time ago." She stared at something far away that only she could see. "Besides, my lover is dead now."

"You told me you caught Phil with his best friend's wife." Her mouth was a grim line in her face. I was losing her cooperation. "Who was she?"

"Fuck you! This is too goddamn personal," she growled. Then she slumped back into the deep cushions of her chair. Her last sentence had extracted all the fight from her. "Oh hell—what's the difference anyway? Barbara Siegel," she said, spitting it out. "Jack Siegel's wife."

• • •

It was bizarre to even consider Jack Siegel with suspicion. He was one of those adolescent geniuses who barely looked up from his studying to offer an opinion about anything. Now he had a motive for murder. The Siegels had seemed a happy couple, even indulging in some sexy joking Friday night. Jack probably didn't like Phil. It was no big deal at the time. Now, it took on a new scent and color.

But according to Adrienne Kohn, there were several other betrayed husbands out there feeling the same way. I wondered if I could find them.

I called Jack where he worked at NASA and invited him to have a drink with me after work—but I didn't tell him why.

My next stop was Bernie's. He'd inherited his parents' home in Beachwood, where they'd moved while he was still in college, and he hadn't sold it yet. It was a nice-sized house that appeared alone and lonely on a fairly long street. Bernie opened the door wearing gray sweatpants and sneakers, and a dark-blue sweatshirt imprinted with the legend: SO MANY BOOKS—SO LITTLE TIME. He was wearing a strange, soft cap on his head, but it didn't look like a yarmulke. It might have been from the Middle East.

He invited me into the kitchen, where he was making tea. A large window admitted the winter sunshine into an old-fashioned room with exposed brick walls. Everything Bernie did, from talking to making eye contact to fixing a cup of tea, seemed hyper—some things never change. He removed a whistling kettle from the range and poured boiling water into a mug over a peculiar-looking tea bag. The resultant liquid was bright red and smelled like drying roses.

"It *is* roses," he said. "Rose hips, anyway. Can I fix you a cup? I have it imported from Egypt."

"No, thanks," I said dubiously.

He loaded his mug with three sugars, and when he stirred it some tea slopped onto the counter and stained the tile. "Isn't this a beautiful kitchen, Milan? My mother designed it herself. She was a magnificent cook. This kitchen always looked as if *House Beautiful* would drop by any time and take pictures. I missed every minute I was away from this kitchen and away from her." He sighed, lost in reverie for a moment. "It was scary knowing she was living here all by herself, an old lady." He slid open a drawer, the kind in which most people would keep their spoons, and pulled out an object that looked like an exotic weapon from the original *Star Trek*. "This is a stun gun," he said. "A Taser. I bought it for her the last time I was home to visit her. She couldn't fire a gun, but she could pull the trigger on this in case anyone broke into her house. That happens a lot to older people. Young kids, punks, they break into elderly people's homes, beat them up and rob them—ah, well, I guess you know that." It was a depressing thought, but he seemed to brighten up right away. "The good news is that Mom never had to use the damn thing anyway."

I knew one of the merchants who sold stun guns locally, Willard Dante. I'd bought some electronic equipment from him myself, and the last time we had lunch together, he told me that Taser sales to elderly homeowners had risen nearly 50 percent in the past few years. The world has gotten hard and tough—Bernie had made a wise purchase for his mother.

Bernie, as I recalled from the old days, was *always* prepared. He'd been a Boy Scout for only a short while but had managed to collect all the survival equipment that would save him if he got lost in the wilderness—even if there isn't much wilderness around Cleveland. He even earned a few merit badges before he tired of the whole Boy Scout thing and moved on to other, more intellectual pursuits.

"Come, let's sit, Milan," he said cheerfully, putting the stun gun back in the cutlery drawer, "so we can talk."

We sat on side-by-side stools at a built-in bar, the top nicely covered with a blood-rust tile that made me think of somewhere in the Middle East from centuries ago. Bernie slurped the tea loudly and with gusto, and it made his upper lip pink.

I told him I worked for Wiggins's lawyer and was checking out everyone who'd been at the Friday mixer. "This is just routine, Bernie."

He nodded.

"You and Phil were friends back in high school, weren't you?"

"Well—we were both Jewish, and there weren't that many Jews at St. Clair, so we were drawn together. But I wouldn't call us real friends. Would you call it a friendship?"

I didn't offer an opinion. "After graduation you didn't stay in touch?"

"No. We went to different schools and lost track of each other. By the time he finished medical school, I was living in a kibbutz in Israel, teaching. Did you know that, Milan? I got married there—well, I guess you didn't know that. That's where I got the offer to teach in Florida. I've been there ever since—even after I got divorced. I never contacted Phil."

"Did you talk to him on Friday?"

He shook his head. "I never got around to it. I had nothing to say to him."

"Bernie, do you remember the Christmas dance our senior year? The Holly Hop?"

"Vaguely." He slurped some more tea.

"Tommy Wiggins and Bitsy Steinberg were crowned King and Queen."

His face lit up with a smile. "You have a good memory. You're right—it's coming back to me in dribs and drabs. It was a hell of a short dance—almost like an afterthought. It lasted about an hour, didn't it? Everyone had some of that godawful Kool-Aid punch and those holiday cookies that looked like Christmas trees or bells. Then we danced a few dances to Christmas records . . ." He chuckled. "God—Bing Crosby dreaming of a white Christmas. Remember that? Then we went home. It was nothing big like the prom or the senior picnic."

"The senior picnic," I said. "We went to the zoo."

Bernie's eyes went dreamy. "I stayed with Alenka all that day," he said, "even when we went to the reptile house. Yuck, I hated reptiles. So did my mom. Of course, she didn't much like animals of any kind. I never had a pet because she didn't want a dog to dirty up the house—but she warned me that if I even *thought* about bringing a pet snake home to play with, we'd both be out on the street." He leaned across the table at me and changed subjects without a pause. "Did you get a chance to talk to Alenka at the party Friday night?"

"Briefly."

"What did she say? About *me*, I mean."

This was hardly what I'd come to his home to talk about. "Bernie—let this Alenka business go. She's married."

He looked offended. "She's separated."

"Who told you that?"

"I heard it around."

"You were just kids," I said. "It was a cute little romantic crush—it didn't mean anything."

"It did to me. Things happen when you're young that you never get over. Look at you—you dated Lila in high school and then married her."

"I divorced her, too," I reminded him.

He pushed the mug toward me, and the rose-scented fumes drifted up into my face, smelling like a homemade cough medicine. I leaned back to get as far from it as I could. "Everything's different now. My mother is gone." His face stretched into a mask of anger. "Fucking doctors, they should be lynched, the way they treated her, like they didn't know what a goddamned heart condition was!" He forced himself to take a breath and calm down. "Sorry, I get worked up. Anyway, after my mom passed away, religious differences went right out the window for me. My own marriage is over, so that's not a stumbling block. I've got this nice house, all paid for, and I can move back to Ohio permanently. I can land a teaching job, and if not, I have a small trust fund that gives me about sixty thousand a year. I want to spend the rest of my life with Alenka."

"Bernie—she's just not interested."

His face reddened; even his protuberant ears flamed. "Then she *did* say something about me."

"Just that you made her uncomfortable."

He pouted. "I thought you were my friend."

"I am. That's why I'm giving you some good advice."

"I don't want to hear it." His lips tightened stubbornly. "There hasn't been one day in forty years I haven't thought about her."

I was growing tired of Bernie Rothman's unrequited love. "That's between the two of you, then. I have to do what I'm being paid to do—and it's about Phil Kohn's death."

He stood up and rubbed his hands together, washing them.

"I'm sorry what happened to Phil, but he was nothing to me. There are more important things on my mind—as I'm sure you know."

He showed me to the door, making me promise to keep in touch so we could have dinner together—and he reminded me to bring a date so we'd be a foursome with him and Alenka.

As I walked down the steps outside his house, I tried not to accidentally step on the Easter Bunny.

CHAPTER FIVE

Jack Siegel—*Doctor* Jack Siegel, who'd earned his Ph.D. in engineering—wore a parka over his brown suit and beige pullover sweater when he slid into the booth at the little West Side bar near the NASA Glenn Research Center at five-thirty that evening. I think he needed a few more layers, because it was another cold and blustery day. He ordered a Diet Coke and I nursed a beer.

He was losing his dark-brown hair even faster than I, his receding hairline a contrast to his full-cheeked, almost cherubic face. As a kid he'd always appeared red-cheeked and blushing. The years hadn't changed that.

"How did you get involved in this murder business, Milan?" he said. "I'm surprised."

"I work for Tommy Wiggins's attorney. Tommy seems to have emerged as the prime suspect."

"Why is that? Do you know?"

"I'm trying to talk to everyone who was there Friday."

Jack looked uncomfortable. "If you're going by alphabetical order, the *S*'s must be pretty far down on your list."

"They were—until Adrienne Kohn told me what happened between Phil and Barbara."

His humiliation rose from the bottoms of his feet to the tops of his ears. He flushed, darting looks around the small bar to make sure no one else was listening. "Jesus Christ, Milan."

"Adrienne said she called and told you about it."

"Adrienne"—he pronounced her name as though it was a vile word—"evidently shared a lot of things with you. But that was years ago. It's ancient history—all water under the bridge now."

"Still, you must have bad feelings about Phil Kohn."

"I won't lie. I hated his guts. But it's not something I go around advertising."

"Was that the end of it? Their affair?"

His shoulders were so hunched they looked to be up around his jawbone. "The end of the affair, the end of the friendship. Adrienne and Barbara haven't spoken to each other since. As for Phil and me—well, what do you think?"

"No violent confrontation?"

"God, no! I'm not violent, I'm a geek. Sure, I had violent thoughts at the time. I still do. I was mortified. I told him just what I thought of him, but I wasn't violent."

"How did he respond?"

"With arrogance and amusement—but that was it. Barbara and I spent a decade trying to put it behind us, to put the marriage back together. At first we said it was for the kids—we have three, you know. But the kids are grown now and it wound up being for us—the healing. It's the best thing we ever did."

I nodded. "The two of you looked happy Friday night."

"We are happy. But it took a lot of effort and a lot of sad years." Jack played with the moisture on the outside of his Coca-Cola glass, running his finger up and down. "We almost didn't come to the reunion at all. We figured Phil would be there. We didn't want it to be awkward—picking at an old scab."

"Why *did* you come?"

He stuck his lower lip out in a kind of sulky pout—feeling around for the right thing to say made him look five years old. Finally he said, "I wouldn't give the son of a bitch the satisfaction that I was hiding from him."

"Did you talk to him Friday night?"

"No. Neither did Barbara. We looked at each other across the room—but we never talked."

"Other than that you haven't seen him for ten years or so?"

"No. Well, yeah, we ran into him one night at the Cleveland Play House about seven years ago," Jack said, "and once somewhere else I don't remember. We didn't speak either time, and we didn't speak Friday. Look, I disliked the prick with everything that's in me—but I've worked hard at getting past all that. If I'd wanted to kill him, I would have done it back then." He turned his hands palms upward, showing his innocence. "But I'm a scientist, not a murderer."

"You're not exactly grieving his death, are you?"

It took him a long time to answer. "No. But I don't give him all the blame for what happened. It takes two." Now he leaned forward. "I never wanted to hurt Barbara. I love her with all my heart, and I busted my ass to make our marriage work again."

He sneaked another furtive look around the bar. It was a popular after-work hangout for NASA Glenn people, none of whom probably knew anything about Jack Siegel's troubled marriage, and he wanted to keep it that way. "I hope you're not going public with this—about Barbara and Kohn."

"Who would I tell?"

"The police, for one."

"You should tell the police yourself."

He recoiled. "For God's sake, why?"

"It'll go easier for you if they don't find out themselves," I warned him. "And they will."

He looked miserable. "This will open up the whole can of worms again. It's so degrading—having people know that adultery almost broke us to pieces."

"It happens, Jack. To more people than you might imagine. Whoever said marriage was easy must have been a lifelong bachelor. Call Sergeant Bob Matusen in Homicide and talk to him. He's a decent man."

He closed his eyes. "I'll have to talk it over with Barbara." He jerked nervously, moving his hands across the top of the table as if he were sifting through dried navy beans looking for pieces of shell. "I suppose after a while Barbara felt like Phil had . . . betrayed her—and betrayed me, too, which of course he did. Adrienne had told me he'd slept with a lot of different women—mostly other men's wives. So Barbara didn't think of him with warmth—but we never discussed it between us."

His face glowed with perspiration. He'd have been more comfortable if he'd taken off his parka before he sat down with me—and more comfortable not talking about his wife's perfidy, even though it was a decade old. It's a Mars–Venus thing, I guess—men and women react differently when betrayed. When a woman's husband cheats on her, she becomes enraged. She tells her friends, her family, her therapist, and the rest of the world, looking for a little sympathy. But when a man's wife cheats on him, it eats out his guts inside, and he prays nobody else finds out and then looks at him with pity or, worse, contempt.

Jack checked his watch. "I should be getting home . . ."

"Sure, Jack. I appreciate your taking the time."

He stood up. "There's no need to mention anything to anyone, is there?" His voice had turned into a pleading whine.

"I can't think why I would. It was a long time ago."

His fingers fluttered over the toggles as he buttoned his parka. "Right," he said. "It was a long time ago. Lots of things happened a long time ago, Milan. I think you'd be a better, nicer person if you didn't hunt around for those old things in somebody else's garbage—especially your friends."

He left me sitting there nursing a stale beer and the stinging of my conscience. I couldn't help but pity him because I know how he felt. Statistics say 60 percent of married men stray outside their marriage, and 40 percent of married women do, too. But it's always a gut shot when it happens to you—the horns of a cuckold are an uncomfortable fit.

Tommy Wiggins had nurtured a rather silly hatred for forty years. Maybe drenching Phil Kohn with a drink had finally exorcised that rage.

Or maybe not.

Either way, here I was on the West Side at six o'clock in the evening with a now-empty beer bottle, a hollow empty hole inside my belly after talking to Jack Siegel, a long and difficult job to do, and some extra time to do it.

I pulled out my cell phone and called Alenka Tavcar.

Olmsted Falls is a small village less than half an hour from downtown Cleveland, and it drips charm in the same way quaint

Northeast Ohio villages like Hudson and Chagrin Falls do. It boasts historic houses and a delightful business district called Grand Pacific Junction, with a delicious bakery, interesting and unusual shops, and an amazing French restaurant, Bistro du Beaujolais. About a block away is the local library, and the waterfall just behind it gave the town its name. Olmsted Falls shivers and vibrates as trains pass directly through downtown blowing their ear-shattering whistles, but otherwise the village feels rural, quiet, and almost turn of the twentieth century.

Alenka Tavcar lived just north of the Grand Pacific Junction district, renting a small carriage house on the property of a rambling mansion that looked as though someone had several times added on to it over the last fifty years. When she let me in, she kissed me on the cheek and told me she'd moved there six months earlier, when she and her husband separated. He still lived in their own, much bigger house—and they'd put it on the market.

"One of the other realtors in my office is handling the sale," she said as we sat in front of a cheery fire and drank red wine. There were small tea candles burning all over the living room, too. "I'm too close to it to do it myself. Imagine showing a potential buyer through my own house and they say something like 'Who designed this ghastly kitchen?' I'd take it personally." Casual and easy, she slid from her overstuffed chair onto the floor and leaned an elbow on the cushion. "What can I tell you about what happened Friday, Milan? I frankly don't know a thing."

"Most people don't, Alenka. Do you remember anything you saw or heard at the hotel—even small and insignificant, if that's all you've got? What Phil did, what he said, who talked to him."

She rubbed stiff muscles at the back of her neck. "I was so shook up by what Bernie Rothman said to me in the course of two minutes, I hardly knew where I was. I remember seeing you afterward—and Gerry Gabrosek, when she finally tore herself away from the registration table." She smiled again. "She only gave up that seat because she simply *had* to pee—because God forbid anyone would come in and not notice her before they saw anyone else. We talked a little before she disappeared into the ladies' room. We were in International Relations Club together—and in Senior Hostesses."

"Anyone else after that?"

"Um—Bitsy Steinberg—and a few others."

"Not Phil Kohn?"

"I wasn't paying attention to Phil Kohn. Why would I?"

"Sometimes," I said, "we remember more than we thought we did."

She smiled without warmth. "I've seen this scene on TV too often, the witness going into a trance trying to remember. I think it was *Law & Order*. Shall I close my eyes?"

"If it will help."

She put her glass down on the floor and leaned her head back against the chair, shutting her eyes. "I feel silly doing this."

"Just relax."

It took more than a minute—I thought she might have fallen asleep. Finally she said, "I recall seeing Phil, standing by the door talking to Gary Mishlove." She thought some more. "Later I saw him with Ilene Silver and her husband—and a few others." She opened her eyes. "I talked to him for a few seconds, and then he broke away from me for a very hush-hush chat with Stupan Godic. The next time I noticed him, he was right in the middle of the ballroom and Tommy Wiggins threw the drink in his face."

"That's all?"

She nodded. "I don't think I saw Phil again."

"Did anyone there have a grudge against him besides Tommy?"

She puffed her cheeks and blew out a tired pocket of air. "He's always been a jerk, but just because somebody shot him doesn't mean it's one of us. He must have had other enemies—because of work or his personal life." Her eyes narrowed and the sky blue in them turned wintry ice. "He was a slut, Milan. He once actually tried to hit on my daughter."

"When was this?"

"My older daughter—I have two of them—is a doctor. When she was in medical school she worked part time at the hospital where he was head of the cardiology unit. She knew we'd gone to school together and she introduced herself—and right off the bat he asked her for a date. She said she hoped she'd get an internship there, and he told her if she was *nice* to him . . ." Her shoulders quivered, and she shook her head to rid herself of the memory. "Must I explain?"

She wrapped her arms around herself as if she were cold, even though she was only about six feet away from the fire. "What a disgusting son of a bitch." Her demeanor had changed. She was a hell of a lot more angry at Phil Kohn than she'd let on.

"Alenka, is your daughter still at the hospital?"

"No. She's interning in Syracuse—she wanted to get as far away from Phil Kohn as she could." She clambered up from the floor and loomed over me, fists planted firmly on her hips. "You don't suspect my daughter, do you?"

"If every woman shot every man who put an unwanted move on them, there wouldn't be any men left," I said. "Probably me included. But it gives me a little more insight into Phil."

"I'm so glad to be of help." Her sarcastic tone was as flat and cold as Arctic tundra.

"Don't be mad at me, Alenka. I'm just doing my job speaking with everyone who was there. Trust me—I didn't suspect you for a minute."

That softened her. "You didn't?"

I shook my head. "You're a good person. You always have been."

"You think?"

"You were bright and sociable, on top of being one of the prettiest girls in high school—and none of that has changed much. You're one of my all-time favorite people from way back when."

She cocked her head; her smile was genuine. "Really? Then why didn't you do something about it? Way back when."

I felt my cheeks flaming. It's pretty embarrassing to blush like a bashful schoolboy when you're almost sixty years old. "I thought about it, frankly—but you and Bernie had a sweet little romance going. I wasn't going to break that up, no matter what."

Bitterness shadowed her eyes, but only for a split second. "Bernie's parents did that very nicely, thank you, without your help or anyone else's. Besides, you were hot and heavy with Lila in your senior year. You wound up marrying her."

"I got two great boys out of that, Alenka. As for the rest of it—chalk it up to mistakes."

"Everybody has those," she said.

The evening was rapidly heading to a close, so I took my leave, feeling a sense of loss as I did so. I'd always liked Alenka Tavcar, and even though I hadn't kept in touch with her after high school, I'd thought of her often, and warmly.

We stood in the doorway. There was a covered porch outside that kept most of the wind and cold at bay. Then she said, "Thanks for coming by, Milan—and thanks for your vote of confidence. I can't tell you how much I appreciate it." And she put one arm around my neck and pulled my head down for a kiss. It was a gentle kiss, very friendly and very way-back-when—except for a whispering taste of her tongue just before she pulled away.

She cleared her throat. "Whatever you're up to, on Tommy Wiggins's behalf, I hope you get the job done," she said. "Maybe it'll give you time to relax."

I had to think about that.

I don't generally make friends on the job—it's the nature of my business—but I was glad Alenka and I had renewed our friendship. This investigation had already cost me other friendships. Most of my old classmates, living plain, vanilla lives, were uncomfortable with their sudden proximity to a murder. Especially those who, it turned out, hated Phil Kohn's guts. I was churning up some smoldering embers.

In the unlikely event of another St. Clair High School reunion I would probably not get invited.

If I do—I damn sure won't go.

CHAPTER SIX

The next morning I shaved and had a cup of tea and a toasted bagel while listening to John Lanigan and Jimmy Malone doing their crazy bit on the radio. Their producer, Tracey Carroll, not only had a soothing and sexy voice, but she was easily able to stand up to those slightly insane radio personalities who generally woke me up in the morning with a smile.

I got to my office early and was putting some order into my schedule when Stupan Godic walked through the door. I'd phoned him the day before, and he'd promised to stop by to talk, but he'd been nonspecific about the time. Eight-forty A.M. was too close to the crack of dawn for my comfort.

Stupan had been small in high school, and forty years hadn't added to his height. He was a skinny little guy with nervous tics. He was several days past his most recent shave, and his hair was even more unkempt than it had been on Friday—complementing today's wardrobe, which was an army surplus jacket with someone else's name on it, worn unzipped over a khaki shirt, and tattered jeans bloused into a pair of filthy combat boots. It's often the uniform of choice for middle-aged Vietnam War veterans who are still traumatized thirty years after their in-country tours.

"Sorry to catch you so early," he said. "I hope it's okay. I couldn't sleep—as usual."

He landed hard in one of my desk chairs and immediately lit a Camel, exhaling the smoke upward. I didn't tell him that after

I quit smoking I'd spent six months getting the stink of my own cigarettes out of the office. I smelled the sharp odor of marijuana all over him, too.

Stupan slouched back in the seat on the end of his tailbone, his hands trembling noticeably. "After I came home from 'Nam I was through with death and killing, Milan. But I never figured out how to get to sleep after that. So I do shit to put me to sleep and do other shit to keep me up. It raises hell with my nervous system, I tell you."

I reminded him that I'd called because I wanted to speak to him about Friday night.

"Oh, man," he said, sounding shocked. "What happened to Phil—Jesus, it got me spooked."

"It has everybody spooked."

He hacked a cigarette cough. "What's your end of this, anyways?"

"I'm making inquiries," I said.

He seemed content with the non-response. "I was talking to him at the hotel. Phil. That was right before he took a couple a caps in the head. I was actually talking to him."

"What did you two talk about?"

"I can't remember—I was pretty wasted." His laugh was self-deprecatingly sardonic. "But then I'm always wasted." He gulped down more smoke and let it out in short bursts. "Oh yeah—he asked me if I do drugs."

"Phil?"

"Yeah. I think it's the first thing he asked me after hello."

"Strange topic, isn't it?"

"I guess he took one look at me and knew—being a doctor and all."

"So you are doing drugs?"

"It's the way I get through my days," Stupan said reasonably. "Crystal meth, mostly. Oxycontin, sometimes Percodan. Oh yeah, I smoke pot, too—all day long." He seemed perfectly happy to confess it to me, as if taking drugs was a hobby like stamp collecting. "I did a doobie today before I got out of bed. I did another one in my car before I come up here."

"That's what you and Phil talked about? Drugs?"

"Ya."

"Nothing else?"

He shook his head. "It's not like him and me have much in common. His family was rich, so he prob'ly got a nice cushy draft deferment in college, while I got shipped out right after graduation to get my ass shot at." He took another drag and held the smoke in his lungs for a long time before expelling it. If I hadn't seen him shake an unfiltered Camel out of his pack, I would have sworn he was smoking a joint right in front of me.

Stupan's smile was gentle, beatific. "He wanted to talk about drugs with me—but I wanted to talk to him about my father."

"Your father?"

"When I came back from 'Nam," Stupan said, "I was pretty much a mess." He grinned pleasantly. "I still am. Anyway, my dad got upset with me, me being unemployable and a stoner and all when I come back home, and with all the stress, he started having heart problems."

"What kind?"

He shrugged. "It was too complicated for me. I knew Kohn from the neighborhood, so I talked him into seeing my old man about it. Kohn was a cardiac resident, running a sort of test program on some of his heart patients, and he talked my dad into being one of the subjects. As it turned out, he was giving half his patients a drug called—Jesus, I can't even remember the name. But a lot of that group got better."

"What did the other control group take?"

"I dunno what they call it—but they got sugar pills of some kind that didn't do a damn thing for them."

"Your father was getting the real thing, Stupan—or placebo?"

He looked lost. "Placebo—what's that?"

"Uh—phony pills. Pills that don't do anybody any good." He looked even more lost. "Sugar pills."

"Yeah, right," he said. "My father was gettin' them. So he took them and he just got worse and worse. Finally we pulled him out of there and sent him to a different doctor in another hospital—but he was all fucked up by then. He lived another seven or eight years after that, but he never felt right again. About his heart."

"Did you and Phil argue about that Friday night?"

He ran his hand through his hair, making it more disheveled than when he'd come in. "He told me I didn't know a fucking thing about drugs except the kind I buy from guys on the street—and he said that's why I was being an asshole to him about my father."

I asked the next question carefully. "Did that make you feel like killing Phil Kohn Friday night?"

"Ah, Milan—my dad's been gone for almost twenty years now. It was too late for me to get mad."

I sat back in my chair. "How do you make a living these days?"

"Not doing much. I'm on 80 percent disability. I stretch that out a little by doing some car repairs and carpentry jobs—I get paid under the table so the Feds can't fuck me up. It's not what you'd call a career." He grimaced. "Not like big-shot doctor Phil Kohn."

"He's not a big shot anymore," I said.

"Nope. He's one dead-ass motherfucker." He squashed out his cigarette butt in my ashtray. "I wonder which one of us *did* take him out Friday." He cocked his head almost prettily. "Was it you, Milan?"

Stupan left soon after, presumably to disappear into the drug haze in which he functioned, and I was left with my lists of phone numbers and my thoughts. He'd been open with me, as open as he was able. He let me know he'd disliked Kohn as much as the rest of us.

For a guy who said bye-bye to the police force a decade ago, I've been involved in all sorts of things, up to and including murder. In each instance, though, I'd been in the wrong place at the wrong time, or involved in a harmless-seeming situation that turned deadly, or even had someone carrying my phone number with them when they died. But I'd never before been officially included in a group of suspects with motives.

Thanks to Lieutenant Florence McHargue, then, for this current honor.

The rest of the graduating class? Let's see: Danielle Webber Magruder, a long-ago high school flame of Phil Kohn's. Jack Siegel, wearing goat horns Kohn had fitted him with. Bernie Rothman? Alenka Tavcar? Bitsy Steinberg? The strange, unsettling Ted Lesnevich with his hatchet face, all cruel angles. There were probably several others I hadn't spoken to yet. Phil Kohn hadn't spread around very much goodwill in his lifetime. Even Alex Cerne or Sonja Kokol could have quickly slipped into the hotel garage to squeeze off two rounds into Kohn's skull—as unlikely as that seemed.

And why had they both been so dead set against my going to work for Danielle's husband, Ben Magruder, to clear the name of Tommy Wiggins?

I wondered about something else, too. The zonked, burnt-out Stupan Godic, who'd just weaved out of my office and nearly fallen down the stairs, was hardly the most reliable of witnesses—but if his memory of Friday night wasn't too fuzzy, what was Phil Kohn's great interest in his recreational drug taking?

I made furious notes on my yellow pad, realizing I had too many classmates to interview. It would take more than a month to run down all the revelers—assuming all of them would be willing to talk. I needed some trustworthy professional help. Hell, Tommy Wiggins would pay for it.

I flipped open my Rolodex and reached for the phone.

Elizabeth Steinberg Miller, known in high school as "Bitsy," was wealthily married and bored. She filled her days running an antique shop on Larchmere Boulevard in Cleveland, just over the boundary from Shaker Heights. Nearby Shaker Square has become rejuvenated in the past few years, and Bitsy's business enjoyed some collateral success because of it. When I walked in, three browsers were circulating through the narrow aisles between antique displays, examining the kind of ugly glassware my Auntie Branka used to have in her cupboards back in the fifties. Now they were priced ridiculously high.

Bitsy was speaking earnestly with another customer at her ornate desk, but looked startled when she saw me. She bounced back quickly, though, smiling and waving while she schmoozed her customer until a sale was made of a ghastly brown lamp with a fringed shade, from a Victorian home near the turn of the last century. I'd worry if I had to die in a room with a lamp in it like that. I couldn't see the amount of the check the customer wrote, but whatever she paid for the little monstrosity was too much.

When Bitsy finally came over to greet me, her eyes were confused. I hadn't called in advance to tell her I was coming.

"What a nice surprise, Milan," she told me in a tone indicating it wasn't a nice surprise at all. "I didn't know you're interested in antiques."

"I'm not," I said. "Is there someplace we can talk?"

She put her left hand to her cheek. Her engagement and wedding ring set looked heavy enough to use as a paperweight. "Is something wrong?"

"I'll tell you about it in private."

Her little office in the back of the store was furnished in Spartan fashion—an old thrift-shop desk with an assembly-required chair from OfficeMax, a metal folding chair opposite, and an Apple computer. This was not for the customers to see. We sat down and I told her why I was there and for whom I was working. That raised her eyebrows.

"My God," she said. "I know the police treated us all like suspects, but I had no idea they were zeroing in on Tommy Wiggins." She chewed most of the lipstick off her lower lip, leaving a light pink stain on her teeth.

"Did you know Phil Kohn pretty well in school?"

"I guess so," she said. "Phil and I were both Jewish, so we ran in the same crowd. Just like I imagine most of your friends at St. Clair were Serbian."

"Slovenian," I said, annoyed. "Do you remember Phil being popular?"

"He was an abrasive kid, even back then. No one was particularly enamored of him."

"Anyone he hung around with, especially?"

"Gary Mishlove and Jack Siegel, I think. They wound up working in science in one way or another. Phil wasn't really good pals with geeks like Gary and Jack, but they helped him with his science homework. He always asked them the answers to homework questions. Even me. Studying seemed beneath him."

"Because his parents had money?"

That got a laugh out of her. "Phil's father owned a business, but that didn't make them rich."

In the land of the blind, I thought, the one-eyed man is king—and that made Phil Kohn's late father a crown prince at the very least.

"Phil was too short for most sports," Bitsy said. "But he was on the swim team, I remember that."

Good for Bitsy—I had *not* remembered. "Any of the swim team there Friday night?"

She patted fussily at her hair. "You don't really expect me to know everybody on the swim team forty years ago, do you?"

"I can check the yearbook and find out who they were—if I can find the yearbook."

She drummed her carefully manicured nails on the top of the metal desk, making the clicking sound of a Chihuahua running across a linoleum floor. "Is that it, Milan? For the questions?"

"Just a few more, Bitsy. Do you remember the Holly Hop? The Christmas dance in our senior year?"

She blushed prettily. "I was Queen of the Holly Hop—except nobody voted. They just picked my name out of a hat. But I loved it anyway."

"And Tommy Wiggins was the king."

She paled under her makeup foundation as she riffled through her memory files. "Gosh, that's right. I'd forgotten all about that."

"Friday night, did Tommy seem okay to you?"

"I didn't know him well enough to tell if he was okay or not. I didn't pay that much attention." She looked at me directly, her eyes flinty. "What do *you* remember about the Holly Hop?"

"Not much," I said. "But I wasn't wearing a crown to get my picture taken. Did you dance with Tommy?"

"One dance," she said, "as the King and Queen. He couldn't dance at all, the Irish klutz. I danced with several guys that day—Jack Siegel and Gary Mishlove . . ."

"And Phil?"

"I don't think so. I danced with Maurice Paich, too." She giggled.

"What?"

"Maurice. He was really 'on' that day. He was quoting Shakespeare all over the place, hoping people would notice him."

"Shakespeare?"

"Oh yes, stuff about kings and queens he thought was appropriate, I guess. Us girls all remember when he recited some line about grabbing a circumcised dog by the throat and stabbing him."

I knew which quote she meant—from *Othello*—but I didn't explain it to her. I think she really believed the stabbing victim *was* a circumcised dog.

"Maurice always quoted from plays with an English accent," Bitsy Steinberg continued. "He was so damn dramatic. He was good-looking back then—he still is, I guess—and very talented. But he was such a goddamn flake! I mean, what high school senior goes around quoting Shakespeare all the time?"

"He and Tommy Wiggins were the two arty types in our class, Bitsy. Both of them stayed in show business—Maurice on the radio locally and Tommy, naturally, on the Broadway stage. He's been more successful than anyone imagined."

"Oh, yes!" she gushed. "It's fun knowing someone famous, isn't it?" she preened. "He won a Pulitzer Prize."

"After he threw that drink in Phil Kohn's face, I'll bet Tommy's wishing he wasn't quite so famous."

She immediately sobered. "Right." She rubbed her upper arms with her hands and stood up. "Well, what happened was awful, and I hope they catch whoever did it," she said, but her thoughts were suddenly elsewhere, and I immediately got the idea I was being politely dismissed.

Larchmere Boulevard isn't that far from my apartment at the top of Cedar Hill in Cleveland Heights, so I stopped home, made myself a peanut butter and jelly sandwich and a cup of tea, and then rummaged around in my closet until I found a dusty copy of the *Forum*, our high school yearbook. I took it back to the office with me to peruse after my two o'clock appointment. I wanted to see who had been on the boys' swimming team with Phil Kohn.

CHAPTER SEVEN

Like me, Suzanne Davis is a private investigator. We don't see each other often, because she plies her trade in Lake County, northeast of the city. She's a very attractive woman in her fifties, and today, in my office, she wore one of the pleated miniskirts she favored to show off her excellent legs, accompanied by black tights and a dazzling red sweater. She's wise-cracking, hard-nosed, has a black belt in karate, and is highly skilled at her job. She's a lot more like the stereotypical fictional private eye in popular fiction than I am.

A few years ago she'd helped me on a case I couldn't have cracked without her, although at the end we'd disagreed about how to resolve it. I was hoping she'd back me up this time.

She seemed to enjoy the view from my office. My nearly floor-to-ceiling windows overlooked the river, Tower City, Progressive Field (which used to be named Jacobs Field and is still referred to by everyone as "The Jake"), and The Q. Suzanne didn't like sports complexes, but she loved watching the gulls flying in graceful circles, then dipping madly into the water and rising again with a flapping fish.

"It's dumb, Milan," she said.

"What?"

"Everybody calls those damn birds out there seagulls."

"So what?"

"We're about seven hundred miles from the nearest ocean."

"What are we supposed to call them, then? Lake gulls? River gulls?"

"Why not just gulls?"

"Because," I said. "*Gull* is a verb meaning to cheat or lie. It's also a noun—someone easily tricked or cheated. You think those birds are screwing with you?"

Suzanne laughed. "Somebody always is." She tilted her head a little to look at me. "You just got a haircut, didn't you?"

"Last Thursday."

She sighed. "Why does every man in the world always look like a little boy right after his haircut? So, what's the excitement? Have you met another in your long, dreary parade of 'right' girls?"

"Don't start in on me, Suzanne. Let me tell you why I called you." And I brought her up to speed on the Phil Kohn killing, including the sad tale of the Holly Hop, and Tommy Wiggins rising to the surface of the police department's soup as the primary suspect.

"I read about it in the paper," she said. "Just your luck, huh, Milan?"

"Trouble is like mosquitoes—it always finds me and takes a bite."

"The paper missed reporting that Tommy Wiggins was involved," Suzanne said. "It said he was there, but there was nothing about throwing the drink."

"That's because he hasn't been arrested."

"Yet." She shook her head, curls bouncing. "He actually threw his drink in Kohn's face? That was pretty baroque, wasn't it? What was he thinking?"

"Probably not that Kohn would get shot an hour later."

"Who's his lawyer?"

"Ben Magruder."

"I know about him. He's an asshole."

"He's my employer, temporarily," I said, "and married to one of my classmates, Danielle Webber. She was the school's reigning belle—Kohn dated her in high school."

"Was Kohn a hunka-hunka?"

I laughed. "Not even close. He was short and pudgy."

"I'll bet he was taller when he stood on his wallet. Ah, well—for every man there's a woman." She uncrossed her legs and then recrossed them the other way. "So, what is it you want me to do?"

I'd prepared two rosters of those who'd attended the reunion, divided evenly into two lists. "My fellow alumni," I said, handing her one list. "Find out if they had a relationship with the deceased, and whether they noticed anything Friday night, even if it seems unimportant. There are damn few people in the world who liked Phil Kohn—and he was a real player, which might have made someone furious."

She nodded. "The curse of the loose zipper."

"You know the drill. If anybody seems hinky, tell me."

"Is this on your dime? I don't like taking money from you, Milan."

"The client will pay for it."

"Right—Tommy Wiggins. With all his plays and movies and Tonys and Oscars, he must be raking it in."

"He didn't win an Oscar," I said. "He was only nominated."

She folded the list and put it into her already-bulging purse. "I suppose you want these answers yesterday?"

"One of life's great truths," I observed, "is that everything has to be done yesterday."

She stood up. "I might wind up talking to the killer."

"It's possible."

She didn't look a bit frightened. "Whoop-de-doo," she said.

When I told Ben Magruder on the phone that I'd engaged Suzanne's services on his client's behalf, he didn't sound enthused. "You had no right to bring someone else in on this case. You should have checked with me first. You can't just spend other people's money."

"You do," I said.

He didn't like that. "You hired her, you fire her."

"All right, I will. But if I have to do all the work myself, by the time I'm done your client might have spent several years in the Graybar Hotel. He's worth about five million bucks on the hoof—spending a few thousand more to clear himself of a murder charge sounds like one hell of a bargain."

He sounded wounded now, and sullen. "Who is this Suzanne Davis broad anyway? I never heard of her."

"She knows who *you* are," I said. I was glad he couldn't see me grinning. "And if you refer to her as a 'broad' where she can hear you, she's going to remove your left kidney with her car key."

His beleaguered sigh rushed through the receiver. "Deliver me from liberated women. Have you come up with anything yet?"

I recounted the meetings I'd held in the past two days. When I finished, Magruder said, "I'm getting a feeling about Jack Siegel. I mean, Kohn was screwing his wife."

"Not for the last ten years he wasn't."

"Ten years or ten minutes—when a married man has been that deeply injured and betrayed, he can carry the rage around with him for a long time."

I started doodling what I've always doodled since I was a teenager: gallows. I never draw anyone hanging from them, though—not even jerks like Ben Magruder, who was sounding vaguely betrayed himself.

"So a ten-year-old affair is a good motive for homicide?" I said.

That seemed to fluster him. "There's a hell of a difference between calling a guy a fag and sleeping with a guy's wife."

"Either way, isn't it a direct assault on a man's sexuality?"

He didn't answer for a moment, which got me wondering about his wife's longtime flirtation with Kohn and whether it had lasted after her marriage to Magruder.

Finally he said, "How about Kohn's wife? What's her name again? Adrienne? She sure as hell had a motive."

"She wasn't at the reunion."

"No, but she knew where he was going. She could have followed him there, waited in the garage . . ."

"The garage will have a videotape of what cars went in and out. But why that particular night?" I said. "I've already talked to her at length, and she says she's known for years that he was cheating on her. Why wait until his class reunion and kill him in a public place?"

"Maybe *because* it's public."

I made the noose on my most recent gallows look thicker with several more pencil strokes, hoping the rope could support a big, heavy man. "You may have something there, Mr. Magruder."

"Ben," he said with emphasis. "Please, all right? Call me *Ben*!"

"Sure," I said.

"You just don't want to entertain the idea that the perp is one of your classmates, do you, Milan?"

"I don't want to, but I'll keep looking anyway."

"I'm glad to hear that. Keep me informed." Barked out like an order. I don't like orders.

"Of course I will," I said. "I'm working for you."

I hung up, but didn't move from my chair until I finished the last doodle. I had seven different gallows scrawled on my yellow pad, each one slightly different in size. Some of them were drawn from the left and some the right. For a good forty years I've been wondering why I grew up doodling a gibbet in the first place. I've yet to arrive at an answer.

I do know that whenever I scrawl them while on the phone—and I never do when I'm off—it's because something is eating away inside me, scratching to get out. After our most recent conversation, I wondered whether Ben Magruder, Esquire, might be himself overwrought over whatever extracurricular activities his beautiful wife Danielle might have indulged in.

That made me squirm because years before, my wife Lila had cheated on me with the man she wound up leaving me for, and inviting to share her home—*our* home—and bed.

I remember the night she confessed her affair to me along with her plans to file divorce papers the next morning, saying I was too strong a man for her tastes, too rigid, too uncompromising—and that she was tired of arguing with me all the time. "You're a good person, Milan," she said, "but I just can't deal with you anymore. Joe and I never fight, and he never insists on getting his own way. It's easier with him."

It was easier for Lila, I guess, because they've been together for more years than Lila and I were married. Was it easier for Joe? I didn't know.

I didn't care.

So Magruder wanted me to find a better suspect for Phil Kohn's killing than the famous and talented Tommy Wiggins, and he'd been at the reunion Friday night himself with his wife Danielle—a woman who'd dated Kohn when they were both sixteen. I doubt he even realized it, but Magruder was every bit a suspect himself.

Sorry—Ben.

Ted Lesnevich's bio listed him as the CEO of Erieside Enterprises, whatever that was. His office was in a squat old building on Superior Avenue near East 18th Street, not far from the glittering red-brick-and-glass headquarters of the *Plain Dealer*. It's one of those industrial buildings, formerly a factory or warehouse, that gives Cleveland its patina of working class and Rust Belt. As old and reliable as it is, parts of the city look as if they're about to crumble into dust. I love Cleveland, but it's a black-and-white town, especially in the wintertime. Its look—full of old buildings like this one—represents its work ethic and pride and, lately, loneliness.

Since I'd be in the neighborhood, I decided to ring up my pal Ed Stahl at *The Plain Dealer*. He's a veteran reporter and columnist and a Pulitzer winner, and despite his personality quirks—he's cranky and irascible about 90 percent of the time—he is one of my best friends. I arranged to meet him for a drink later.

Ed is smart as hell, and what he doesn't know about the movers and shakers of Greater Cleveland isn't worth knowing. He'd had several days to catch up on whatever juicy Kohn murder news might be circulating. Maybe he could point me in a novel direction.

You never know.

But I had to talk with Ted Lesnevich first. Part of the job.

When I stepped off the creaking elevator and through the door of Ted Lesnevich's office, with the firm's name in old-fashioned gold lettering on a pane of opaque glass, I saw immediately that he was not only the CEO of Erieside Enterprises, but the all-purpose employee as well. The office consisted of one room, meanly furnished with a scarred wooden desk and a computer cart. The only other illumination besides gray light leaking through the dirty window came from a fluorescent table lamp with a green glass shade that made Lesnevich's hard-planed features look like a death mask. He sat in shirtsleeves behind his desk, a cigarette bobbing at one corner of his mouth. The whole room stank of stale tobacco. However he made a living in that office, he probably didn't have many visitors.

When I came in he was on the phone. He looked at me and said into the mouthpiece, "I'll call you back," and hung up, slowly and deliberately. He leaned his elbows on the desk; he wasn't surprised to see me.

"I figured you'd be around," he said. His lips were pulled back into a sneer, and many of his teeth showed when he talked. The canine teeth were pointed, and made him look as though he devoured little children for lunch. "A high-profile guy like Phil Kohn gets iced, and an even higher-profile guy like Tommy Wiggins looks good for it to the cops—and guess who's there when it happens? You, Milan—playing hero like you always do, hoping to see your name in the papers. That's just the kind of thing a media suck like you always gets your nose into, hoping for another one of those stories on the front page of the local section with a fifteen-year-old picture of you. Now you're looking to hang the murder on me, right? Because I was never one of the 'in' crowd."

"I can't figure why you dislike me, Ted, considering I haven't said more than two words to you in my life."

"It's *because* you never said more than two words to me in your life." He motioned to a chair. "Go ahead, take a load off your gumshoes. I know this isn't a social visit."

I unbuttoned my parka and sat down. The manufacturers had said in an enclosed brochure that it wasn't a parka at all, but a "cold weather system" with a heavy metal zipper. I don't know about that, but I was certain it would keep me warm chasing penguins in Antarctica.

"I hate being backed into a corner," I said.

He shrugged. "The best defense is a good offense."

"What are you defending against?"

"You—because you bore the shit out of me. So ask your questions and then go home."

"If you insist. How close were you to Phil Kohn in school?"

"As close as Seattle is to Key West. He was a Jew with a rich father and I was a poor Slovenian with a mother who drank too much and no father at all. How close do you think we were?"

"Did you see him since we all graduated?"

Something in his face changed imperceptibly, transmuting his expression into a lupine grin. "I saw him around."

"Often?"

He shrugged again.

"Once a week?"

"No."

"Once a year?"

"More."

"How much more?"

"Gee," he said, fumbling with his papers to impress me, "I have to look in my diary."

"Where did you see him?"

Lesnevich gave me an eighth-note laugh, just one short burst. "Around."

"Friendship or business?"

"I don't have friends, Jacovich."

"I can see why. What business are you in?"

"I told you the other night—sales."

"What do you sell?"

He rubbed his left knuckles with the fingers of his right hand, his brows lowering over his eyes. "Recreational products."

"Like athletic equipment?"

This time his laugh was more of an arpeggio. "Sure. Jockstraps."

"How many more guesses do I get?"

He cocked an eyebrow. "Smart guys shouldn't need more guesses."

"Then I'd have to say you're either a drug dealer or a pimp."

He flushed with irritation. "Pick the one you like."

"Drugs, then," I said. "Because even hookers have some standards."

His eyes turned dangerous, shadowing his sharp cheekbones. "No more games. We're done talking."

"Would you rather talk to the police? That can be arranged."

Lesnevich chuckled. "Send the National Guard over here if that's what floats your boat. I'm a legitimate businessman—and you can't prove different. My books are clean. So don't threaten me with cops—it doesn't scare me. It just makes my ass ache."

"Then why don't you just cooperate with me—for old times' sake?"

He jerked his head back to get a strand of his messy slicked-back hair out of his eyes. "You don't get it, do you? You and I don't *have* any old times. And I don't give a rat's ass for Tommy Wiggins one way or the other. What did either of you ever do for me?"

"Is everything a quid pro quo?"

"That's how the world works, yes."

"Okay, then. Do you ever go to the movies?"

"No," Lesnevich said. "The smell of popcorn makes me gag."

"I thought you might have seen a few of the movies Wiggins wrote and they made you laugh."

He shook his head. "*You'd* make me laugh if you weren't so annoying—you and your poor, harassed millionaire."

"You have something against millionaires?"

"Not a damn thing," he said, cocking his head as though he were adding up his assets. "I happen to be one myself."

Now I *was* impressed. "Business is that good, huh?"

"When wasn't it?" He squished the butt of his cigarette into an already-brimming ash tray. "I don't have a problem in the world. I only showed up Friday night to tell a few people—arrogant, better-than-thou guys like you—just how much I resented them all these years."

"Did you tell Phil Kohn off, too?"

"Nah. I told him off years ago." He seemed to be enjoying the memory. "That one was particularly sweet."

"Why?"

"Because the snotty little rich kid who turned snotty little rich doctor—until somebody iced him—was a stone junkie."

That made me sit up a little straighter.

"Surprised, are you?" he went on. "Amphetamines. The guy was a speed freak—and one of my most valued customers."

"A doctor has access to all the drugs he wants."

"Not really. Hospitals keep track of drug supplies. Even a doctor can only write himself so many prescriptions until a red flag goes up."

I assimilated the information. "How often did he buy?"

"Every few months—in small quantities. Mine wasn't the only store he patronized."

"Who else?"

"Who cares?"

I put my hands into the pockets of my parka. "That doesn't look good for you, Ted. Maybe he owed you money."

"Nobody owes me money," he said smugly. "My business is strictly cash-and-carry. No checks, no plastic, no paper trail—not with anyone. So send the cops up here, because they won't find a fucking thing." He leaned back in his chair and smiled past my shoulder. "It'd be a real bad idea if you did that, though."

"That sounds like a threat."

"I don't threaten. I don't have to." His eyes drilled right through me. Then he lost interest and picked up the phone receiver. "Call it a little friendly advice," he said without looking at me, dialing a number he knew by heart. "You know—for old times' sake."

CHAPTER EIGHT

I've been hanging out at Vuk's Tavern on St. Clair Avenue near East 55th Street my entire adult life. I still go there sometimes, even though I don't live in the neighborhood anymore. On my twenty-first birthday I had my first legal drink—a Stroh's beer, no glass—at Vuk's long mahogany bar. My first beer after returning home to Cleveland from Vietnam was at Vuk's bar, too. Vuk, the owner/bartender, had named the establishment after himself, and although I've never popped in there at seven A.M. when it opens for business, I'm certain he opens and closes the place, too. He's in his seventies now, but he still has all his hair, and he still wears it in the same style. He sports the same bushy walrus mustache, too—and the "pacifier" he keeps behind the bar, an old Reggie Jackson Louisville Slugger, has been there as far back as I can remember.

You don't go in there and order a grasshopper or a margarita—not if you want to stay healthy. Vuk doesn't serve "cocktails"—he pours booze, and nothing fancy or expensive, either. The front room always smells of beer, even though he mops and cleans it himself first thing every morning. Vuk's Tavern is a living, breathing reminder of Cleveland's good old days.

His full name is Louis Vukovich, but everybody has always called him Vuk except his mother, who referred to him as "Lou" or "Louie," and sometimes "Little Louie" because he was named after his late father. She's gone now, passed on at the age of ninety-one—and his first name is barely a memory.

Ed Stahl doesn't come into Vuk's unless he's with me—he prefers his own favorite joints downtown. On this particular evening he was at the far end of the bar nursing a Jim Beam, which is his poison of choice. I use the word *poison* advisedly because any alcohol was toxic to his chronic ulcer, but he didn't seem to care. He'd shrugged into one of his trademark rumpled tweed jackets—hardly the attire of a Pulitzer Prize–winning journalist. His hopelessly 1940s horn-rimmed glasses were set low on his nose, giving him the appearance in the *Plain Dealer* newsroom of a dissolute, too-old Clark Kent. He dourly ignores the new law against smoking in public, and smoke from the ever-present pipe clenched between his teeth rose into the air and blended with the tavern atmosphere. Above Ed's head the white pipe smoke made it look like the College of Cardinals just elected a new pope.

I don't know anyone else who still smokes a pipe.

I took the stool next to him, and he grunted at me as our eyes met in the mirror behind the bar. Ed is always the proverbial Gloomy Gus, and today was no exception. He was well into his Jim Beam, and for all I knew, it was not his first of the day. I just nodded at Vuk and he brought me what I'd always drunk at this bar.

Ed was glancing dourly at the small TV set at the end of the room as it broadcast the six o'clock news. He had a withering disregard for television journalism, especially the local variety, although he admired the striking beauty of the Channel 12 news anchor, blond and regal Vivian Truscott, who at the moment was smiling down at us like a kindly Madonna wearing a high-fashion suit. Ed said, "Was that your high school reunion the other night where somebody got killed? I thought it might be. You actually went to it? Jesus, Milan. And you're involved?"

"Peripherally." I proceeded to spin out the Tommy Wiggins story. The papers and TV newscasts had mentioned him, St. Clair's most famous graduate, as a reunion attendee, but nobody had outed him as the police's favorite murder suspect.

Ed listened without expression. "Throwing a drink in a man's face?" He gulped at his Jim Beam and grimaced when it hit bottom and watered his ulcer. "That was pretty pissy. Why did he do it?"

"This isn't for publication, Ed."

"Fine."

"Back in high school—at a Holly Hop Christmas dance—Kohn accused Tommy Wiggins of being gay."

"Is he?"

"Hardly."

Ed laughed once—his laughs were always short, blunt, and to the point. "So Phil Kohn called him a queer and he waited forty years to do something about it?"

"It looks that way."

His pipe tobacco was almost dead and he sucked at it manfully until it got hot again. The dottle inside the stem rattled around like a backed-up sink drain. "I thought Wiggins was married to some sex kitten movie star."

"He was. Not anymore. He's spent his whole life proving to the world that Phil Kohn was wrong."

He gazed at me over his glasses. "You want background from me?"

"If you have any."

"I always have background—it's how I make my living. When the story broke Monday I did some research—to see if I could get a column out of it."

"And?"

"Not enough there for me to write about. But I found out the late Dr. Kohn was a jerk. I hope he wasn't a friend of yours."

"I hardly knew him."

"Okay. Then he was a double jerk."

"Why?"

"The gals who cover the society beat all knew him, and they say he was pretty arrogant. But I specifically refer to four medical malpractice lawsuits filed against him, the most recent sometime last year. He's a cardiac guy, so you can imagine what those suits were like."

"Did he lose them?"

"I don't know if they were dropped or settled quietly, but none of them ever got to court." He puffed up more malodorous smoke—Ed must pack his worn leather tobacco pouch with pencil shavings. "Malpractice is a bitch kitty to prove. They say doctors always bury their mistakes."

"I thought his medical reputation was pretty good."

Ed shrugged it away. "His reputation was good as a society doctor. He and his wife went to all the right parties and benefits. He was—visible. That's how one gets oneself known." He cleared his throat. "I'm told he also fancied himself a ladies' man."

"You're told?"

"He actually made a move at one of the reporters at a Heart Association benefit a few years back. A crude one at that, she says—with Kohn's wife five feet away at the time. Maybe he thought our reporter would write about him more. As it turned out, she never mentioned his name again in the paper."

"Which reporter was that?" I said.

"Give me a break, Milan—I work with her. But from the skimpy picture I got from the files, there's no dearth of suspects in Kohn's killing."

"Dearth?"

Ed grinned. "They pay me good money to use good words like that."

"Good," I said, taking a long pull at my Stroh's and waving at Vuk to get his attention and perhaps another Stroh's. "It makes my investigation tougher when there's a dearth."

I grabbed a quick, satisfying dinner at Sterle's Slovenian Country House on East 55th Street, not far from Vuk's. The restaurant has been there forever, serving Slovenian comfort food, and on weekends, you can polka your heart out to a small but effective polka band. Then I made my way eastward, to a brick house that once was almost as familiar to me as my own, and rang the doorbell, hoping my welcome would at least be civil.

Matt Baznik still lived in the city of Euclid, where he'd moved more than twenty-five years ago. He and I, Marko Meglich, Rudy Dolsak, Sonja Kokol, and Alex Cerne had been close childhood friends, and our relationships had lasted into adulthood.

Part embarrassment and part paternal guilt made Matt quit

talking to me after his son's problems, and our friendship ended like a cracked ping-pong ball falling off the edge of a table. Except for Friday evening, when he and his wife had studiously avoided me, I hadn't seen him since.

I approached the Baznik home with trepidation. I needed their feedback. I could have let Suzanne Davis talk to them, but I chose to view it as an opportunity to try reconnecting.

Rita Marie Baznik looked stunned when she saw me on her front porch. Apple-cheeked and prettily plump, she'd been doing the supper dishes, and she wiped her hands nervously on her apron. She still wore an apron in the kitchen, like a Norman Rockwell mom who had time-traveled from the 1950s into today's world of fast food and microwaves.

"Milan," she whispered.

"Hello, Rita Marie. How are you?"

She was too flustered to answer.

"We didn't get a chance to talk Friday," I said, not pointing out the obvious—that they'd ignored me. "So I'm taking the opportunity—even though I'm here on business."

I heard Matt from inside the house. "Who is it, hon?" he said, and then appeared behind her. He looked bewildered when he saw me. His eyes darted around, searching for an escape hatch. "Uh—hiya, Milan."

"Hey, Matt—good to see you." I stuck out my hand and he took it tentatively, perhaps worried where it had been before. "I hope I didn't catch you in the middle of dinner."

"No," Rita Marie said. "We're finished."

I stood on the porch, a cold wind skirling around my ankles, forcing its way into the collar of my cold weather system parka. "Mind if I come in for a few minutes?"

Rita Marie flapped her apron, embarrassed. "Where are our manners? Sure, come on in."

In the vestibule I hung my parka on the antique wooden tree just inside the front door and moved into the living room, remembering that I'd entered here more than a hundred times before—back when I was welcome. I lowered myself onto the sofa—the overstuffed corner easy chair was reserved for the man of the house. Matt perched on its edge in case he had to get up suddenly. Rita Marie stood in the archway between living and dining rooms, fussing with her apron.

"How's Paulie doing?" I said.

Matt's face closed up; I'd picked open the scab again. "He's okay."

"He's working at Murray's Auto Store on Mayfield Road," Rita Marie added. "And taking night courses at Tri-C."

"That's great," I said. I waited for one of them to ask about my kids, but apparently it didn't occur to either of them.

Matt was trying to think of something else to say. Finally he came up with: "So, uh, what's the deal?"

"I'm working for a lawyer who's involved with the Kohn killing."

He frowned slightly. "How do you fit with that?"

"Did either of you see when Tommy Wiggins threw the drink at Phil?"

"Oh, my!" Rita Marie said. "That was so awful."

"Did you talk to Phil at all on Friday?"

Matt looked away. "I don't remember."

"Sure we did, Matt," his wife chimed in. "We said hi to him just before the drink thing happened. We were over by where the DJ was set up."

"Oh. Yeah, right." He looked at me fiercely. "But that's all we did, say hello. We didn't hang out together, so I didn't pay no attention to him. I wasn't looking; I didn't know there'd be questions."

"I'm just wondering if you saw or heard anything that can help me—or Wiggins."

"Nah." Matt, head down, almost swallowed the sound he made.

"I saw him talking to Maurice Paich too, Milan," Rita Marie said. "Briefly—and then to Byron Hoogwerf. What's her name again, Matt? Byron's wife?"

"Heidi." He offered the information grudgingly, as if it cost him something. "Her name is Heidi."

Rita Marie pushed an errant lock of hair from her forehead. "It didn't seem like a pleasant conversation, either."

"They were arguing?"

She shook her head. "I wasn't close enough to hear. It was their—what do you call it, their body language? They looked mad."

"Okay," I said. I didn't write anything down because my scribbling would have spooked them. I was taking mental notes like crazy, though.

"Look, we don't know anything, Milan. You know?" Matt leaned forward, agitated, ready to pounce—except that wasn't part of his personality. "We seen what everybody else seen. That's all."

Too close to a dismissal. I stood up. "Well, thanks for talking to me." Matt stood up, too. Nobody said anything.

A few years ago an Ohio couple returned home one evening to discover a black bear in their living room, and while they didn't want to kill him, all they wanted was to get him out of the house. Matt made me feel like that bear.

"It was great to see you both," I said.

"Yeah." Matt stuck his hands in his pockets to avoid another shake. "Well, take it easy."

I shrugged into my parka. Rita Marie took down a heavy sweater from the clothes tree. "I'll walk you out."

"Rita Marie . . ." Matt said.

She whirled on him, blue eyes snapping. "I'm walking him to his car! We're not having an affair between here and the curb, for God's sake."

Stung, Matt turned on his heel and stalked silently into the kitchen.

"Rita, you don't have to walk me—"

"Come on, Milan!" she ordered, and her tone brooked no argument. We descended the steps and carefully made our way down the icy walk, Rita Marie wrapping the sweater around her shoulders. When we got to my car she turned and put a hand on my chest. "It was good seeing you."

"I miss you guys."

"Matt's a proud man," she said, her voice chattering from the cold. "He's humiliated that you saw him at his weakest, and embarrassed that he needed your help."

"That was a decade ago, Rita Marie."

"It's as good as just yesterday to Matt."

"He acts like he hates my guts," I said.

"Oh, he doesn't. We're both grateful. It's hard for him to face you." She took her hand from my chest and hugged herself against the icy wind.

"It's been a lot of years."

"I know—and it might be more. But you and Marko were his oldest friends. Just wait—someday he'll invite you over to watch a game or something, and I'll cook one of your favorite dinners like I used to. Like Segadin goulash. Remember?" Her eyes were bright, and I could tell she was close to crying. "Give him time, Milan."

"I have to," I said, my half-frozen fingers fumbling with my car key. "I don't have any choice."

We've all felt rejected sometime, haven't we? When someone to whom you're mightily attracted says he or she isn't interested, or worse, ignores you—when you're turned down for the job you wanted or for the team you were born to play for—or when someone who was once your friend treats you like a half-grown rat they've found in their kitchen, that's when rejection hurts.

Matt Baznik had figuratively slammed the door in my face. I understood his inappropriate pride and humiliation—I'm sometimes guilty of the same thing. Still, it hurt like a sonofabitch. I wish I'd never knocked on that door at all.

I drove through the mini-storm that had kicked its way into town that evening. When I was about ten minutes from home my cell phone chirped like an annoying canary. It took me three rings to claw it out of my pocket.

"Glad I got you," Suzanne Davis said. "I spent an interesting day."

I wanted to keep the conversation short. I dislike talking on my cell phone when I'm driving, and I hate other people who do, too. They're as much of a road menace as drunken teenagers.

"I'm still in Cleveland," Suzanne said. "Buy me a drink and I'll tell you about it."

"Sure."

"Nighttown in half an hour?"

I'd already spent an hour in a bar with Ed Stahl, and I was sick at the idea of it. "I've got plenty of booze," I said. "And all I want to do is wear my slippers. Why don't you come up?"

"Your apartment?" Her voice was playful, teasing. "Will you try to seduce me?"

"No."

"Rats!" she said.

CHAPTER NINE

Suzanne Davis walked into my apartment thirty minutes later, all business chic, in a gray pinstripe suit and medium heels, lugging an ostrich-leather executive attaché case and looking like a big-time senior executive. We must have seemed an odd pair, since I'd changed into sweatpants, a Kent State sweatshirt, and a disreputable pair of slippers with the heels run down in the back. It's the only pair I own, and I constantly walk around the apartment squishing the heels because it's too much trouble to bend down and adjust them—but then I've never considered myself a fashion plate.

I already had a beer, half finished. I poured her a bourbon on the rocks.

"I talked with some of your old schoolmates," she said, opening her case. "It was weird."

"Weird?"

"Meeting your school chums made me think of them as gawky, pimply teenagers from forty years ago." She giggled. "I guess I started thinking of you that way, too."

"Don't squeal to the principal that I'm drinking beer."

"A blue-collar high school usually turns out a cookie-cutter group. Your crowd is—eclectic."

I recounted to her all the people I'd interviewed that day. Some had been good friends, which made me uncomfortable. Then she pulled a notebook from her attaché case, settled back, and tucked her legs under her.

"My turn," she said. "I started this morning with Geraldine Bokar—Gerry Gabrosek to you." She scanned her notes. "Did you know she and her husband were world-class volleyball players? They have a load of trophies in their den. Some years back Gerry was rated the number 178th female volleyball player in the *world.* She said the New York Yankees' right fielder then . . ." She ran a finger down the page until she found the name she was looking for. "Paul O'Neill, I think—was rated 178 in Major League Baseball. So she must have been pretty good, ratings-wise."

"I never want to hear anything good about the New York Yankees," I cautioned. "Did the Bokars ever play volleyball with Dr. Kohn?"

"Hardly. But a few weeks before the reunion Kohn asked Sonja for a list of all the classmates who'd accepted—he wouldn't commit to showing up until he knew who else would be there. Then he called again last week to find out the names of the late registers. No other alum did that, Milan. Just Kohn."

"Maybe he wanted to come only if he knew someone specific would be there."

"Or," Suzanne said, "if someone specific *wouldn't* be there. Did you ask Kohn's wife?"

"She made a concerted effort not to know her husband's plans. He was a womanizer."

"Gerry Bokar said that Friday night when Kohn registered, he looked ready to dive into her tits."

"You should have seen her dress," I said. "Ignoring her tits is like ignoring the Grand Canyon."

"Yeah—but Kohn made an obvious and uncouth pass."

I turned the bottle in my hand. "I heard he was into younger women."

"For affirmation of his own sex appeal? It didn't really matter—young, old, fat, thin—he was an equal opportunity cock-hound. He could get the bird nineteen times in a row, but on the twentieth try—he shoots, he *scores!*" She flipped over a page. "I heard that from Heidi Hoogwerf."

"Who?"

"Byron Hoogwerf's wife. She was in a tight group with other married women Friday night, so you probably never met her."

"She didn't even go to St. Clair High with us. She was a West Side girl."

Suzanne sipped her bourbon—Maker's Mark. I'm not a bourbon drinker, but I always keep some in my apartment for visitors. "They'd met socially when Byron Hoogwerf sold Phil Kohn a disability insurance policy a few years ago."

I couldn't believe it. "Kohn nailed Heidi Hoogwerf?"

"She didn't confess because her husband was right there with us. But I have instincts about how she looked when I mentioned Kohn. Was it a long affair, a one-night stand, or something in between? Who knows? But I'd bet the farm that it happened." She pointed to her stomach. "I just feel it—here."

I let a sip of Stroh's roll around on my tongue like an oenophile tasting a 1964 Château Margaux—but it didn't taste any better than it always has. The late Phil Kohn, I was learning, lived an interesting life. He might have been a hale fellow well met in some other town, perhaps a sophisticated city like Chicago—but in Cleveland he'd crossed an invisible no-no boundary with married women.

There are different Cleveland rules for things like that. In Los Angeles everyone tries to fuck everyone else. In Las Vegas they'll fuck *anyone* else. In New York—at least in Manhattan—fucking is often connected to wealth or power or prestige. But despite Cleveland's roughhouse blue-collar image and the wealthy citizens' drive to make even more big money, anyone, male or female, who spends an inordinate amount of time hunting for a variety of sex partners, especially married ones, is generally regarded as a slut.

"Damn," I said.

"What?"

"A lot of my classmates are popping up as suspects."

"That's a good thing," she said, chuckling. She threw back the rest of her Maker's Mark. "Magruder hired you to take the cop heat off Tommy Wiggins and lay it on someone else. Be glad nearly everyone hated Kohn's guts as much as Wiggins. We've got an entire ensemble of Maybes."

"You think?"

"Do *you* think so? Is your conscience sticking in your throat when you're poking a stick at people you grew up with? Or are you glad you're doing a good job reconnecting with old school pals and turning up lots of would-be life takers?"

Even Suzanne was gouging me about upending the apple cart of my life—and somehow that hurt as much as the disdain I was racking up with my friends. I tossed down the rest of the beer, such a big swallow that it made my eyes tear.

"Delighted," I said.

When I arrived at my office fifteen minutes before nine the next morning, my voice mail light was flashing at me. I played back the single message, logged in at 8:07 A.M. The caller didn't have to identify herself. I'd recognize Lieutenant Florence McHargue's menacing voice anywhere.

"Jacovich, if I don't see your ass here within the hour, I'm going to set it on fire—personally."

Click.

Nice message. All the warmth of an Antarctic penguin who somehow missed out on the long march.

I didn't even take off my parka. I got to her office at the Third District just in time to save my ass from burning.

Having spent several years in blue and several more after I left the force just visiting, I'm as familiar with the Third District precinct house, on Payne Avenue and East 21st Street, as I am with the house in which I grew up. The station, built in Federalist style early in the twentieth century, had slowly but steadily fallen into disrepair, and was contemptuously called the Rock Pile until it was spiffed up enough to look clean and inhabitable to commuters who drove past it on the way downtown in the morning. The inside, however, still stinks of a century of lawbreakers and frightened victims, and to most cops it remains the Rock Pile.

There was a time when the Cleveland gangsters hanging out in the Third were glamorous, exciting, and even romantic in the literary sense—colorful, charming guys like Irish mobster Danny Greene and his Hungarian rival, Shondor Birns. They had good friends in the rich and fashionable social crowd as well as their pals from the criminal side, and athletes and entertainers, too.

The outlaws laughed, rollicked, and partied downtown in safety on the east side of the Cuyahoga River, and bought drinks for anyone who even said hello to them at places where they made their home away from home, like the Hickory House, and the Theatrical Grill on Short Vincent Street—both just memories now. Everybody had a good old time with the smiling tough guys, who had style and class all their own. That's why they used to call the police precinct the Roaring Third.

Danny and Shondor died thirty years ago, in separate car bombings—Shondor on West 25th and Lorain on the bank of the river, and Danny in a Beachwood parking lot where he'd spent his last afternoon with his dentist—and when the smoke cleared there was little left of either of them to mourn. That's why the Third District doesn't roar anymore. Today the criminals who are escorted through the Third District doors are pond scum with gold teeth and gold-plated Caddys, and their imaginations begin and end with violence. They've forgotten that when you're rich, powerful, and celebrated, you're expected to give back some of the money you've cadged and chiseled and stolen from honest people.

I was a patrol cop back then, not much more than a rookie. I'd met Birns and Green a few times—moments always strained with cops-and-robbers tension. But oddly enough I miss them today. They were part of the lively, colorful Cleveland history that's quietly faded away.

Florence McHargue—I never heard anyone refer to her as "Flo"—hasn't faded away, nor is she quiet. She rarely raises her voice, but her words are acid, and sound worse than yelling.

When I walked into her cluttered office she checked her watch. "You're a lucky man, Jacovich. You're about six minutes away from big trouble."

"Good morning to you, too, Lieutenant." I sat down.

She noticed, and her tone got even more sarcastic. "Please *do* sit down. Make yourself comfortable."

"I've got things to do today," I said. "So can we just cut the small talk? You can get to the business of chewing me a new one and then you can send me on my way."

"You're on *my* schedule. I'm not on yours."

Florence was a nice-looking woman when she wasn't snarling. She was in her mid-forties, and had dropped about ten pounds since I'd last seen her. Her straightened hair was always done up in a severe bun, but long enough to fall below her shoulders if she let it. Her burnished skin was coffee-colored with a dash of cream, and her eyes large and brown behind her glasses. With more attention to her hair and makeup—and a concerted effort to smile occasionally—she'd be really attractive.

But she hadn't earned her lieutenant's badge by being cute. Her bad temper on the Job, and perhaps off the job too, made sure she kept the rank—and the power. You can tell she enjoys the power.

"Jacovich, the way you're running your own investigation makes you seem like you look under beds the way old ladies do," she said. "You not only compromise this department's investigation, but you deny you're also a potential suspect in the murder of Philip Kohn."

"I'm not denying anything," I said. "So I guess I am a suspect, even if you know damn well I'm not."

"You're working for Ben Magruder." She mulled that over. "He was at the hotel Friday too, along with Wiggins. Now he's paying you to take the heat off his famous new client, who is a suspect too."

"So is everybody," I said, "including about a hundred hotel employees who were there that night, and the St. Clair grads who didn't show up at all. For all we know, it was someone from the medical community or the country club Kohn belonged to—or maybe an out-of-towner none of us has heard of. Come on, Lieutenant—give me some slack."

McHargue said, "You've been off the Job and out of a blue uniform too long. Did you forget police officers don't *give* slack—especially to hotshot private tin like you who get off on making us look bad?"

"How do I make the police look bad?"

"Let me count the ways." McHargue raised three fingers and began ticking the reasons off, starting with her index finger. "Showing up places you're not supposed to. Our people have to interview a witness or suspect who's pissed off and wrung dry because they already talked themselves out to you." After a pause the ring finger went down, too. "You find things out that might be important to our investigation—but you don't share them with us. Makes us look like holy asses."

The only finger still erect was the middle one—make of it what you will. "And when you *do* crack a case, which you can't legally shove your way into, your name hits the papers, and suddenly every mouth breather in town who believes half of what they read starts thinking you're the Caped Crusader—and that us real cops spend all our time eating free Dunkin' Donuts and taking kick-backs from guys we should throw in jail anyway."

I watched with perverse fascination as she mercifully lowered her middle finger. "Is that all?" I said.

She shuffled some papers around on her desk. "No it's not. How is it, Jacovich, that at your big-shot reunion Friday night, the only people of color in attendance were the waiters and bus people working for the hotel?"

I blinked. "Jesus—that didn't occur to me. I didn't really notice a lot of things Friday night, and after the squabble and then the report of Kohn's murder, I didn't even think about it anymore. So—I don't know why none of them showed up."

"There were *no* blacks in your school forty years ago?"

"There were a handful, yes," I said. "I played football with two of the guys. I have no idea why none of them joined us for the reunion. Maybe you should ask the people who sent out the invitations."

"Like Sonja Caruth?" she said. "The former Sonja Kokol?"

I nodded.

"I'm too busy, Jacovich. *You* ask her."

"Me?"

"You. Just out of curiosity—*my* curiosity."

"I'm too busy right now to take up valuable time easing your curiosity."

McHargue didn't smile. "You know what they say—if you want something done right, ask a busy person."

"That sounds suspiciously like an order."

"I don't care if it sounds like a Muslim from Baghdad singing 'Ave Maria' in an Orthodox synagogue. I *give* orders—that's why I carry a gold badge. The people who didn't show up at that reunion are just as suspect as all the ones who did—and that includes your strangely absent black classmates. So don't argue with me—for a change. Just do what I tell you."

I fought vainly to avoid any expression on my face, but it wasn't working. I felt my features changing, hardening—and I saw her watch them change. "Am I dismissed, Lieutenant?" I said.

"Just one more thing," McHargue said. "You stink on ice, Jacovich, and I don't like the best part of you."

"Just for that, you're out of my will."

"When they read your will, I'll be smiling. Look, this Kohn case is a visible fuck-up. A doctor is murdered, and some famous playwright is a prime suspect. It made newspapers in New York and L.A. on the weekend—even *Entertainment Tonight* mentioned it. There are visiting newsies in town from the coasts and Chicago to find out what's going on with big-shot Tommy Wiggins. Do you think with all the aggravation on my plate I need *your* shit, too?" She pushed her desk phone closer to me—an old-fashioned black phone that had probably been on that desk since the fifties. "You know Ben Magruder's number? Make me happy—call him and bow out. It's none of your goddamn business anyway."

"It *is* my business, for several reasons." I held up my own three fingers. "I have to make money to eat—and lawyer Magruder is paying me handsomely. You don't consider it ethical, but it's legal and you'll have to live with it." I dropped my index finger. "Kohn's murder is getting pushed on Wiggins. He's an old acquaintance, so I'm taking it personally. I work for what I care about."

I pushed my ring finger down toward my palm, but only left the middle one straight for two seconds. I didn't dare stretch my luck *or* my sense of humor with Florence McHargue. "Cleveland's my town. You may not have noticed, but unsolved crimes take place here. Some of them happen to little girls and boys, and some of them to adults. We all remember the Sam Sheppard case, the torso murders of Kingsbury Run, the Amy Mihaljevic disappearance—and the little girl, Shakira Johnson, found dead in a vacant lot. Until now, nobody's been nailed for her killing, either, and there are lots of others who never made the nightly news."

It wasn't the first time McHargue and I had butted heads—but I never stood up to her before. I think she was stunned.

"It's still early days," I continued. "But I'm damned if Phil Kohn's killing ends up in a box in the Cold Case room. Not my schoolmate, and not on my watch. If you want to lift my license, call Columbus and put in the paperwork to take it away from me—if you think you can. In the meantime—"

I stood up and moved to her door. "As I said earlier, I'm busy. My job might not be important to you, but it's vital to me—and to Tommy Wiggins, too."

I'd watched her face grow still, almost resigned while I talked. Now her expression had turned to controlled fury. "Don't forget what I asked you to do."

"I'll remember it with every beat of my heart—just because it's you."

"You think you're one pretty tough son of a bitch, don't you, Jacovich?"

"I don't just think so," I said.

CHAPTER TEN

I hadn't been introduced to Heidi Hoogwerf at the reunion. She was about ten years younger than our St. Clair graduating class and almost resembled her husband Byron, who was also pleasant looking without being anyone's idea of a hunk. He was that way in high school, too—forty years earlier, and maybe thirty-five pounds ago.

I got to their house in Richfield at about eleven o'clock. I hadn't been to Richfield in years. At one time the Cavs played there at a huge arena, the Richfield Coliseum, which was abruptly torn down after they moved downtown to The Q. A few blocks away there used to be a great restaurant, the Taverne of Richfield, with a great piano player in the lounge—but that's gone now, too. Richfield is a long haul south of Cleveland and not many people visit the way they used to—but it's still a pretty, peaceful suburb. From the look of the Hoogwerf house on a large, tree-filled lot, I could tell Byron had done well in the insurance business.

Heidi Hoogwerf opened the door, looking very distracted. I'd interrupted whatever she'd been doing on her laptop in the dining room.

"Sorry we didn't meet the other night," she said, slightly frazzled. I couldn't help noticing she dyed her hair too black and had chosen a makeup base that was too orange. "I wasn't sure who you are, but I asked Byron for his own memories about you, and I read your reunion bio."

"There wasn't much to tell."

"I googled you on the Internet."

"I don't think anybody ever googled me before."

"Really? There are lots of articles about you—you should get with the twenty-first century and look them up. You'll mostly get a kick out of them. You have a computer, don't you?"

"I do," I admitted, "but it never dawned on me to google myself."

"Well, did you google *me*?"

"All I know is that you're Byron's wife."

She frowned, not liking that. "The woman who works for you—for Milan Security? Suzanne Davis? She's been here already. I said all I had to say to her yesterday." She tossed her head.

"I want to check a few things with you again."

"You knew Byron in school, not me. Talk to him."

"This won't take but a few minutes, Heidi." I knew it would be uncomfortable for both of us. Since I'd spoken to Suzanne, I'd searched my conscience in vain for a way to ask Heidi Hoogwerf an invasively personal question in a kind way.

She looked longingly at her laptop. "I don't have all day. I work from home."

We installed ourselves on either end of the sofa. I'd forget the room the moment I left it. It was, like Heidi, neat, pleasant in an unassuming way, and wouldn't catch anyone's attention.

"Byron and Phil Kohn weren't close friends when they left school?"

If I hadn't been looking closely—as I always do—I wouldn't have noticed how her lips disappeared at the mention of Phil Kohn's name. "No. They went separate ways."

"How did Byron happen to sell him a policy?"

"Selling disability policies is Byron's field. He does particularly well with doctors. He saw Phil's picture in the paper after one of those benefits, and he called him."

"That's when they became friends?"

"Acquaintances. I told Ms. Davis this last night."

"Were you friends with his wife, too?"

"*Acquaintances!*" she said raggedly. "How many times must I tell you?"

"I just want to find out how well Byron knew him." I waited until she met my eyes. "And how well you did."

Her cheeks reddened beneath the foundation. "Are you asking a rude question?"

"A straight one, that's all."

"I wonder where it came from. Is that how you get your jollies?" She was working her way into a fine keen anger. "You study other people's shit, asking personal questions, and then go home and jerk off thinking about it?"

I shook my head sadly. "Wow, Heidi," I said.

She sprung up from the sofa, stalking the room slowly for a minute, not looking at me. Tigers confined in too-small zoo cages pace in exactly the same frustrated way. Then she stopped and crossed her arms protectively across her chest. "I don't want to be an item in a gossip column." Fright and loss rumbled low in her throat.

"I don't collect gossip," I said as gently as I could. "Or pass it around, either. I'm sorting out Phil's relationships—that's all."

"Every relationship affects every other relationship—like water rings emanating out from a tossed-in pebble. Is that how you figure?" Her rage was deserting her, leaving her only feeling trapped. "Will you shoot your mouth off to everyone? Like my husband?"

"Not unless one of you shot Phil."

She snorted nastily. "Not likely."

"Then probably not."

Her sigh was deep enough to ruffle the fronds on a potted palm near the window. "What the fuck," she said, and, coming out of her mouth, the obscenity shook me. "Okay—fine! So Phil and I had a very quick fling, if you must know. Three times? Four? I can't remember—it was about twelve years ago."

"Does Byron know?"

"I don't know. I doubt it."

"Were you in love with him, Heidi?"

"Are you kidding me? Phil Kohn? That sawed-off little putz?" Heidi rewarded me with a short, mean laugh. "I was in lust—with his money. No, no—it wasn't his money. Byron has money. Not as much as Phil, but he does okay. No, I think I loved Phil's power. A hell of a lot of doctors—cardiologists, brain surgeons, oncologists—they all have a God complex. Every time they put on a white coat, they hold someone's life in their hands. After a while they start believing they *are* God—and acting like it. My marriage was okay—but Byron's a little dull at the best of times. So . . ."

"So you thought it might be fun to sleep with God."

This time her laugh was genuine. "Very good line—write it down. God, however, dumped my ass after a few weeks. He said it would be too difficult since both of us were married to other people." She pushed her hair off her forehead. "He got laid, he got bored, and he bailed out—the fucking sleazebag."

"Do you hate Kohn?"

"I don't even think of him anymore. He was a jerk—but it's not like he threw me under the wheels of a bus." Heidi plopped onto the sofa again. "I don't hate him enough to kill him, if that's what you're wondering."

"One of the things I was wondering," I said. "The other is if Byron finally found out about the two of you and decided to get revenge."

"When Byron wants to get revenge—on me, anyway—he sleeps on a futon for a few nights in what once was our son's room."

"You have a son?"

"Freddy. Well—Fred. He manages a restaurant in Pittsburgh. He married a Pittsburgh girl. And now he roots for the Steelers. We're considering disowning him."

"A Steelers fan? I don't blame you, I'd disown him too." I stood. "Thanks for taking time for me. What you've told me is strictly confidential."

"Unless one of us killed Phil Kohn." Heidi sighed. "Then it won't matter anyway."

She walked me to the door and shook my hand. I held it for a long moment. "By the way, Heidi—your earlier question?"

"Which one was that?"

"Whether asking personal questions gets me off. I get my kicks in many different ways. But everybody—*everybody* masturbates now and then."

She sighed again, taking her hand back. "Tell me about it," she said.

• • •

I heard the phone ringing in my office while I was still on the stairs, and I hustled to get to it before my voice mail picked it up. I was out of breath when I answered "Milan Security," but the voice on the other end almost made me gasp.

"Hello, Milan. How are you? It's Victor Gaimari."

Just like that. It's Victor Gaimari. I would have recognized his voice anywhere. For a large man, his voice was fairly high pitched.

Victor is a stockbroker and financial advisor, with an elegant suite of offices in the Terminal Tower and a beautiful estate in the eastern suburb of Orange. He serves as a trustee for several non-profit institutions, he has season luxury boxes for both Browns and Indians games, and he rarely misses an opera, especially one composed by an Italian—Verdi or Puccini. He's a true gentleman in many senses of the word.

He's about my age, with a neatly trimmed mustache and dark good looks that remind me of the Latin Lover movie star of the 1940s, Cesar Romero. Witty, charming, single, and very rich, he shows up at many banquets, benefit parties, and elegant galas, always squiring one or another of the most beautiful women in Ohio. His taste—in cars, clothes, food, and women—is admittedly superb.

He's also the acting godfather of the Cleveland mob.

You're surprised? Don't be, at least not yet. The mob isn't the feared powerhouse it used to be. After a century of Cleveland dominance, complete with shocking assassination headlines every few years, the crime world changed like everything else. Now, law enforcement has more things on its mind than a bunch of aging Italian guys from Murray Hill in Little Italy. The old-time Mustache Petes—unless they actually moved away to places like Youngstown and Warren and Niles—live pleasant and unexciting lives these days, watching *The Sopranos* so they can point out and laugh at the show's mistakes, and refuse to admit, even to themselves, that it's mostly fiction.

Victor Gaimari's uncle on his mother's side is Don Giancarlo D'Allessandro. The Don ran the Cleveland mob from the time I was a small child, and for many years kept his "business" as clean as possible, meaning that despite his control of gambling, prostitution, labor racketeering, and political chicanery, he didn't allow illegal drugs to be peddled in Northeast Ohio—at least not by his extended family. He's almost ninety now, and he's scored more heart attacks than Dick Cheney, so he passed his power and skill along to his nephew, Victor.

A few years back, Mrs. Regina Sordetto, the Don's lady friend of almost forty years, who loved him, cared for him, and ensured he didn't eat anything that wasn't good for him, passed away quietly. Now he doesn't do much of anything.

Don Giancarlo has always liked me, and so does Victor. I've never understood why.

Do I like them, too? That's a toss-up. I very much like the old man, who used to invite me to dinner. He frightened a lot of people because of who he was, but he never scared me at all. I admired him completely—almost loved him, Mafia godfather or not. Even though he is small and elderly now, he's always briskly entertaining, sometimes kind, and wise in many ways. I've learned much from him, even when he pisses me off.

As for Victor and me, we started out badly. Almost twenty years ago, he threatened my family, so I invaded his Tower City offices and punched him in the nose—and to this day his loyal secretary doesn't even speak to me. He retaliated by sending two lurps to my apartment to deliver a beating. Ever since then it's been remarkable how often our paths have crossed in business. He's helped me when he could, and I've helped him, too. He's a crook, but there's decency to him, a gentleness that attracts and repels me at the same time.

Victor and his "family," though, are still a force to be reckoned with. I always handle him carefully and with respect.

I hadn't seen Victor for a while, perhaps more than a year. Despite what one might term our friendship, we don't hang out together or run into each other very often. I wondered why he was calling me.

"I just finished my lunch," he said cheerfully. "I wanted you to join me, but apparently you weren't in the office, so I didn't leave a message. You should have a cell phone, Milan, so people can get hold of you more easily."

"I have a cell phone—but I only use it to call out, not to receive. I hang on to what little privacy I have left."

"You're such a Luddite, Milan," he chided. "Do you have something important on your plate right now? I'd like to chat with you. I'm still at the Blue Point Grille on East 9th Street, but I can be in your office in ten minutes. Our conversation won't take long—and I'd appreciate it."

Whatever I might have "on my plate" at any given time, I never say no to Victor. I'm not sure why I don't refuse, except that his charm gets to me every time.

I hung up my parka and straightened my desk as best I could. It took him more than ten minutes to get to my office from the Blue Point Grille—but not much more, and he entered as splendid as ever. He always wore a cashmere overcoat in cold weather—but the passing of years changes all of us, including our personal styles, because today he was in a caramel-colored leather trench coat, his scarf almost the same color. I noticed for the first time gray streaks in his jet black hair. He was aging handsomely and gracefully.

Despite all the things that have gone on between us, I felt a flush of affection when he came into my office. When we shook hello, he took my forearm with his other hand, and I felt he was happy seeing me again, too.

"It's good getting together, Milan." He unbuckled his trench coat to reveal a dark-blue suit with subtle windowpane pinstripes, and a medium-blue necktie vivid enough to remind everyone he's not just a boring, everyday stockbroker.

"I have to admit you look sensational, Victor," I said. "Are you taking good care of yourself?"

"I try to. I'm eating more sensibly, drinking less, and I do about five half hours a week on my elliptical at home. Also I spent all January getting good sun and better golf in Naples. No Cleveland tanning booths for me."

"And how is the Don?" I said.

He flattened his hand and tipped it back and forth. "*Mezzo*

mezzo. He has good days and bad days. At nearly ninety, it's not so easy for him. He can't take care of his house alone anymore, so I put him in a nice apartment near Beachwood Place," he said. "A practical nurse lives there full time and takes care of him—takes him out to lunch every day except when the weather is miserable. Of course I look after him personally whenever I can."

"Is he happy?"

"He watches videos all day long. It doesn't make him happy, exactly, but it fills up his time. He watches *The Sopranos* over and over again. Ha ha."

Victor Gaimari never really laughs. Whenever he attempts it, it comes out a spoken "Ha ha."

"Please give him my sincerest regards, Victor."

"I wish you'd visit him yourself, Milan. He asks about you."

"I will," I said, meaning it.

Then Victor said, "Tell me how you're involved with the murder case of Dr. Phil Kohn."

No warm-up, no change of tone. Victor was in a hurry. I tried not to look surprised. "Is that what brought you here?"

"One of the things."

"I was at the reunion when it happened. Kohn was a high school classmate."

"Ah," he said.

"Yes."

"So you're working for a client?"

"I always work for clients, Victor. Or attorneys."

"Ben Magruder."

Son of a bitch! I neither admitted nor denied. I'd be damned if I'd let on to Victor. He knows everything that goes on in this town.

"Who is Magruder's client?" he said.

"That's privileged information."

He just waved a hand at me. "Okay, I'll find out anyway."

"Is that why you're here?"

"I'm here," Victor said, "mainly to reconnect with my old friend Milan whom I haven't seen for more than a year—and we should set up a dinner sometime. But there's another reason. Someone

I'm acquainted with called me and said you're harassing him. He wants to know why."

"I don't harass people. I'm conducting a private investigation. If your buddy isn't comfortable with that, too bad."

"We're not buddies. And he's not uncomfortable—just curious."

"Your people get curious a lot," I said.

"He's not 'my people.' As a matter of fact, he's one of *your* people—a Slovenian."

It took me milliseconds to figure it out. "Ted Lesnevich."

Victor nodded. "The D'Allessandro family doesn't deal in drugs, as you know. We never have. But—we live and let live. We have to, because we know people in all sorts of businesses. We've known Ted Lesnevich a while."

"So he calls you out of the blue," I said, "and whines because I asked him a few questions?"

"It wasn't out of the blue." Victor looked down at his legs for a moment, preparing to cross them. Then he changed his mind, deciding it would ruin the crease in his blue pinstripe pants. "About six years ago, the Don had a major heart attack."

"I know," I said.

"After his bypass surgery he started seeing Phil Kohn regularly as his cardiologist. I'd met Kohn a few times socially, but when he took over my uncle's medical care I got to know him better."

Something nibbled at the edge of my awareness, but I let Victor lead me wherever he was going.

"I learned to know him too well," he said, "because he asked me where he could buy his recreational chemicals."

I frowned. "He thought all you stockbrokers know things like that?"

"Milan, Milan." Victor shook his head. "Be polite. Kohn ordered a triple bypass on my uncle's heart, and observed in the OR while it was done. You think he was too stupid to know who Giancarlo D'Allessandro is?"

I ignored the jab. "What did he want? Amphetamines?"

"Correct—but we're not in that business. So I sent him to someone not connected with me in any way."

"Ted Lesnevich," I said.

"It doesn't bother me how Ted earns his living," Victor said. "But Phil Kohn is another story altogether. I stopped trusting him, so much that I changed heart specialists. I didn't want drug addicts ministering to the Don—too dangerous."

"So you hadn't seen Kohn since?"

"No—just across the lobby in Severance Hall at a concert."

"And Ted Lesnevich?"

"From time to time. But we never talk business. That's off limits."

"Victor, are you warning me to stay away from Lesnevich?" My own voice took on a sharp edge. "I don't respond to threats."

"Has anything I've said sounded like a threat?"

I mulled that over. "No, it didn't. I apologize."

"You've come to me many times over the years, Milan, looking for help or information, and I've given it to you freely—when I had it." He smiled pleasantly. "I've come to you, too, on occasion, haven't I? That's how it works in life—friends help other friends. And there were no threats or demands on either side, were there?"

"Only at the beginning," I reminded him.

He put his hand up and gently felt his nose. He remembered, all right. "At the beginning," he said, "we weren't yet friends. Now we are. Aren't we?"

CHAPTER ELEVEN

Tommy Wiggins could easily afford his suite in the Renaissance Hotel, which was spacious and elegant. Its windows looked out at busy but snowy Public Square and the hulking silhouette of the nearby Key Tower rising against an iron-gray February sky. The conference table in the main room could seat twelve, and there were more sofas and overstuffed club chairs than I used to have in my old four-bedroom house. The bathroom was larger than most Best Western hotel rooms, and the shower stall boasted eight different nozzles coming out of the wall at various heights. There was enough space in that stall to throw a medium-sized party, depending on how well you might want to get to know your guests.

In the sleeping quarters the bed was super-king-sized, in case an overnight tenant wanted to invite several good friends for a sleepover. Tommy Wiggins, our most celebrated schoolmate, was rich and famous enough to live high off the hog.

Except for the fancy suite and the room service and his trips out to excellent restaurants downtown like Lola and Johnny's, and Sans Souci right there in the hotel, he wasn't living that well during his enforced stay in our city. He was bored out of his mind.

"I'm so sick of watching HBO by myself every night," he whined. "And I don't want to go downstairs to the lobby bar and get shit-faced all by myself. Jesus, Milan, what do you do for fun in this town?"

"We don't *have* fun in this town," I said.

I didn't give him a chance to ask another question, but started in on him about Phil Kohn and his extracurricular activities as a drug addict.

"I swear to God," he was saying, "I had no idea Kohn was a junkie. I mean, like him or lump him, he was a doctor."

I'd gone to see him shortly after Victor left my office. It was not quite four P.M., but Tommy was already sipping on a martini he'd mixed from the generous array of booze bottles ordered from room service—Grey Goose vodka with two olives.

"If I'd known about his jones for drugs—well, I wouldn't have baptized him with my drink. The poor fucker was pathetic enough."

"What about you, Tommy?" I said. "Are you taking drugs?"

His little innocent laugh was charming, as if he were confessing whether he drank Coke or Pepsi. "I smoke a joint once in a while, or maybe drop something to keep me going if I hit a writer's block when I'm working on my play. But I'm a million miles away from being hooked."

If that was a million miles for Tommy Wiggins, it was beyond the boundaries of the universe for me, because never in my life did I spend a nickel for illegal drugs. I smoked two joints when I was in college, shared with a Kent State short-term date who had grass around all the time. I decided then that marijuana was boring and made me sleepy, and never touched drugs again. But I realize I'm practically alone in my part of the world.

"Was your beef with Phil only about the Holly Hop?" I asked him. "Or was it something to do with drugs, too?"

"It had nothing to do with drugs—or with anything else except what he said to me forty years ago."

"Don't get mad, but your reputation with younger women is pretty much an open secret, if one reads the gossip columns."

He bristled, negative *New York Post* headlines dancing in his head. "So what?"

"So Phil Kohn had the same sort of rep. Did you and he run into each other somewhere one of you shouldn't have been? Did you have sex with one another's girlfriends?"

Tommy shook his head vehemently. "I live mostly in New York and Los Angeles. I haven't been on a date with a Cleveland woman since our prom."

I tried not to smile. "Who did you go to the prom with, anyway?"

That seemed to amuse him. "Slipped your mind, did it? I went to the prom with Ilene Silver."

"Wow," I said.

"Ring a bell?"

"I was out with her once or twice, too, as I remember."

"Except for that prom night, I never went out with her at all," he said. "I didn't have a date for the prom—of course, I never dated in those days—and as I remember, she didn't have a date, either. So some mutual friends set us up for the senior prom and we went together—and it cost me a goddamn fortune for a tuxedo, and a corsage for her. That was it."

"No romance?"

"Here's to romance." Tommy lifted his martini in a weird toast. "We kissed at the end of the evening because that's what you did on prom night—but it never went beyond that."

"I seem to remember kissing her too," I said, "sometime or other."

"Did you feel her up?"

I laughed. "No."

Tommy Wiggins almost preened. "I did," he said. "I got my hand down the front of her prom dress but I couldn't seem to budge that tight wired-up bra."

"Congratulations, you're one up on me."

"I wonder if Phil Kohn has been with her," he mused. "Maybe he was one or two up on both of us."

"So you don't know anything about Kohn's love life and you didn't know he was a drug addict."

Tommy Wiggins wandered over to the window to enjoy the panoramic view his twelfth-floor suite afforded him. He wouldn't meet my eyes. "I wouldn't quite call him an addict."

"What would you call him?"

"A recreational user—like everyone else in the world."

"Not quite everyone."

He spun around to confront me. "What's this got to do with me anyway?"

"Your attorney hired me to find a better suspect than you, Tommy. I'm hoping you don't qualify."

He sounded offended. "Are you on my side?" he whined. "Or do you hate me because I'm rich and famous?"

"Do you always refer to yourself as rich and famous?"

Now I was *sure* I'd offended him, because he pouted. "I'm famous for doing *good* things and making people laugh—you'd know that if you'd seen one of my plays."

"I've seen most of your plays," I said. "But I'm not a drama critic, and I'm not laughing now." I got up and followed him over to the window. The closer I got, the louder my voice became. "I don't hate you because you're rich and famous, because frankly, my dear, I don't give a damn. Help me, Tommy—don't make it tougher on me because I'm on your side. Now—when you and Phil had your argument, was it because of what he said to you at the Holly Hop? Or was it about drugs?"

"You already asked me that." His mouth was dry. Then he drank the rest of his martini and popped both olives into his mouth to chew up. "Why are you in my face? I won't pay to get pushed around like this."

"You're paying," I reminded him, "for me to get the cops to *stop* pushing. I'm trying to determine that there are more valid suspects with a better excuse to kill Kohn than you. But if you're not honest with me, you're wasting your money and I'm wasting time—so I'll go home for a beer and you can hire someone else."

"Maybe I should," he said, but he was more sulky than angry.

"Fine. They can go interview all our classmates again. That'll work out well for you, because nobody was thrilled about it in the first place."

He slumped down onto the sofa, one hand trailing the empty martini glass beside him. "Shit," he said.

I waited in silence.

"One thing has nothing to do with the other," he said.

"Tell me why."

His chin was practically on his chest. “Milan, Friday night I was going to make a scene.”

“About the Holly Hop?”

Tommy nodded. “That’s all it was—at least that’s how it started. Afterwards I was going to walk away. I wasn’t going to throw any drinks.”

“But . . . ?”

“The ensuing—conversation—took other directions.” His confident manner had been slowly disappearing since I got to his hotel. Now it was almost nonexistent.

“I told him what I thought of him. I reminded him of the Holly Hop. He just laughed. And then,” Tommy said, frowning as he remembered, “he looked at me and came up with a brand-new insult.” He shook his head sadly, thinking it over. “He said, ‘Congratulations. I see you’ve traded in corn-holing for dope.’”

“Phil made you for a user?”

He twitched his nose a little and moved into the center of the room, putting down his empty glass and shoving his hands into the back pockets of his khaki slacks. “He said that doctors can tell things like that.” He spoke more quickly now, looking around. “He also said it takes one to know one.”

“Tommy, you’re walking on thinner ice every minute you talk to me.”

“I keep telling you I’m innocent.”

“Tell that to the police again. But don’t talk about drugs unless they ask you, or they’ll yank you out of your fancy luxury suite up here and fix you up with a nice efficiency unit over at the Justice Department.”

He looked disoriented. “Why would they do that?”

“Because you’re a murder suspect,” I told him. “And you’re a junkie—even one who does grass and then takes uppers to get over and around your writer’s block. To a cop, that’s a lot more interesting than being rich and famous. Isn’t that right, Tommy?”

Don’t you sometimes wish you were back in the 1950s or 1960s again, when life was simpler and a lot less difficult to figure out—

especially on TV and in the movies? Your mom would clean the house wearing a cocktail dress and a string of pearls like Harriet Nelson always wore. Your dad would wear his dark suit and tie all day at work and keep it on all evening in the house while he ate a family dinner, read the newspaper, and spooled out pearls of wisdom to Wally and the Beaver, like Ward Cleaver did. And really famous people like John Wayne and William Holden and Harpo Marx would be kind and understanding to you the way they were when silly-but-lovable Lucy Ricardo made them stumble all over themselves so the world laughed.

But then this isn't the fifties anymore, is it?

I'd shifted all Suzanne Davis's interview notes on my classmates to my computer. Then at my office early the next morning, I typed up my own notes. I was convinced Wiggins didn't kill Phil Kohn—but as for his life, he struck me about as innocent as Machine Gun Kelly.

It's always been my modus operandi to transfer the names of all my possible suspects onto three-by-five cards and then move them around on top of the desk trying to discern the relationship between all of them, hoping to discover who is connected to whom and why—but I had our entire senior high school class to deal with, and most of their spouses or significant others too. That was too many cards to fill out and shuffle around. Instead I carefully sketched a border around the top yellow sheet of my legal pad and then filled it in with the side of the pencil while I thought. It came out looking like a rustic frame, but I had nothing to put inside it.

Marko Meglich was our classmate, too, and I thought as I obliterated the shaky frame I'd sketched that if he were still alive and had been at the Friday night get-together, he would have solved the mystery by now. He was a good cop—a great cop, really. My guess is that if the Sundance Kid were on the job, Ben Magruder and Tommy Wiggins wouldn't have asked for my help in the first place.

It was about nine-thirty and I was adjusting the shade on my big window so the sun wouldn't shine across the river and directly into my eyes when I heard the downstairs door open and shut and heard two sets of footsteps ascending the stairs. From the sound, I gathered they were hardly lightweights.

Two big men walked in the door of my office. The one in front was a few inches short of six feet, about thirty-five or so, with a neck like a rhinoceros. His overcoat was a few years too old and out of style, but his girth was impressive, and he didn't appear fat. The bulge under his left arm stretched the coat and was as easy to read as if he had a big sign around his neck announcing he was carrying a piece. He actually sported a hat—Borsalino-style Italian, black with a frivolous green feather in it—and he was smoking a cigarette, letting it dangle out of the side of his clean-shaven mouth. He probably imagined he looked tough, but to me he resembled a too-old Hollywood producer who hadn't worked on a movie since the last time they filmed an Andy Hardy. The one behind him was younger, and big enough to block out the sky. He had at least three inches on me, anyway—and I don't meet many men I have to look up to. His short leather jacket was unzipped because it had grown too small for him.

"Mr. Jacovich?" the older one said. "We're from Morris Kepler's office."

It was a familiar name, from my cop days. Morris Kepler doesn't *have* an office. He's a longtime bookie who operates on Cleveland's fringes, moving around every day and doing all his accounting in his head so no one can find anything for which to blame him. He makes a lot of money taking bets on horse races or football and basketball games, but he never books Major League Baseball because he says it's too erratic. In this modern age he has a variety of cell phones in every pocket of his suit—he always wears a suit—so he doesn't have to take bets in a Walgreen's phone booth or on a street corner. He's hardcore when it comes to lox, bagels, chicken soup, and the like, and he can usually be found in one of several excellent Jewish delicatessens in the eastern suburbs. He's a successful little man, now in his seventies, and he frequently employs muscle to collect delinquent payments from his clients.

Muscle like the big guy standing a little to one side behind the one in the Borsalino hat.

"And to whom am I speaking?" I said.

"Whom? You talk very fancy. My name is Orloff," the older one said in one of those raspy voices you can't listen to without hoping the speaker clears his throat. "And this is Mr. Shaffran."

I looked to the big guy. He was only in his late twenties, but his name was familiar to me too. "Are you any relation to Bruce Shaffran?" I said.

He nodded. "That's my father."

Orloff said, "The thing is, he's Bruce's son, Leonard. We call him Leo."

I nodded. "I knew your father from way back, Leo. I used to be on the Job, and sometime in the nineteen eighties I put him in prison—for about two years, I think."

"Twenty-six months," Leo said. "For fraud. I was a baby then."

"Are you here because you're pissed off about that?"

Leo shook his head. "No, it's okay."

"Good. How is your dad?"

"He passed away a few years ago," the kid said.

"My sympathies, then. He was a nice man."

Neither of them made an effort to sit down so I didn't either, but came around to their side and leaned lightly against the desk. At my size, I didn't lean very lightly. "What can I do for you today, gentlemen?"

Orloff put his hands in the pockets of his coat. He wanted to look like an old gangster movie villain but he was falling short of it. "I understand you're working for Dr. Phil Kohn."

"You understand?"

He nodded.

"Where do you understand it from, Mr. Orloff? Dr. Kohn is deceased."

"That makes no difference. The thing is—he owes Morris Kepler a lot of money."

"Did Dr. Kohn bet on horse racing?"

Orloff thought about that for a while. "Mostly basketball."

"I see."

"The Cavs," Orloff said. "He liked to bet on the Cavs games all the time because of LeBron James."

"LeBron James is a hell of a player."

"Yes. The thing is," Orloff said, "the Cavs don't always win."

"No."

"And when they lose, Dr. Kohn loses, too."

"To the tune of?"

"Excuse me?"

I sighed. "How much does he owe Morris Kepler altogether?"

"Around thirty-seven thousand, give or take a few bucks," Orloff said.

"Including the vigorish."

"Yes."

"That's impressive," I said. "Why should I care?"

"Because," Orloff said, "you work on behalf of Dr. Kohn."

"I work on a situation that involves him—I can't work on his behalf, since now he's dead. I'm not working for him or representing him."

Orloff looked at Leo. "The thing is, that's close enough," he said.

"For?"

"His unfortunate passing doesn't negate the fact that he's in debt—and since we can't get it from him we have to discuss the situation with those closest to him. So here's the thing, Mr. Jacovich—we give you a week to come up with Dr. Kohn's money he owes to Mr. Kepler," Orloff said, "or at least half of it. That's fair, right?"

I nodded my understanding. "Half of it."

"Yes. The other half we give you an extra week. Of course then we add more vigorish."

"Fascinating."

"Excuse me?" Orloff seemed to employ "excuse me" and "the thing is" with monotonous regularity.

"I have nothing to do with Phil Kohn," I told Orloff. "Until last Friday I hadn't seen him for forty years. Now that he's dead, I have no connection with him whatsoever. So you've made a trip here for nothing, because I'm out of it."

"Mr. Kepler doesn't accept losses, okay? Since we can't reach the late Dr. Kohn, we're forced to deal with those close to him—like you." Orloff's voice was like a low-powered radio station reaching you through lots of static.

"I'm nowhere near close to him," I said, and stopped. Orloff wasn't listening. He had in his head that I owed his boss thirty-seven grand, and that's all he knew—or wanted to. "You'll have to look somewhere else—not here."

"I can't do that. Look, we're being straight-up. We're giving you a week. After that, we come back here to discuss it some more—and you won't like it."

"I don't like it now," I said.

"You don't want Leo to have to hurt you, do you?"

"You don't want me to hurt Leo, either. Or you."

Orloff chuckled mirthlessly and hitched his shoulders, his hands still in his coat pockets. It was a corny, 1940s kind of shoulder hitch, and I thought about what actor from that period he was trying to look like. It wasn't Cagney or Edward G. Robinson, I was sure of that. Not Bogart, either. Ah, then I got it—George Raft.

"You used to be a tough guy, but you're not so tough anymore," Orloff said, hitching his shoulders again. "The thing is, you're too old, okay? You can't bring it the way you used to."

"The thing is—try me," I said.

He clucked his tongue like a little old lady. He seemed to have a remarkable repertoire of movie characters he kept channeling—first George Raft, now Gabby Hayes. "Take the week like we asked you and come up with the money. Mr. Kepler would prefer it."

"I'll be busy next week," I said, "straightening out my sock drawer."

"A wise shit. Dumb, too." He sighed, turning to Leo. "Remember, he's an old guy, Leo. Don't hurt him too bad, okay?"

Leo nodded and started moving toward me slowly, flexing his hands, popping his knuckles like castanets. I didn't pay much attention to him—I was busy looking at Orloff. Orloff was calm about whatever was next, even though Leo seemed delighted with anticipation. He doubled up his fists.

When Leo got close enough to me, just before he took his first swing with those big meaty hands that might have driven me through the hardwood floor, I leaned my ass back against the desk, hard, and kicked him in the scrotum.

The expression on Leo's face registered more surprise than pain, which was too great for him to deal with logically. The sound he made was like a horse stepping into a groundhog hole and breaking an ankle. A huge man, he clutched his crotch, his upper body narrowing itself into a triangle shape. He deflated slowly, first to his knees and then collapsing onto his side and rolling around on my floor.

Orloff's hand was only halfway to his chest before I stopped him. "Hard to draw a piece from underneath a buttoned-up overcoat, slow-ass," I said. "Get your hand away or I'll dislocate your shoulder."

He considered his options and then decided it was a bad idea. He dropped his hand to his side, and then hitched his shoulders again to make sure they were still operative.

"Go help Leo stand up," I said. "Then we can talk civilized."

Orloff squatted down next to Leo, helping him sit up straighter on the floor. The boy's face was virginal white.

"Jesus, those shoes of yours must weigh ten pounds each," Orloff said, looking at my boots. "You might have killed him."

"If I wanted to kill him, he'd be dead right now." I pushed one of the chairs over toward them. "Let him sit there until he feels better."

Leo crawled his crooked way up into the chair like a broken-backed beetle, not looking at me, believing that if he kept his eyes averted I wouldn't hurt him again. He continued moaning, though—softly, the sound he made high in the back of his throat like a mewling kitten. He put his head back and closed his eyes.

"Orloff, you want to tell me what this is really about?"

Orloff sounded less confident than a few minutes earlier. His hand was at the back of Leonard Shaffran's neck, gently patting and stroking him with genuine maternal concern. "I do what I'm told. It's nothing personal between us—or between Leo either."

I decided not to lecture him regarding the grammatical use of "between Leo." "Who told you to do it, then?"

"I work for Mr. Kepler."

"And who told Kepler to send you after me?"

He shrugged, moving a hand from Leo Shaffran's neck to his shoulder, massaging and squeezing it like a football coach bucking up his quarterback after he'd been sacked and injured. "You'll have to ask Mr. Kepler."

"I'm going to do just that, Mr. Orloff," I said.

CHAPTER TWELVE

The radio station at which Maurice Paich plies his trade as a house announcer isn't one of those upscale corporate outlets that are part of a huge conglomerate owning stations halfway across the country and deciding in their boardrooms what songs should be played on the air. It's independently owned, taking up half of one floor of an old building on the edge of the Warehouse District, about a block from the Cuyahoga River. If you're lucky enough to be the program director your office overlooks the water. Every other midlevel executive there who even has an office is forced to stare out the window at the brick wall of another building nearby, and the sales department—a group of harried-looking young people who aren't being paid enough money—works in prairie-dog village cubicles in a large central room.

Maurice Paich shared an office with two other radio personalities who worked different shifts. Their three desks took up about 90 percent of the room space, but Maurice was alone there when I kept our appointment later that morning. He was still as good-looking as he'd been when we were both seventeen, but like everyone else, he'd suffered the attrition of passing years. The skin on his face was flaccid now, and the overhead light exposed his wrinkles.

"I wish you and I'd gotten more of a chance to talk last Friday," he said. His resonant radio voice was confident even though the rest of him wasn't. He looked uncomfortable that I'd invaded his workplace, and during our conversation he seemed nervous that the boss might pop in and catch us. "But it's not exactly the right time today, Milan. I'm on the air every hour—all day."

I checked my watch. "We have about forty minutes. I won't even need half of them," I assured him. "I just want to run a few things by you."

He didn't like the sound of that. "Run a few things by me?"

"I've been hired to get some information and flesh out the picture of our own peers who were at the reunion party—before Phil Kohn died."

"Oh. Hired?"

"Yes," I said. "Tommy Wiggins is considered what the cops refer to as a person of interest. He'd like that not to happen, and his attorney hired me."

"Who's his attorney?"

"Danielle Webber's husband."

He laughed without mirth. "It's a small world, isn't it? I remember Danielle very well. She was so pretty—she still is, from what I saw of her Friday. I never talked to her much when we were teenagers—but I was good friends with Tommy. As much as I was friends with anybody in school, I suppose. We were the only two . . . artistic types who were around back then."

"Did you talk to Tommy on Friday?"

"A little. Believe it or not, I was intimidated. It's been a long time since high school—and now he's one of the most famous playwrights in the world. Wow."

"Did you spend time with Phil Kohn on Friday, too?"

Maurice allowed his brow to lower into a frown. "I talked to Phil for less than two minutes at the hotel. That's about it."

I nodded. "What did you talk about?"

He shifted in his desk chair and tried to laugh but it came out phony. "What did any of us talk about that night? Small talk—cheerful bullshit. It wasn't much more than a hello and how're you doing."

"Were you and Phil good friends in high school?"

"Not particularly. I was an artistic dreamer then—and he didn't have much use for me."

"Did you know him well in later years?"

He tapped the left side of his chest. "He was a cardiologist. A few years back I went to him so he could look and listen to my heart. He just told me I should take Coumadin every day. He wrote me a prescription and left me sitting there in his office without saying goodbye."

"Coumadin? What did he say was wrong with you?"

"Atrial fibrillation. When you get into your fifties, you become more aware of your body, and I started worrying about my heart because I get short of breath. I went to Phil because he had one of the best reputations in the city for cardio, and the tests they took showed that I sometimes have an irregular heartbeat. But he didn't spend much time with me. Maybe it was because I was an old school tie and he wasn't as interested in me as he was in super-rich people, like Arab emirs and sheiks and shahs." Maurice shrugged sadly. "There are more sheiks who visit Cleveland than almost any other hospital—especially the ones with heart problems. Did you know that?"

"I'm not up on the comings and goings of Arab sheiks," I said. "Phil made a good living that way, anyhow. How about socially? Did you spend time with him when it wasn't about your heart?"

"Cleveland's a small town, when you get right down to it—everybody sees everybody once in a while."

"When's the last time you saw him, then? Before Friday."

He gazed up at the fluorescent light fixture in the ceiling while he considered it. Nobody looks good under fluorescent lights, at least when they reach our age, and I could see Paich wore a light coat of coverage makeup, blended in skillfully around the corners of his mouth and eyes, that made him look fifteen years younger than I do—unless one looks too closely. "A few months ago, I guess," he said. "Maybe October or November—in the late fall."

"You and your wives had dinner together?"

He compressed his lips before he answered. "No. Just the two of us met for a drink—Phil and me."

"Is your wife friendly with his wife?"

"Not really." He was working hard at seeming casual.

"Maurice, did you and Phil Kohn have any problems or disagreements between you?"

His answer was airy and unimportant-sounding. "If you know somebody all your life, you get into disagreements sometimes. It's not a big thing."

"It's a big thing when someone you know all your life gets shot in the head," I said.

"Come on!" he whimpered, going on the defensive. "I didn't shoot Phil Kohn in the head!"

"Somebody did. That's why police are asking questions. They'll be asking you sooner or later. Tell me first and save yourself some grief."

His face suddenly grew sad, and he leaned one elbow on his desk and cupped his chin with his hand. "Damn it," he said. His radio voice still sounded resonant, but it was much softer now. "Why can't people just mind their own business, Milan? Why does it always get fucked up?"

"Things are like that," I said, and waited.

After about thirty seconds he got up and closed the door to his office, then sat back down. "This is between us, all right?"

"Unless it isn't, Maurice."

I hated the direction in which this conversation was heading. I sensed it would be painful for Maurice Paich—and painful talks with people you've known for forty years often become unbearable. I waited for his sad sigh, which was forthcoming.

"I got involved with Kohn without wanting to," Maurice said. "So what I wound up doing was illegal—but it never touched me, I swear to God. Never."

"What didn't touch you?"

He put his hand over his forehead, as if shielding his eyes from the sun, and gently rubbed it. He seemed to be getting a headache. Without looking at me, he said, "I had to go out and get Phil Kohn drugs—with his money—at least once a month. Sometimes more."

"You were buying illegal drugs?" I hardly believed what I was hearing. "You swore it never touched you."

"It didn't! I never messed with drugs in my life." He glanced once more at the door to make sure no one was listening "He was a famous, successful doctor—and he didn't want it getting around town that he was such a heavy doper. He didn't even want his dealer to know how much he was taking. That's why he made me do it for him."

I wanted to ask why he didn't just say no. My next question obviously got to Maurice and bit deep. "What did Kohn have on you to make you keep running that kind of errand for him?"

His cheeks flamed and he looked away from me. "Please don't ask me these kinds of questions. It's not fair . . ."

It was never fair, especially to my long-ago classmates who were suddenly enmeshed in a murder investigation. So when I told him that he was better off talking to me first than to the police so I could ease their pressure on him, I did so with a heavy heart and a generous dollop of guilt. I felt lousy about it.

The warring emotions on Maurice's face revealed his struggle with a big decision. Finally, sadly, he made it and, after a long, deep breath, confessed to me that despite the silly old argument between Phil Kohn and Tommy Wiggins that started all the ugliness at the reunion, it was he himself who was gay, not Wiggins.

"I never did anything about it in high school." He was close to tears, lowering his mellifluous voice so no one beyond this room could hear him. "Back then we didn't even *know* what to do about it. You won't believe this, but I ignored it, Milan, I ignored the feelings I sometimes had for other men. I only had one actual homosexual experience before we graduated, and I put it out of my mind, actually pretending it never happened. For many years after that, I wouldn't even consider those feelings. It wasn't until I was in my late thirties that I actually came out of the closet—that I admitted I was gay, even to myself."

"That's nothing to be ashamed of," I said.

"It is when the far right hears about it. This is a socially conservative town, despite its politically liberal leanings. It's fine if you're open about your sexual preferences if you're an actor or a painter, that's fine, and even accepted. But it would raise hell with my life if some of those important people found out the truth about me—the people whose homes I come into when I talk on the radio every day, and especially the far-right conservatives who own this radio station. I could lose my job and never get another one in the Greater Cleveland area. Where else in America could I go, at my age and gay, to snag a radio gig?" He sniffled. "So Phil

Kohn made me buy drugs for him or he'd blow the whistle on me. I didn't have much choice, did I?"

I started feeling my own headache beginning. "How did Phil find out about your . . . sexual preferences . . . in the first place?"

His complexion went from a rosy red blush to white anger and his lips were a nearly invisible line. He nervously twisted his wedding ring around on his finger. "Oh, he had his ways, the son of a bitch," he said. I think it sounded lame even to him. I just looked at him and waited.

"It embarrasses me to say this, Milan."

I waited some more.

"Phil—found out about me from Meredith."

"Who?"

"Meredith is my wife," he said mournfully. "They had a little affair about three years back."

I was never introduced to Meredith Paich, but I remembered a glimpse of her across the room at the Friday night reunion. She was somewhat younger than Maurice, pretty in a hard-looking way, and flirting her ass off with every man who came near her. With my new information, direct from a discomfited horse's mouth, Maurice's news wasn't surprising me.

"When Meredith is drinking—she's *always* drinking, that's just one of her weaknesses—she'll blab damn near anything, especially to somebody sharing a bed with her," Maurice said. "So—she told Phil about me." He rubbed his forehead even more aggressively now, but still being careful not to smudge the Cover Girl makeup smoothing out his wrinkles. "That's her idea of pillow talk."

"You didn't fight with Kohn about that?" I said. "Him talking pillow talk with your wife?

"I didn't fight with any of the other men Meredith slept with, either. Hell, why would I fight? I haven't had sex with her in about eight years—so I don't really care what she does in bed, or with who." He flushed, embarrassed, but his voice once again grew strong and clear. "I've had a committed relationship with another man for the past four years now."

That took me aback. "I didn't think you were totally out of the closet."

"I'm not," he said. "This man is—well, he appears very masculine, so everyone who knows me thinks he and I are good friends. You've never met him, I don't think. He's an art broker here in town, but you'd never know he was gay by talking to him. We even go to Indians games together sometimes, and drink beer, eat hot dogs smothered with Stadium Mustard, and hoot at the other team and yell at the umpires—so I'm not one of those queens flitting around from one man to the next."

"As long as you're happy, that's what counts," I said. "How long have you been Phil's go-between for drugs?"

"Ever since his affair with Meredith—three years ago. Closer to four, actually. They only fooled around for about three months, but even after they stopped, Phil never quit pressuring me for the drugs." He slumped back in his chair and closed his eyes against the ghastly glare of the fluorescents.

"Kohn told me where to go. He bought drugs from the same man himself, but he made me swear I wouldn't mention to the pusher that I was buying for him, not myself." He took a long, deep breath, finally met my eyes, and spit out the name.

"It was Ted Lesnevich," Maurice said. "Remember him from St. Clair High?"

I gritted my teeth, remembering him, all right. "Phil Kohn was blackmailing you—making you take illegal chances for him and threatening to expose you if you didn't. You had a pretty good motive for killing him."

He breathed loudly through his nose for a moment. "Why in hell would I kill him? Sure, he was blackmailing me. But every time I bought dope from Lesnevich, Phil—how can I say this? He actually tipped me."

"Tipped you?"

"Whenever I made a buy for him, he'd give me a few bucks. Maybe even a hundred or more, depending on his mood." He ducked his head, more embarrassed about his extra income than about his sexual preferences. "What the hell, Milan—nobody like me ever got rich working in local radio."

Jack's Deli, on Cedar Road just off Green in University Heights, is my favorite place in Cleveland to eat a great corned beef sandwich, blintzes, or potato pancakes, or even a breakfast of matzo brei. It's usually crowded in there from noon until two, but by the time I arrived that afternoon—I'd already checked out another deli, Corky and Lenny's on Chagrin Road, with no success—it was during that lull between lunch and dinner when only the elderly hangers-on hadn't gone home, and were still at their table chatting and drinking coffee. They'd probably been there since breakfast because the deli was a second home—their own living room.

Morris Kepler was obviously one of the regulars. He seemed at ease. He was ensconced in a large booth, wearing an inelegant suit that was either metallic blue or metallic green—I couldn't tell exactly, especially when he moved around and it changed colors under the lights. Along with Mr. Orloff, one of my earlier unwanted visitors that morning, Kepler was surrounded by four men even older than he was, who were listening carefully as he held court and waxed magisterial about something or other—a habit he indulged in often. Whatever his judgment of the subject, it inspired everyone else at the table to argue loudly, with great waving of hands. I could tell from across the room that it was genial squabbling—between old friends.

I walked up to the edge of the booth and stood there listening to the debate until Orloff noticed me. Then, looking troubled and almost frightened, he leaned over and whispered something in Kepler's ear. The old man raised his head slowly to examine me, making a sour face, but there didn't seem to be much anger behind it. We hadn't seen each other for at least twenty-five years, but there was a kind of strange recognition between us. Maybe we'd met before, in another life—or perhaps even in heaven, frolicking around together amongst the angels and cherubs.

I have a big oil painting of *that* ever happening.

"This is Mr. Jacovich, I presume?" he said.

"That's right."

"I hear about you, Mr. Jacovich. Mr. Orloff here mentioned to me that you're a cruel and vengeful man. You not only refuse doing business with me, but you attacked poor Leo this morning, and he wound up going to the doctor. The *urologist,* for God's sake, and I had to break my ass trying to get him like an emergency appointment! That was unkind of you."

"I attacked Leo before he attacked me," I admitted. "But have it your way—I'm not a very nice human being. We have to talk, Mr. Kepler."

He shrugged. "Here's how it works: put your money on the table. Then I'll talk to you."

"My money?"

"Thirty-seven thousand dollars, I believe." He took a ballpoint pen out of his inner pocket. "I haven't added today's vig yet."

"I should put thirty-seven grand on the table? Do I look that dumb?"

"Ask me no questions and I'll tell you no lies," he said, but his eyes twinkled. "You expect to just walk in here and interrupt a pleasant chat with my friends, just to talk with me?"

The other old men mumbled their dissatisfaction. They glared at me, their eyes hostile.

"Your flunkies—Mr. Orloff here, and Leo—interrupted *me* this morning," I said. "And it was in my office, too—not in Jack's Deli. Fair's fair, no?"

"Life isn't fair, Mr. Jacovich. Your father never told you that?"

"My father lived it."

Kepler sighed loud enough that other customers heard him halfway across the restaurant. "I'll give you a few minutes," he said. He made a shooing gesture with both hands at the two men on his left, who scooted out of the booth to allow him an exit. "We'll go to a table by the window."

We crossed the dining room and sat down, and immediately a waitress was there, probably wondering why we'd moved. She asked if anyone wanted more to eat. I wasn't hungry, but I ordered a bowl of matzo ball soup—just so I wouldn't sit there taking up space.

"You really think," Kepler asked when we'd been left alone, "if you hurt poor young Leo because you're too chickenshit to come up with my money, that there aren't other people who'll go over to talk to you?"

"I hurt poor young Leo before poor young Leo had a chance to hurt me," I said. "I think you should know Leo is too young to be any good as a hurter. He's too eager, and he doesn't think to protect himself. He'll get over it, I imagine."

"Getting kicked in the balls he's going to get over?"

"I was being charitable," I said. "I could have broken his neck just as easy—and he'd never get over that. Look, I don't owe you any money, and I don't even know what you're talking about. But if you send anyone else around to rough me up, I'll not only send them to the doctor, but then I'll find you and send you there, too."

That didn't frighten him. It didn't even cause him a tremor. "Are you threatening an old man like me?" he said quietly, half-smiling.

"As I explained, I'm not a nice person." I shifted my chair closer to the table so I could lower my voice. "What the hell made you think I was working for Phil Kohn? I haven't seen or talked to him in years. I had no idea he was playing the horses with you."

"Basketball," Kepler corrected me. "Phil Kohn bets basketball with me. *Bet,* I should say—wrong tense. Football, too—he still owes me from the Super Bowl, and that was weeks ago—but mostly basketball. I'm sorry he's gone—I'll say a kaddish for him, a prayer for the dead if it'll help—a nice Jewish man like that. But I want my money."

"I'm sure you do," I said, "but you won't get it from me, because I had nothing to do with him. You can believe that or you can call me a liar—but either way, if anyone comes around to lean on me, I'm going to get angry and hurt them."

He looked at me for a long time. "You just might—a big guy. I didn't realize what a big guy you are. You're an old *pischer* like me, but you look mean."

I laughed. "I'm not nearly as old a *pischer* as you are—but I can be mean as a snake," I said. "Still, hurting anyone for no reason is pretty silly, don't you think?"

"It's no reason if I believe you."

"Why wouldn't you believe me? Who told you I work for Kohn anyway?"

His old brown eyes twinkled again. "I have my sources."

"Your sources are full of shit then."

He actually smiled; his teeth were perfect. "I don't s'pose you'd make good for Kohn's thirty-seven large anyway—just to be on the decent side."

"Nobody is thirty-seven-large decent," I said. Kepler was turning into an amusing old fellow. "And if they do happen to make good, it's not paying off somebody else's debt. It's charity. You don't strike me as a charity case."

He tried one last attempt. "Would you feel differently about it if I forget the vig?"

"Better that you forget about *me*. Think about your source, instead. He told you all wrong."

"He did, eh? *He* did."

"Apparently."

The waitress brought my steaming matzo ball soup, the bowl surrounded by packets of saltine crackers. I wanted it, but I feared I would look like a fool slurping soup alone while he went back to his own table and all those men would stare resentfully at me while I ate. I took a few delicious tastes and then opened a pack of saltines and crumbled them into the soup.

He took the pressure off me. "Eat, enjoy," he urged me. "I'll stay here with you."

"All right," I said.

I tackled the matzo ball soup with gusto and he watched me, amused. "You look like you maybe played football when you was young?"

"High school and college, yes. I was a nose tackle."

"Not one of the glamour positions, eh?" His look and tone grew manipulative, and he inched ever closer to where I was sitting. "So yourself—do you bet, Mr. Jacovich? Bet money on football?"

"Hardly ever."

"Hardly?"

"When and if I do," I said, "maybe next year when there's another season, I'll call you first. How does that sound?"

"I'll even buy your chicken soup today." The old man snatched up my check. "There, I got it. Now it's a promise."

"Thanks for the soup. That's very nice of you."

"I'm always nice," Kepler said pleasantly, without bragging. "That's the way you do business."

CHAPTER THIRTEEN

Sonja Kokol Caruth worked for Cuyahoga County. She had always been a very smart woman, and if she'd finished college, she'd probably be *running* the county, not slaving for it. After two years at Cuyahoga Community College—Tri-C, everyone calls it—she chose to enter the work force instead. Now she's an executive assistant to one of the county commissioners—which means that she manages his office as efficiently as she put together the reunion.

Sonja looked surprised to see me, and I could tell she was still annoyed. In our youth, I couldn't remember her ever staying mad at me for more than a day. I shouldn't have bothered her, should have let her cool down in her own good time—but it was late in the afternoon, and I had the idea she wasn't too busy to answer a question.

So I asked it.

We'd walked into the coffee room—not furnished with much more than three inexpensive tables and stained plastic chairs, a couple of vending machines, and a coffee pot obviously used for most of the day but not yet washed out. It was okay with me—I didn't want coffee anyway. Not *that* coffee.

The plastic chairs were as uncomfortable as hell, and mine felt sticky and nasty to the touch, so I didn't waste any time. When I asked her why there were none of our African American classmates at the reunion, Sonja looked like she had just been hit on the forehead with a sledgehammer.

She finally managed to say, "What the hell kind of a question is that?"

"There were approximately thirty black graduates in our class," I said. "I played football with five of the guys—one of them got a four-year scholarship to Grambling because he was a hell of a linebacker. I recall three black girls got together, wore sensational red dresses, and sang 'Ain't No Mountain High Enough' just like the Supremes at our annual talent show that last year—and sounded terrific to everybody. I was probably in one class or another with all of the black kids over the years. Yet not one African American attended the reunion Friday night, and none of their bios appeared in the reunion booklet, either. Did you invite them along with the rest of us?"

Her face took on that noncommittal look. "Why would you ask that?" she said. She didn't even try being pleasant.

"Just curious, Sonja."

"I *did* invite them," she said, but she didn't sound very convincing and I just looked at her until she continued uneasily. "I started to, actually."

"And?"

She licked her lips as if her mouth were dry. "Well, one of the black guys that graduated with us got killed in Vietnam."

"I know that. So did two white guys who graduated with us. Your point?"

Her speech was growing more clipped and irritated. "I tracked down one of our black classmates, and her mother said she moved out of town—to Seattle or someplace. One of them . . ." She stared at a vending machine as if she expected it to spit out a gourmet meal instead of the stale Glad-wrapped sandwiches. "One of the guys is in prison, you know."

"Two of our white classmates are, too. I'm still trying to find out—"

"Oh, for Christ's sake!" she snapped, her eyes flaring anger and several other emotions, too—one of which was guilt. "Where was your head all those years ago besides up your own ass? Don't you realize the black kids stuck together and didn't hang out with us—

and vice versa? We didn't mix. Everybody socializes with their own kind, and that's the way life is whether we like it or not."

"That was forty years ago—"

"It was forty minutes ago! You and I are Slovenians. How many black seniors did we hang with? Were there any Jewish classmates we bonded and became friends with? How many Italians, or Hungarians, or Croatians were good friends with our parents, or had us over to their houses for dinner? America's been a segregated society in one way or another for the last two hundred and fifty years, and it didn't stop for a time-out that year we were all St. Clair seniors."

"There are African Americans working right in this office, Sonja. Don't you get along with them?"

"Sure, I get along with them. I get along with them fine. They're nice people, good workers, pleasant to talk to, and we have no work problems—on either side." Sonja's face was setting into granite. "But are they my good friends? Do we go out to lunch every day together? Do we go out shopping on Saturdays? Do we gossip and borrow each other's clothes? Do they and their spouses come to my house for a casual dinner, or do I go to theirs? No, Milan! Because that's the way things are in our world."

"In our world?"

"You better wake up and realize it. Look, I was going to invite all of them anyway, but when I called Shareeka—"

"Shareeka?"

"Shareeka Washington. She's married to James Worthman now—he works for the Board of Education. You remember her—she was one of the real brainiacs in our class. I think she was valedictorian."

"Salutatorian," I corrected her. "She was our number two genius, right behind Jack Siegel."

"Whatever," Sonja snapped. "When I asked on the phone if she was coming to the reunion, she told me off. From what she said, she doesn't have much use for white people—she never did, I guess, but now she's finally old enough to say so out loud."

"That doesn't sound right."

"That doesn't *mean* it's not right. I heard her loud and clear, so I just saved myself the trouble of calling any of the other ones."

I felt my backbone go soft, but I feared that if I leaned back against the plastic chair my jacket would get sticky with whatever someone had spilled on it. "That's really shitty."

"Not inviting blacks to a reunion?" Her eyes almost disappeared. "They never invited me to anything, either."

"They?" I put enough acid behind the word to really get to her. It worked, because the smattering of friendliness still left in her face disappeared like the sun during a lunar eclipse. Quickly, she stood up, brushed off her skirt, and looked at her watch.

"I have things to do," she said severely. "So do you. But ask yourself while you're doing them how many black people—or African Americans, or whatever the hell you're supposed to call them this year—you actually call *your* friends."

I stood up, too, madder than hell. "I guess I should rethink exactly who *are* my friends."

She got dangerously quiet, her jaw jutting aggressively forward. "Are you calling me a racist?"

I moved toward the door. "Look the word up in your dictionary, Sonja," I said. "I wonder if you'll find your picture next to it."

Damn it! The wind coming off Lake Erie turned the brisk February wind into steel wool against my face as I pulled on my gloves. For all I knew, my lifelong friendship with Sonja Kokol Caruth had breathed its last moments ago. The way I felt, ending the friendship was not a bad idea. Whatever might come of my argument with Sonja, I didn't think it would ever revert to the way it had been.

I thought about one of the last things she said to me and I ran through my friends and acquaintances in my mind. Dr. Reginald Parker, the current principal of St. Clair, is a black man, an Army Ranger combat veteran, and an intellectual tough guy who's saved my life not once but twice since I met him years ago. I'd call him one of my best friends. I still keep in Christmas-card touch with several men who'd shared my military police experience in Cam Ranh Bay in Vietnam, white, black, and brown—to me they were just my team, my buddies, my friends. None of them lived in Greater Cleveland now; only one of them was from Ohio, just north of Cincinnati. My short-term life on the Job with the Cleveland P.D. hadn't garnered me any close friends either, black or white—except for Marko Meglich—and that was so long ago.

Jesus, I thought, was I as much of a racist as Sonja?

My mental "No!" was so firm, I almost said it aloud as I fought my way through the punishing wind toward the parking lot where I'd left my car. If I had been sending out the reunion invitations, instead of Sonja, I would have made damn sure everyone, no matter their ethnicity, race, or attitude, had been contacted and cajoled—just like I had.

Yet I couldn't remember Sonja ever saying anything the least bit bigoted—until now. I had to wonder, then, what tension arose on the phone between her and the woman who told her off and refused to attend the reunion—Shareeka Washington Worthman.

I had no idea where she worked or lived, and it was too late in the day for me to start looking for her. Besides, I had a dinner date—with my new partner, Suzanne Davis, at Nighttown.

Nighttown—named after the redlight district in Dublin that James Joyce immortalized in *Ulysses*—is right at the top of Cedar Hill at the western edge of Cleveland Heights. It's about a block and a half from the apartment in which I've lived ever since my marriage collapsed, and there were more nights than I can remember during those early suddenly-single years when I sat at the Nighttown bar and drank quietly until closing time. The booze was good and the food wasn't bad, and then a real live Irishman named Brendan Ring bought the place and improved the food to excellent, built a covered outdoor patio, and turned Nighttown from a neighborhood bar into what's now one of the best jazz clubs in the entire world. For all the improvements, it's still a comfortable joint.

Suzanne and I met for dinner at 6:30 so we could eat, talk, and compare notes before the evening's entertainment took over. We sat in the smallest of the dining rooms, tucked right behind the bar, occupying a corner table where we could chat without tempting anyone sitting nearby to eavesdrop on us. Our preprandial cocktails were Jameson's Irish whiskey for Suzanne and a pint of Guinness Stout for me. It was still more than a month before St.

Patrick's Day, but many people feel that when in Nighttown they should drink something Irish, whether they like it or not.

She was wearing her hair in a loose bun, with wispy tendrils escaping on either side. "Sorry I look like hell," she said. "Before I left this morning, I couldn't find my hairbrush. Do you believe that? I can't imagine where I left it. I looked all over the house. I finally gave up and combed my hair with my fingers and put it into this messy bun."

I laughed. "I comb my hair with my fingers every day—because there's not enough there to worry about a hairbrush."

"Maybe I ought to invent a hairbrush on a rope to hang right next to the front door—that way I'll never lose it and then I won't walk around town looking like the Wicked Witch of the West. And I'll make millions off my idea, too."

"Your hair looks fine, as always," I said. "But I love finding out you're so disorganized."

"My personal life is always disorganized," she said. "Not when I'm working, though. Then I'm as together and professional as they come. It's like I'm bipolar that way."

Before we ordered dinner, I told her about my unpleasant meeting with Sonja Kokol.

"Wow," she said, "that must have been rough. She's one of your oldest friends."

"I hated every minute of it—but I don't feel too kindly towards her right now. It ticks me off to think someone I've cared about since we were kids has turned into this kind of person."

"I don't get it." Suzanne agitated her glass so the ice cubes clinked. "Unless Lieutenant McHargue is making a statement about race relations in this town, and at your old school, too—which ain't her job—why does she give a damn that no blacks were invited to your reunion?"

"It *seems* to be a statement. But it makes her think—makes both of us think—that a racial snub could have turned bad feelings into a murder." My thoughts were jumbled as I studied my tall dark-brown Guinness. "That's why she made me ask Sonja in the first place."

"Where are you going with this, Milan?"

I shrugged. “My next move is to talk to the woman who got into Sonja’s face on the phone.”

“That’s not going to be a day at the beach.”

“Only crazy Clevelanders go to the beach in February.”

“Good luck,” she said. “I had a busy day, too. I talked with Gary Mishlove this morning.” She opened her notebook. “My guess is that he weighs in at around three hundred and fifty pounds.”

“Looks that way,” I said.

“He admits he had a spirited discussion with the deceased at the reunion—all about his weight.”

“Really?”

“Dr. Kohn lit into him about taking off at least a hundred pounds or he was going to drop dead.”

“Was Gary his patient?”

Suzanne shook her head. “He says no. He doesn’t even have heart problems. But the minute Kohn saw him Friday night, he started scolding him about his health, and how stupid he was to allow himself to get so obese.”

“All doctors yell at their patients,” I said. “But they rarely yell loudly, and never at a public event with two hundred of your former classmates looking on.”

“Mishlove was still pretty angry, even though he seemed upset that Kohn is dead. Do you think that public scolding humiliated him into feeling murderous?”

“I doubt it, Suzanne. Gary Mishlove must know how out of shape he is. His showing up at the reunion was announcing ‘I’m-fat-and-I-don’t-give-a-damn’ to everybody. He might have been mad at Kohn, but hardly murderous. And why would he bring a gun to the reunion?”

“When I questioned him,” Suzanne said, “he swore that there was no bad history between them.”

“Was your questioning of him gentle?”

Her eyes sparkled. “I can do that sometimes. I can interview possible subjects like a pussycat—when I’m not being a hard-ass.” She flipped over a page. “I visited with—um—Amalia Turkman. The one with the dogs.”

“Welsh corgis.”

"Yes, whatever. She said she didn't know Phil Kohn very well in high school, and she's hardly ever seen him since then. But she wasn't exactly broken up about somebody taking him out, because she's pissed off with him."

"She's hardly seen him in forty years but she's pissed off?"

"But good."

"Why?"

She tasted her Jameson. "Do you remember a few months back there was a huge stink about some doctor at the hospital trying to get his bosses to buy some sort of medical device from a company in Maryland? He set up a demonstration of sorts—with a dog they'd bought from a kennel, for research. This doctor sent a message to all the other doctors and hospital buyers to attend the demonstration because, as he said, it might be a lot of fun." She tried not to shudder. "Fun!" she said. "When the demonstration started they used the instrument on that poor dog—I forget what breed it was and so did Amalia Turkman. They were administering a series of heart attacks and then bringing him back. They were literally torturing him to death—and everyone there who wanted a turn *got* one! The hell of it was, there was no reason to actually torment this dog over and over just to show off an obscure medical instrument. Eventually, when everyone had their turn zapping the poor little guy right there in the conference room, they had him destroyed."

"I read about that in the paper," I said. "It made the television news shows, too. Gruesome."

She nodded. "Well, Amalia is an animal rights advocate in Northeast Ohio, and she finally found out who the doctor was who arranged it—even though none of the papers or the news stations used his name."

I shook my head. "Don't tell me."

"I won't," she said, "but the Josef Mengele doctor's initials are Philip Kohn."

That made me whistle.

"So," Suzanne continued, "Amalia Turkman and her husband—" She checked her notes. "Her husband Augie—they're both into raising Welsh corgis into champions, and have them in dog shows all the time—were furious with Kohn."

I chewed on that. “He killed a dog for no reason, so now the Turkmans kill him?”

“I don’t think so,” she said, “but I’m not sure of anything. Maybe you’d like to drop by and try to pry more information out of Amalia Turkman.”

“I think I will,” I said. “Tomorrow.”

“Good.” Suzanne took another belt of her Jameson. “I love dogs too, y’ know.” She turned another notebook page. “I talked to three other people today, Milan, but I didn’t get a rise out of any of them. They didn’t know Kohn all that well, so their distress didn’t last very long—they’ve all moved on to other things.” She pushed the notebook toward me, turning it around so I could read her notes. “You can reinterview them if you want, but I think it’s a waste of time. I’ve got lots of other old pals of yours to chat with.” She cocked an eyebrow. “Unless you think Tommy Wiggins actually did commit the Kohn murder.”

“No—I think I’m reading him right,” I said. “Besides, he has more millions in the bank than I have fingers and toes. I can’t imagine him hunkering in the shadows of a public garage with a weapon in his hand, cocked and ready.”

“Maybe,” she said, “he spent a few of those hoarded dollars paying somebody else to do it for him.”

“Possible. But my job isn’t nailing his ass—it’s nailing somebody else’s.”

“Then pray you do,” she said. She opened her menu and studied it for a moment. “What’s good here, Milan?”

“Just about everything,” I said.

“What’s a Dublin Lawyer?”

“I couldn’t tell you the recipe, but it’s Nighttown’s specialty—cooked lobster in heavy cream and Irish whiskey, served over rice.”

“It sounds interesting. You had that?”

“A few times. It’s good.”

“Maybe I’ll try it.” She closed her menu and smiled across the table at me. “I dated a Dublin Lawyer once.”

“You did?”

“Yep,” she sighed. “But he wasn’t an Irishman. He came from Dublin, Ohio.”

• • •

After dinner, when Suzanne drove home to Lake County, I walked back to my apartment, well fed but thinking hard about all the things I did that day. I was afraid what I had told Morris Kepler—that I'm not a nice human being—was the truth, because except for Suzanne and my significant other, Jinny, everybody I knew was mad as hell at me. I didn't blame them. If I were on the other side of all these personal, intrusive questions, I'd be mad as hell at me, too.

The long years in my profession have taken a bite out of my ass. I've become cynical and suspicious of everyone—and now I had a long list of suspects, all of whom I'd known since we were fifteen, and their wives and husbands.

I started up the outside steps, digging into my pocket for my key, when a movement by the door caught my attention. I had to look more closely as the figure began to shiver forward into the pooling overhead porch light. It was Bernie Rothman, almost buried in his own parka with the hood up, nearly covering the red skullcap perched on his head. I knew he wasn't homeless, but I'd never seen anyone huddling outside in the bitter cold without somewhere specific to go. He'd obviously been waiting for me.

"Bernie, what are you doing out here in the cold?" I said, but he didn't answer me. He took a few more steps out of the shadows, straightened up inside his bulky parka, and drove his fist toward my jaw. Bernie Rothman obviously hadn't thrown too many punches in his life and this one was ineffective, especially coming from a man so much shorter than I am. It took me by complete surprise, so I couldn't block it, but I instinctively moved my head to one side so that his fist bounced harmlessly off my shoulder.

He almost whimpered a curse and then backed away from me. He was lucky I had no intention of hitting him back, anyway. One swing from me would have knocked him all the way back to Florida.

"What the hell is wrong with you?" I said.

"You bastard!" His voice approached a shout, too loud for the doorway of a residential apartment building but nearly swallowed up in the wind. "You sneaky goddamn bastard!"

"Lower your voice, Bernie," I warned, "or I'll lower it for you."

He stopped, gulped, and cringed, leaning against my front door. He was quite a pathetic figure.

I took my right glove off and fished in my pants pocket for my keys. "Come upstairs and tell me what's gotten into you," I said, "before you take another crazy swing at me and wind up falling down the steps."

"I don't want your goddamn hospitality!"

"Well, I'm not going to stand out here and discuss anything with you. So come up to my place and talk to me or stay here in the cold by yourself all night. Whatever you decide, though," and I grasped his shoulder and moved him forcefully from in front of my door, "get the hell out of my way."

I unlocked the door, swung it wide, and walked through. I wasn't sure if he'd come in, nor did I, at this point, care. However, without looking backward over my shoulder I heard his footsteps follow me, climbing up to the second floor.

Once inside my apartment, I took off my outer clothing and hung it up. Bernie Rothman stayed bundled the way he was, the hood of his parka drooping around his head, both hands stuffed into his pockets. He looked pretty ridiculous standing that way in the middle of my living room.

"Do you want a drink, Bernie? Or some coffee or tea?"

"I don't want anything of yours," he snapped.

I sat down in one of my more uncomfortable chairs, hoping he wouldn't stay long if I didn't get too comfortable. "Are you going to tell me why not? Or do I guess?"

His eyes narrowed to slits. "You moved in on Alenka when I wasn't looking," he accused. "You're making a play for her—trying to sneak in and steal her away from me, you son of a bitch!"

"I'm not doing any such thing."

"I saw you! I saw you kiss her!"

"Christ, are you following me around?" I said. "Have you gone completely crazy?"

His breathing was hard, his face flushed with anger. "I was sitting in my car, across the street from her house. I saw the whole thing. What were you doing there in the first place?"

I'd been sitting down for thirty seconds, but already I was tired of listening to him. I got to my feet. "What I was doing there, or anywhere else, is none of your business. And you're a stalker, Bernie. Alenka doesn't want to start up with you—you creep her out. As far as my sneaking in to take her away from you—I've lived across town from her ever since high school, all the while you were in Florida or Israel or wherever else you've been. It would have taken me a twenty-minute drive to get to her—and I'd have done it a long time ago if I'd wanted to."

His emotion was on rolling boil, somewhere between total rage and bursting out crying. Judging from his behavior at the Friday night reunion, he was prone to tears. "Then why did you kiss her?"

"It was a friendly kiss between two old friends—nothing more."

"Liar!" He literally danced with hatred, feet churning, his hands still in his parka's pockets. "You goddamn liar! It didn't look friendly to me."

"I don't care how it looked to you," I said. "You're over the top. Settle down, and maybe get some help with your anger. You're a smart guy—get hold of yourself."

"I'll get even with you, Milan. Wait and see if I don't."

"Don't threaten me, Bernie—and don't ever take a swing at me again, because next time I'll swing back." He looked frightened all of a sudden, and I tried to take some of the sting out of it. "Now shed your coat, have a drink, and calm down. It's a hell of a lot better than stomping out of here furious. Come on, what do you say?"

He didn't even have to think twice. "Fuck you!" he said hoarsely, putting a space between the two words and hurling them as if he'd never said them aloud before. It didn't bother me. I'd heard it before, and said better, too.

He had trouble getting his fists out of his pockets to wrench open my apartment door. In leaving, he slammed it hard enough that some photographs hanging on my wall went crooked—pictures of my boys. I heard Bernie bang down the stairs, and I moved to the window to see him explode out of the building and onto the front steps, his hood flapping around his ears. He trudged off into the night, his upper body bent forward against the wind, his feet kicking up little puffs of snow with each step—dirty snow piled on the sidewalk near the curb where the plows had displaced it, certainly not what lyric poets call virgin snow.

Bernie Rothman kicked at it viciously, enraged that there were no virgins *left* in this town.

CHAPTER FOURTEEN

I went to Augie and Amalia Turkman's house in Maple Heights first thing in the morning. Augie, of course, was at work, but Amalia was home, her dark hair in a perky ponytail, and wearing a red sweatshirt with a pair of white leggings that look like old-fashioned men's long underwear. Two cardigan Welsh corgis frolicked around her feet. The female was obviously pregnant with the Turkmans' next litter.

"Of course I was furious with Phil," Amalia said after she'd set me up with a cup of tea and sat me down at her kitchen counter. "I hold him in complete contempt. I resent any helpless animal being the subject of a gruesome experiment. I suppose animals can be helpful in testing new procedures or drugs, even though I think it's loathsome and unnecessary." She reached down and scratched the ears of the larger dog. "But this was an infernal machine of some sort—they swear it's an improvement over those paddles—designed to stimulate the heart with a kind of electric tingle, so they kept giving the dog a shot that almost stopped his heart and then jolted him alive again, over and over. It was worse that once wasn't enough. There were about a dozen people in that room, and every damn one of them played around with that poor dog's heart. Then they ordered it put down, and everyone at the demonstration went out to lunch together." She blinked back tears that were threatening to burst from her moist eyes. "It'd be hard for me to eat anything after that."

I nodded agreement, even though I've never owned a dog. My mother was afraid of dogs and never let me raise one—and Lila just doesn't like them.

"The memo Phil sent around the hospital inviting people to join the demonstration," Amalia said, "stated that it was going to be a lot of fun." Her eyes were wet and she sniffled. "A lot of *fun!* My God! The sad thing is, I think the son of a bitch *did* think it was fun."

"How did you find out it was Kohn? The *Plain Dealer* never printed his name."

"One of the lab technicians who works at the hospital in the cardio unit is a customer of ours—he has been since Augie's dad ran the cleaning shop. He came in late that day—the day of the experiment—to pick up his cleaning, and Augie was behind the counter. Of course we have color photos of our corgis all over the store and the customer saw them and got to talking with Augie about what he'd had to witness that morning—and he happened to mention that the doctor who was running the show was a real megalomaniac. Augie asked who, and he told him Phil Kohn."

"What did you do about it?" I said.

She looked helpless, frustrated. "There wasn't much I could do. I wrote several protest letters—one to the head of the hospital, one to the chairman of the cardio unit, and several to various humane societies and SPCA offices, using Phil's name, of course. I also wrote the newspapers. I don't know what, if anything, was done about it."

"Did you contact Phil Kohn, too?"

She smiled. The pregnant corgi stood up on her hind legs and put her front paws on her mistress's lap, and Amalia bent over and kissed her on the top of the head between her two pretty pointed ears. "I saved my angriest letter for last," she said. "I wrote and told him exactly what I thought of him."

"Did he answer?"

"He was probably too busy torturing another dog into cardiac arrest to write me a letter back," she said bitterly. "Or call me."

"You must have hated him for that."

"I hate anybody who enjoys torturing and killing animals. There's *never* a reason," Amalia said. "I suppose, in my wildest and most secret fantasies, I think about all the horrible things I'd like to do to those people—kill them the same way they've killed dogs and cats and rabbits. But it's just thoughts."

The male corgi wandered over to me, more curious than anxious, and I leaned over and scratched his neck as he pressed closer against my hand. Nice dog. "Does Augie share those murderous fantasies with you?" I said.

"I don't know. When you've been married to the same person for nearly forty years, your secret fantasies are just about the only thing you don't share." Then Amalia got serious. "I didn't kill Phil Kohn, Milan. Neither did Augie. I don't think I felt much pain when I heard he was dead—but I didn't do it."

"Tell me something," I said. "How would you have felt about Phil Kohn if he'd performed that demonstration on—" I looked down at the corgi beneath my hand, "on him, for instance?"

"I'd have cut Phil Kohn's balls off with a butter knife."

"Do you have any idea who wanted him dead?"

"None at all," she said. "But I'll bet my boots it was probably someone who loves dogs."

"I like dogs too," I said.

"Do you have dogs?"

"No. I live in an apartment—I couldn't have a dog."

Amalia ruffled the ears of the expecting corgi mother. "If you change your mind, Milan, I'll let you have the pick of the litter."

Scranton Road is very close to my own office in the industrial Flats on the west side of the river. The view isn't very scenic unless you happen to enjoy looking up underneath the bridges that span the various twists and turns of the river. As I drove along looking for a particular address that morning, I noticed some boldly painted graffiti on one of the pylons beneath the bridge's surface. PATSY IS UGLY, it said in highly stylized Day-Glo lettering. Not very nice, I admit, but it looked much better than most of what passes for modern art.

There's not much reason for you to visit Scranton Road in Cleveland. The buildings are all close to a hundred years old, and even though their small parking lots are occupied and there are signs on several of the doors and windows quietly advertising the tenants, today's Clevelanders have conveniently forgotten about them.

It was still cold on that particular morning, but the weather, in one of its many inexplicable caprices, showed up sunny and cheery, so bright I actually wished I'd worn sunglasses on the drive to work. It would have been a bad idea on which to follow through. People don't wear sunglasses in Cleveland in wintertime, unless they're ready to defend themselves.

Every February, Cleveland gets a break. For a day or two the temps hover around seventy degrees and the sun shines. Then we discover Mother Nature was just teasing, because it all goes away and we're slammed with two more months of snow, cold weather, and dark-gray skies. It's almost like what the movie business calls a trailer, a coming attraction. "This is spring—coming soon to a theater near you."

The address I found was a skinny, slightly bowed gray stone building that might have awakened that morning with a backache. A brassy plaque emblazoned with AFRICAN DRM was cemented into the wall beside the front door, the plaque looking nearly a century newer than the building itself. I went inside and climbed narrow steps to the third floor, emerging from the stairwell into a small but bright-looking office, its old-fashioned casement window peering across the dusty old street into the river. The coffee in the machine against one wall smelled fresh and good. A recording of Robert Lockwood Junior was playing softly in the background, too good to be relegated to an office's muted elevator music. Junior was the last of the great bluesmen. He'd died a few months earlier, in his nineties—America and Cleveland will never be the same.

Despite a computer with a large monitor glowing on the front desk, there was no one in the room, so I waited for a few moments, finally calling out a tentative hello. Almost immediately a young man emerged from a doorway. He was in his early twenties, wearing pressed khakis and a blue dress shirt with a mustard yellow tie, and from the way his body looked beneath the clothes and the effortless way he moved, he should've been playing second base for the Indians and not working in an office.

"Hi," he said pleasantly. "Can we help you?"

"I hope so," I said. "I'm looking for Shareeka Worthman." I gave him one of my business cards, and he studied it with more than casual interest. I doubt he'd encountered private investigators too often, especially in his office.

"Mr. Jacovich?" he said, mistakenly pronouncing the *J.* I corrected him.

"Sorry about that," he said. "Just a minute, please." He went back through the door from whence he'd come. I wandered around the confined front room, noting the morning's *Plain Dealer* on one of the tables, along with *Ebony,* the *Call and Post, Newsweek,* and *Time.* It was an upgrade on the reading material in any waiting room I've ever been in. I was impressed.

While I thumbed through the morning's paper I'd already read, Shareeka Worthman emerged from the same door, followed by the young man. Well into her fifties—like the rest of us—she was petite, as I remembered her from high school, and she hadn't added too much weight. Her beautiful hair was the color and texture of brushed silver, worn in a modified Afro, and her dress, deep maroon and vivid yellow, was fashioned from an African print fabric.

"As I live and breathe," she said, smiling and taking off her small glasses for a better look. "Has it been four decades since we've seen each other, Milan? I can't even remember."

We hugged and then she stepped back and looked up at me. "Well, some of the hair has gone in the front, there—but you look pretty fit otherwise."

"You even remember?"

"I remember you best in your football uniform," she said. "You were one of the biggest guys on the team—you stood out."

"That's why they put me on the defensive line," I said. "Coach figured nobody was going to get by me."

"From what I read about you in the papers these days, nobody gets by you now, either." She turned and indicated the young man who'd greeted me earlier. "This is my son, Jamie. Jamie, Mr. Jacovich and I went to high school together."

"Nice to meet you, sir," he said. His handshake was firm and friendly.

Shareeka looked at my business card. “You want to see me about something special?”

“If you have a few minutes.”

“Sure. Come on back into my office.”

There were six offices in the hallway we entered, each occupied by a busy-looking and professionally dressed employee. A few of them waved at her as we moved past their open doors.

Shareeka’s own office was bigger than the others, but not by much. The furniture looked nice, though not expensive. I noticed the framed awards and commendations she’d hung on her walls.

“Not as awesome as they look,” she said cheerily, indicating that I should take a seat on the small sofa against one wall. “All are nice things people have said about my business, and the awards come with a free cup of coffee—no refills. Do you know what we do here, Milan?”

“DRM, I suspect, stands for Direct Response Marketing.”

“Bingo. We advertise other people’s products or services by mail, by flyer, and once in a while when we’re paid enough to afford it, we produce a sixty-second commercial that runs on the off-network stations in the middle of the night. The African part of our company name means we mostly target the African American market, both here and nationally.”

“Nice,” I said. “This is your company, then.”

“Mine and my husband’s, except he works elsewhere so I run it.” Before I could ask anything else she added, “I got a degree in marketing at Bowling Green, and I regularly made the dean’s list. But after graduation, when I couldn’t land a decent job elsewhere in town—this was thirty-five years ago, mind you, and I was damned if I’d tuck away my diploma and spend the rest of my life cleaning other people’s houses—I decided to work for myself. It’s been a long haul, but worth it.”

“Congratulations. You’re making our class look good. I wish I’d gotten to know you better back in school.”

She sat down on the other end of the sofa, and her smile turned sour, even when she didn’t want it to. Her sigh was small and subtle. “Those were different days. So, Milan, what is it you wanted to see me about?”

"I guess you heard what happened Friday at our reunion? To Phil Kohn?"

"I read the papers."

"I'm sorry when Sonja Kokol invited you, you said you couldn't come."

She leaned against the armrest and her expression hardened. "I didn't say that. I said I *wouldn't* come."

"Mind if I ask why?"

"Mind if I ask why you're asking?"

"I'm working for a client who might be a suspect in Phil Kohn's death," I said, "and I'm trying to come up with any answers that will get him off the hook."

"Assuming he's innocent," she said.

"Assuming."

Her shrug was elaborate. "Why ask me, then? I wasn't anywhere near the reunion."

"I'm talking to all the local classmates, whether they were there or not."

"And you want to know why I didn't come?"

I said, "Let's start with that."

She drummed her fingers on her thigh, thinking about it. "I liked a lot of the people we went to high school with, Milan. For instance, when Jack Siegel beat me out and became valedictorian, I was glad as hell for him. We actually exchanged small personal gifts that graduation night. He's a real genius, and I was happy just coming in three percentage points behind him. I also had a tiny little crush on Marko Meglich, who was wide receiver on your team." She allowed herself another genuine smile. "That's a more glamorous position than yours, Milan. He scored touchdowns. Sorry." Then the smile disappeared. "Sorry what happened to him, too. I went to his funeral—but I was sitting toward the back of the church and I guess you didn't see me."

That made me sad about Marko all over again.

"Being a grind like I was," Shareeka went on, "I wasn't much into sports myself, but I was secretary of the Senior Girls Club and president of the International Relations Club. I got along fine with everyone in those groups."

I didn't say anything, because I was anxious to discover where she was going with all this.

"I got along fine with my white classmates—almost all of them."

"Almost?" I leaned forward.

"There was a small knot of girls—and guys, too—who persisted in treating black people as though we were subhuman. Oh, they weren't nasty to us, exactly. They just ignored us like we weren't there—except when they got caught looking at us with contempt to remind us that we weren't as good as they were." Shareeka looked me straight in the eye and took a deep breath. "One of the worst was one of your good friends, Milan. Sonja Kokol."

Now I took a deep breath, fighting off my disbelief. "God, I'm—well, obviously I'm sorry. I had no idea."

"*You* don't owe anyone an apology," she said. "You weren't in that elite group. But when Sonja called with the invitation, I could hear it in her voice—she *had* to invite me but she really didn't want me anywhere near *her* reunion. So I not only told her no, but I called everybody I could find—every African American who graduated with us—and told them to stay away, too."

The phone on her desk rang. She looked over at it with annoyance and then ignored it. After three rings someone else picked it up in another office. "This is the twenty-first century. I've got a college degree, run my own successful business, and am married to a pretty important man in Cleveland. FYI, I drive a new Mercedes, too. I'm damned if I'll put myself in a position where I'm going to feel like crap again, just like I did forty years ago." She drew in a fast breath and then blew it out even more quickly. "And that's it."

"That sucked," I said. "But things have changed. America has changed."

"Not all things," she said.

"Why was Sonja particularly—uh—angry with you?"

"Probably just because of the color of my skin—but it had something to do with the late Phil Kohn, too."

"Phil? He was a friend of yours?"

She threw her head back and laughed—it was more like a bray.

But her eyes weren't laughing. "For a very brief—*very* brief—time Phil and I were good buddies. I haven't seen him since high school graduation," she said. "I've tried not to hear his name, either. When I read in the paper Saturday morning that he was dead—well, I guess I've mellowed after all this time, so I didn't cheer. But I didn't feel particularly bad, either."

"Why is that?"

She looked up at the ceiling, imagining it to be heaven. "Do I have to tell this story again? It's been a long time . . ."

"You don't have to do anything," I said, "but I haven't heard it before, and it'd be helpful."

She thought about it for at least half a minute. Then she got up and closed the door before returning to the sofa. "I don't want anyone else in the office to hear this," she said, her voice lowered a few decibels. "Especially not my son." She leveled a painted nail at me, her hand steady. "I don't want you spreading it around, either, Milan. It's yesterday's news, okay? The day before yesterday . . ."

"I don't gossip," I said.

"A damn good thing, too. Okay." She squirmed around, getting more comfortable, crossed her hands demurely in her lap, and began telling a story. She didn't get too far into it before I began to understand why she didn't want anyone else to hear it—and why she didn't bother coming to the St. Clair High School reunion.

When she was seventeen years old and a senior in high school, she and her older sister were shopping at Higbee's Department Store on Public Square about three weeks before Christmas. They were walking out onto the street, laden with gifts for their parents and cousins, when they ran into Phil Kohn and Gary Mishlove, who were downtown just hanging around the way all teenagers did back then—and still do, I guess, except now they hang out in suburban shopping malls. They all got to talking, and Phil Kohn, who bragged that he often drove his dad's expensive car, suggested that he and Shareeka go out to a movie some Friday night, see a Christmas film, and then go out for a sundae or something afterward.

"My sister warned me not to go out with white guys," Shareeka said, "but I never thought of it as a date. It seemed like a nice thing two friends did together, especially at Christmastime. So I said yes."

I was itching to take notes but I fought the impulse, hoping I'd remember all of this later when I got back into the car.

"My parents seemed okay with it—my mother more than my father—but Phil actually came in the house to meet them, and he was so polite to my father, calling him sir, you thought he was made out of sugar. So we went to a movie—downtown, too. Afterwards, he came through on the rest of his promise and took me to Boukair's for a sundae. Remember that place, Milan? The amazing sodas and milkshakes, and the salad so good they never gave out the recipe to anyone? Anyway—Phil was driving me home and he took the long way, on East Boulevard through Rockefeller Park. We stopped and talked for a while, and he even kissed me. It surprised the hell out of me, frankly—I'd never kissed a white boy before. But what the hell—it seemed like a nice kiss. So I kissed him back."

She'd been looking at me while she spoke, but now her eyes drifted away. I wasn't sure if she was just looking out the window—not nearly as big as the one in the waiting room—or staring at a video screen inside her head, watching a replay of the long-ago past.

I noticed her fingers had grown tense on her lap. "That's when he tried putting his hand up my skirt."

I didn't say anything.

"I pushed his hand away two or three times. Finally I told him to stop it. He didn't want to. He said—" Shareeka stopped, swallowed, licked her lips, and went on. "He said he'd never seen a black pussy before—not in the flesh." She swiveled her head around to meet my gaze. Quiet rage bubbled behind her eyes like a laser. "Phil wanted to know," she said evenly, "if a black girl's cunt hair felt just like a Brillo pad."

I fought down an actual wave of nausea. I managed to choke out: "What did you do, Shareeka?"

"I slapped him hard on the side of the face, and caught part of his ear," she said. "His head must have been ringing for days afterwards. I knocked off his glasses, too, and broke the frames—they cut the bridge of his nose before they fell. He looked pretty shocked—I don't think anyone had ever hit him before." She finally settled against the back of the sofa and relaxed, relieved she'd actually told the story.

"He was furious, though. He reached over, unlocked the car door, and pushed me out before he drove away," she said. "So there I was, in the middle of Rockefeller Park at about eleven o'clock at night. I walked back up to St. Clair Avenue, went into a bar—and you can imagine the looks and the catcalls and the racial crap I got in there—and called home. Thank God my sister answered, and she came and got me. Neither of us ever said anything about it to my dad, or he would've gotten a gun and gone looking for Phil Kohn." She compressed her lips. "He would've found him, too."

She put up a hand to stop me. "I have plenty of white friends, and business acquaintances, too. And like I told you, at graduation I was very close to Jack Siegel—we worked on a physics project together during the last semester. But I never again went out with a white guy, nor was I ever that comfortable being alone with one, just the two of us."

"Did a lot of people know about it at school?"

"I suppose so," Shareeka said. "I'm sure your friend Sonja knew about it because she said something to me about a week later."

"What did she say?"

She compressed her lips even more. "It's not important. But when she called and invited me to the reunion, I just wasn't in the mood to go—not to see her, not to see some of her other friends, and for sure not to see Phil Kohn. So instead of suffering through a boring evening, my husband and I invited two other couples over for spaghetti and wine, and afterwards we played Scrabble." She winked. "I won three games out of four."

"No wonder you won," I said. "You were the salutatorian."

"You want to know something else about my mini-party Friday night, Milan?" Her smile broadened. "One of those other couples was white."

CHAPTER FIFTEEN

It was late afternoon, the winter light disappearing through the window of Florence McHargue's office at the Third District. I was telling the lieutenant and Bob Matusen about my meeting with Shareeka Washington Worthman. Matusen listened intently, jotting down notes. McHargue looked as if she'd just bitten into a rancid peanut.

"Your friends are real pips, Jacovich," she said. "Your black classmates should have stayed at a segregated school. At least they'd be treated decently."

"You're talking about a small minority of my friends," I reminded her. "The points I'm trying to make are that the reunion was de facto segregated even when no one believed it would be, and that African Americans disliked Phil Kohn as much as whites did."

"Maybe," Matusen observed, "someone killed him because they'd been ostracized from that reunion."

"It's tough," McHargue said, "believing anyone killed Kohn over something that happened forty years ago."

"If that's true," I said, "why lean so hard on Tommy Wiggins? He was pissed off at Kohn over an insulting joke at a Christmas dance in high school."

Her glare made her resemble an angry mongoose. "He was pretty mad Friday night, Jacovich, we know that. And he hasn't given any indication why, other than the gay joke. Apparently he'd nursed a grudge his whole adult life, and came back to Cleveland to do something about it."

"To tell Kohn off," I said. "Not to kill him."

That cast a pall over the conversation until Matusen, hoping to start it up again, observed, "Life is strange, isn't it?"

It *was* strange—how something trivial to most people can get under one person's skin so much that they might kill over it. Even things that seem normal to some appear strange to others. This country has been split apart over things that bother some of its citizens throughout all of the still-short twenty-first century. Not just the war in Iraq, which I think upsets most of us in one way or another—but gay marriage and abortion and stem cell research and immigration and sending local jobs to India to pay workers a tiny fraction of what American employees used to make, and whether your car or your neighborhood or your religion is as good as mine. The only thing most Americans agree on is football, assuming they care about it at all—and there are vicious fights every day about that, too, depending on which team you root for.

Sometimes anger doesn't ever go away. Tommy Wiggins had a hate on for Phil Kohn since high school because he'd joked unfairly about Tommy's masculinity. Bernie Rothman never recovered from being in love with Alenka Tavcar. Shareeka Washington never completely let go of the memory of her one insulting senior-year date with Kohn. Ted Lesnevich hated my guts for forty years when I hardly knew he existed—and now that he's a white-collar drug dealer, I still don't know what I did to get on his hate list. Sonja Kokol has quietly nurtured her ugly racial bigotry since she was a teenager.

Matusen was spot on when he mused that life is strange.

When I went to see Gary Mishlove after dinner, I had little idea what kind of relationship he'd had with the late Phil Kohn. They argued at the reunion an hour before Kohn was shot. Suzanne had reported to me from her interview with Gary that it was over his excess weight and the damage it threatened to his heart. I hoped to get a better answer than that.

Gary Mishlove was a salesman for a medical equipment company and spent most of his weeks on the road, so his apartment in Strongsville was dull and unassuming, with little more personality than a Best Western motel room. One of its bedrooms was converted into an office, and the TV set in the living room was a small one bought at least ten years ago. The rest of the sparse furniture looked like it was from Value City. There were no pictures or photos on the walls. The newspapers and magazines strewn all over the living room concerned themselves with sports and entertainment. Gary, I learned, had married in his mid-twenties, and his wife left him four years later because he'd grown too fat.

He stood about five feet, six inches. His dark hair had thinned out considerably and was probably gray beneath the self-applied black-shoe-polish dye. His face was full and chunky, framed by an alarming set of jowls, and the rest of his body had settled into the shape of a squash. When he was standing up it was probably impossible for him to see his own feet. An uncouth young guy had turned into an uncouth middle-aged man. As a teenager he never bothered looking for a men's room when he was outside, but stepped off the curb between two parked cars to relieve himself, and he didn't much care who else was around to see it. My guess was that he hadn't changed.

He was wearing an enormous pair of jeans from a big-and-tall catalog, and a faded sweatshirt with a Cavaliers logo on the front—the old Cavs logo before they changed their uniform colors and their ownership. He was almost panting; rising from his sofa and walking to the front door had run him out of breath.

"I already talked to that other woman working for you," he wheezed. "What was her name, Suzette?"

"Suzanne," I said. "But I wanted to check some things out with you. Is this a good time?"

"Goody, somebody else to talk to. Sure, fire away—I already had dinner." He inadvertently looked through an archway into the small kitchen. An extra-large Donatos pizza box was on the counter, opened and empty. My guess was that it had contained their special Serious Meat Pizza.

"How friendly were you with Phil?"

"I'm friendly with everybody," Gary said.

"In high school?"

"We were friendly in high school."

"You quarreled at the reunion?"

"We didn't quarrel, *he* quarreled. He was in my face about my weight." He threw up his hands. "Like I don't know I'm heavy already."

"Did he do that every time he saw you?"

Gary shrugged helplessly.

"How often was that?"

"Do I look like a twelve-year-old girl who keeps a diary? I don't know—every once in a while."

"But in high school, you were close buddies."

"We were minorities—Jews going to a high school full of Slovenians like you. Along with Jack Siegel and Bernie Rothman and a couple other guys and girls, we stuck together because we were all in the tribe."

"Did you stay friends with them all these years?"

"With Bernie, yes, even though he moved away. We'd get together every time he came back to Cleveland to see his folks. And I was right there helping him out when he lost his mother. He really needed a friend at that point. I see Jack maybe four times a year, too—he's married and I'm single so we have different lifestyles. But Phil Kohn? Not so much."

"You didn't like him anymore?"

"Nobody liked him anymore. When we were kids, living in a very Catholic neighborhood like St. Clair Avenue in the east fifties and sixties, we stuck together because we were all Jewish. When we got older and smarter, it wasn't such a hard-and-fast rule that you stayed friends with your own kind and shut everyone else out."

"I see," I said.

"*You* got along with everyone, Milan—I remember that. Everybody liked you and looked up to you. But your closest high school pals were Slovenian, too. That's how neighborhoods happen. Somebody new in the community finds people just like him and moves next door. "

"You didn't get along with Slovenians?"

"We got along with them fine," he said. "But we didn't hang around together picking out china patterns."

"Same with blacks?"

Gary Mishlove shook his head. "Not exactly the same. To tell you the truth, we hardly associated with them."

"Why not?"

His voice rose in decibels and pitch as it had at age seventeen whenever he got excited. "Because they scared the shit out of us. They probably scare the shit out of you, too, if you're totally honest."

"I *am* totally honest, Gary, and nobody scares the shit out of me, no matter what color they are, unless they're carrying an AK-47 and walking a pit bull."

He slapped his hands to his face like the little brat in the *Home Alone* movie. "*Oy*! Pit bulls yet!" Then he laughed. I couldn't think of a reason why, and I suspect he couldn't, either.

"I guess Shareeka Washington never scared you back in high school."

His smile lost considerable wattage. "She was a real brain then—a smart girl who studied all the time. I didn't know her very well."

"Phil Kohn did."

He shifted his shoulders, and lowered his chin like a turtle sensing nearby danger and preparing to hide inside his shell. "Didn't all of us know everybody back in school?"

"Phil invited her out to a movie date," I said. "You were there when he asked her."

"Yeah."

"And?"

"I didn't go on the date with them—so how the fuck should I know?"

"You started talking to her first—when you ran into her downtown. Is that right?"

His jaw grew fierce-looking, or it would have if it weren't well padded with suet. "Who told you that? Did she say that?"

I ignored the question. "But Phil horned in, right? He asked Shareeka out before you had a chance to."

He wiped his mouth with the back of his hand. "I wasn't gonna ask a black girl on a date. My parents would have killed me. But when it comes to girls, high school guys do that all the time—horning in on other guys if they can. It wasn't a big deal."

"You must have gotten pretty sore at him."

Gary wrinkled his nose. "Yeah, but it only lasted like a day and a half and then it was over. We were best friends back then," he said with a certain bravado. "No chick ever came between two good guy friends—not Shareeka, not nobody."

"From what I hear, Phil's date with her didn't go too well."

He snickered. "She surprised him, he told me. She slapped his face and broke his glasses."

"The way he treated her—did that get you mad?"

"Hell no, I didn't get mad. What do I care? The whole date was a washout, anyway."

"You weren't jealous?"

"All he got off her was a little tit, and that was it."

I couldn't keep my feelings off my face. "Gary, how come you still talk like a sixteen-year-old?"

"Maybe because I never really grew up, Milan," he said with sad innocence.

"When you were all in high school, you and Jack Siegel and Bernie Rothman used to do Phil's science homework for him almost every night, right?"

"Yeah, as I remember, we did."

"So Phil got to be one of the highest-paid cardiologists around here—and you're traveling all over selling medical equipment."

"So what?"

"Does that bug you, Gary? You did all his homework and now he gets to be a rich doctor."

"And I got to be a salesman. His parents could afford to send him to Stanford, and mine scraped by sending me to junior college. Listen, fate works that way sometimes." He looked at his watch as if, dressed like a slob, he had someplace he had to go.

"Can I touch on one more thing?"

"Yeah, but make it snappy, will you, Milan? I don't want to miss *Jeopardy*." He sucked in his basketball-sized stomach as far as it would go—which wasn't very far at all. "I'm great at *Jeopardy.*"

"How come he jumped on you about your weight at the reunion?" I said. "That was odd for him, especially since he saw you several times a year anyway."

He didn't look at me directly while he tried to decide whether or not to tell the truth. Finally he said, "Phil—Phil's department, I should say, and he was the chairman—was one of my better customers, buying sophisticated cardiac equipment. Two weeks before the reunion, Phil's nurse called to let me know they were buying from another company instead."

It seemed every time I talked to another St. Clair classmate, I got stunned all over again. "Is that the company that helped Kohn demonstrate their equipment on a dog—and it made all the papers and headlines?"

"Damn right," Gary Mishlove said, "except they never named Kohn and they never named the company. Even the media wasn't looking for a lawsuit."

"I see," I said, learning more every minute.

"That was a real shot in the ass, pal, let me tell you. But after that, every time I called his office about it—about him taking business away from me and food off my table—his nurse or whoever told me he was out, or with a patient or in a meeting . . ."

I nodded.

"The first time I got to talk to him after that was Friday night. I asked him why, point blank." Gary put his small hands on his spreading thighs and stared at the carpet. "He said I was so fucking fat it embarrassed him when I came into the office—and he was going to start buying from somebody who didn't look like a hog. Okay?"

"That must have got you furious."

"I was so mad at the cocksucker that I . . ." He stopped talking as his face went whiter than usual. "I was mad at him—I admit that. But I didn't kill him. Do I look like a goddamn killer? Come on, give me a break."

I was not certain the police would give him any sort of break at all.

. . .

The Veterans Affairs Medical Center in Cleveland is on East Boulevard, an area with many aged but still handsome mini-mansions on one side of the street and part of the Cultural Gardens in the park on the other. Whatever your ancestral background, you can find it in those gardens if you look hard enough. Many of the ethnic groups haven't worked on the upkeep of their small patches in the past several years, but it's one of those only-in-Cleveland sights for tourists that I love—especially the Slovenian Garden. I'm embarrassed to admit I've never been inside it, but I drive by it all the time and feel a sense of pride.

I arrived at the hospital at about 10:30 A.M. on a February morning as grim and depressing-looking as any day of the year. The VA hospital is hardly cheery, either.

It took me thirty seconds at the front desk to track down Booker Bratton.

Booker and I played high school football together. I plodded away on the defensive line; he was a fullback, short and solid with amazing speed—so talented that he played on special teams as well as on offense, mostly returning kickoffs. He volunteered to go off to Vietnam with the infantry and was shipped back four months later, a grievously wounded quadriplegic with minor brain damage and an injured heart valve. Unable to do much of anything, he took up permanent residence at the VA hospital and has stayed there ever since as his family eventually moved on in their lives or simply died. Shareeka Worthman was the only regular visitor he had—and that says an awful lot about Shareeka in terms of real friendship.

I knew Booker hadn't been invited to the St. Clair reunion to begin with, and it had nothing to do with his race. Except for wheelchair rides around the grounds in good weather, and a few group excursions to Indians games over the years, he never left the hospital. No one imagined he would live this long, and I had the feeling Booker Bratton hadn't expected to either.

He was watching morning television with about a dozen other male patients. Most of them were close to his age, but one looked to be in his early twenties, and I figured he'd been in Iraq within the last few years and something like a suicide car bomb must have blown off both his legs several inches above his knees. He was angrily talking back to *The Price Is Right* in front of him, rocking his wheelchair back and forth, filled with life—and nothing he can do with it and nowhere to take it.

Booker Bratton didn't remember me at first; it was, after all, forty years since I'd seen him, and he and I had both changed. He'd weighed a solid 210 pounds back in his football days—now he was nearly a hundred pounds less than that. His arms and legs had atrophied to awkward sticks. He asked me to wheel him to the other side of the room, away from the TV set and its most vocal viewer.

I pulled a folding chair up next to him and reminded him I'd been in Vietnam too, as an MP, and I explained that I'd become a private investigator. He nodded sagely and said "Yes" a few times, barely understanding a word of it. I finally reminded him we'd played football together at St. Clair High for three years.

"I was a defensive tackle," I told him.

"Oh, yeah. No wonder I don't recognize you," he said, speaking with a difficult slur. "Never saw you 'ithout a helmet—'less you was butt-ass nekkid in the shower." His crooked smile was genuine.

"I wanted to bring you something, Booker," I said, "but I didn't know if you smoked, and I figured the nurses would take away a bottle of booze. So . . ." I gently placed in his lap a fancy box of candy I'd bought at Mitchell's on Lee Road that morning. "I don't even know what kind of candy you like, so this is mixed—dark chocolate and milk chocolate."

His eyes lit up. "Tha's okay," he said, holding the box on his lap with his left forearm. "I thank you, Milan." He ducked his chin and lowered his eyes, almost shy.

"Can I open that for you? You can pick out your favorite."

The sound he made in his chest sounded like laughter. "Don' tell no one, though. The nurses find out I had a candy before lunch they skin me alive."

I ripped off the plastic wrapping and opened the box, extended it so he could make a decision. Finally he said, "That big round milk choc'late one in the corner looks good."

I carefully removed it from the box and moved it up to his mouth. He took all of it between his teeth, chewing it up and almost purring.

"Mmm," he said. "I betcha that one's maple flavor. Oooh, yeah! You go on, take one for you'self."

"That's okay, Booker, they're yours."

He shook his head. "If I have one of these ever' day it'll take me more'n a month to finish it all. You have one."

"Have the nurses pass it around to your friends, then."

He nodded. Then he said, "You know what I really like?" His expression turned sly. "Malted milk balls. Whoppers, you call 'em? I like 'em a lot, an' they's cheap, too."

"Whoppers it is next time."

"That be excellent. So—um—Milan. You come by to ask me 'bout somethin'? Shareeka Washington phoned up and said you was comin'."

Booker still thought of Shareeka Worthman by her maiden name. I moved my chair closer to him. "You know there was a senior class reunion last Friday?"

He chuckled softly. "Yep. I din' go, though."

"Does it make you mad that nobody invited you?"

"Shee-it, no, man. Anybody knows I wouldn' of showed up anyways. Besides, what Shareeka say, it was only white folks."

That hadn't been my choice, and it still ripped my guts out just to hear it. "I remember when we were in high school, Booker—you were friends with just about everybody."

He nodded, his head on the skinny stalk of his neck moving painfully. "I be friends with jus' about everybody now, too. You notice back there, patients sittin' around the TV set is black, white, Mezcan . . . We all diff'rent colors, but we got sumpin' more impo'tant in common with each other. We none ain't ever walkin' outa here."

"Can I ask you a few questions, Booker? You don't have to answer if you don't want to."

"I answer anythin' you ask, man. But I don' wanna get—um—clinical 'bout how I live here, 'cause it be gross . . ."

"Just about the people we went to high school with. You remember Phil Kohn?"

The sunny look on his face disappeared behind a dark overhanging cloud. "He got capped the other night. The Jewish guy."

I nodded.

"I seen him—saw him—'bout eight, ten years ago. He come right here to this hospital for me. He wouldn'a come 'cept Shareeka ask him to."

"Shareeka?"

He tried a smile again but it didn't work out well. "On top o' all the other shit wrong with me—the spine out a condition an' the . . ." He stopped, tried to remember the ten-dollar word, and finally did, pronouncing it carefully. " . . . the aneurysms in my brain—one o' my heart valves sprung a leak." He wanted desperately to tap his heart telling me about it, but he couldn't move his hands anywhere near his chest. "Like you drivin' your car an' one o' your tires spring a slow leak." His smile was crooked and off-kilter. "I think it somethin' like that, anyways."

"So Kohn came here to examine you? He was a cardiologist."

Booker Bratton made a sound suspiciously like a Bronx cheer. "Man, my grammy was a better heart doctor than him. Oh yeah, he examine me—listen to my heart with one a them thingies you stick in your ears. For 'bout half a minute he listened. It take me longer to read the football scores on Monday than him examinin' me. Then he said I should take Coumadin—which I'm already taking—and didn't offer no other advice. Then he skeedaddled outa here fast, like he had someplace more important to go. It was a ten-minute deal. Maybe less. I started out bein' glad he come here to see me, an' pretty soon I felt lousy he wasn't givin' me more'n ten minutes. Dirty bastard. He was always a dirty bastard, even in school." He blew air through his lips, imitating an attempted whistle, but he didn't have enough strength for it. "Damn, he wouldn'a come here at all if it wasn't for Shareeka ask him. And that took lots a balls on her part, 'cause in our senior year he did somethin' real shitty to her which I'm not gonna talk about, an' she never forgive him. Tha's why I appreciate the friendship with her—she worries about me. Otherwise she wouldn'a pissed on Kohn if he was on fire."

I reached over and squeezed his leg warmly, realizing too late he wouldn't feel it. "That tells me a lot, Booker. Thanks for spending time with me."

"Hey, I know your job, an' I—respect—what you do. But I didn't have nothin' to do with Kohn catching a slug." He barely moved the fourth finger on his right hand against the control on the arm of his chair and it jerked forward for a few feet. "I had an alibi." He smiled big. "Know what I'm sayin'? It's too damn hard drivin' this chair through the snow."

I stood up, feeling awkward that I was looming this close to a man who would never stand up again. "I'll come back and see you, Booker—with no more questions. Just like old friends—teammates. I'll bring you some Whoppers next time, too. I promise."

"Tell me ahead of time, okay?" he said. "I'll remind Nursey to put in my teeth."

I did visit him again—probably once every two or three months—and I always brought him a big carton of Whoppers, which made him happy. A few weeks after my fifth or sixth visit, Shareeka called and told me Booker had died. He spent thirty-eight years of his life in that chair, in that hospital, in that hell. I hope he's gone to heaven, if there is such a place, finally running the football again the way he used to, moving relentlessly, joyously forward with his legs pumping high and hard, laughing and joking, and chasing beautiful women.

CHAPTER SIXTEEN

I got back to my office shortly after noon. There were several other cars in the parking lot, most belonging to the owner and employees of the wrought-iron shop that rented my first floor so they can make gates and railings, so I didn't pay any attention to the dark-blue Buick until I locked up my own car and started toward the building. I heard a door slam and looked over my shoulder to see Bernie Rothman heading toward me again. He didn't look quite as cold and miserable as he had on my apartment doorstep, but his facial expression conveyed a different emotion now—it looked a lot like shame. He still worried me, though, and as he scurried up to me, I turned to face him head on, pulling tight the glove on my right hand. Bernie Rothman was a poor, sad little guy I'd give anything not to hit back—but I can't have people swinging roundhouses at me by surprise, and in case it was called for, I only wanted to have to throw one punch.

"Think twice, Bernie," I said, putting out my left hand to keep him at a distance, "before you try another sucker punch. The first time I let it go and blamed it on your emotional state. The second time I won't."

His cheeks flamed with embarrassment. "Please don't threaten me, Milan—I came to apologize. I'm so sorry—that I tried to hit you, I mean. I feel like a total jerk." He whined believably, but I still took note of whether he had his hands in his pockets. A silly, jealous fool carrying a weapon automatically becomes a dangerous fool. However, his hands were clasped in front of him, almost as if he were praying.

He followed me up the stairs to my office, babbling incessantly, trying to explain that when a man is in love—*truly* in love—he can become envious and enraged over the simplest things.

I hung up my coat as he continued: "I don't know if you've ever been in love the way I have for my entire adult life. I couldn't make it happen after high school—with Alenka, naturally—because of my parents. You know what I'm talking about—the religion thing. Then I was living down in Florida and out of touch for a long time, and I didn't know Alenka and her husband were separated until I showed up for the get-together."

"Who told you?" I asked.

That put a momentary plug in his jabbering. "Uh—I can't remember," he managed to stammer, seeming confused. "Somebody I talked to before the reunion told me. Maybe it was Gary Mishlove, but I'm not sure. You know Gary, he blabs about everything."

I wondered if and how Gary Mishlove knew about Alenka Tavcar's love life, but I didn't press further because, frankly, I didn't care.

"Why were you hanging around outside her house, Bernie?"

He looked pained. "This is embarrassing."

"Say it anyway."

He tried to straighten up to his full height, but he still didn't even reach my chin. "I was crazy jealous, Milan. I mean, after I talked to her at the reunion she wouldn't even chat with me on the phone. She told me she wasn't interested, she told me to forget about it. It ripped me up inside. It just ate out my *kishkas,* you know? And I couldn't help wondering whether she was seeing somebody else—some other guy. So I was hanging around across the street from her house trying to find out, and—and then I saw you. It got me crazy, thinking you were dating her—especially after I opened my soul to you Friday night. You understand where I'm coming from, right?" He pointed to me and then to his own chest. "Guys understand things like that."

I didn't understand things like that at all—not after living my own history. I'd been betrayed and then deserted by my wife,

Lila, and after that pain had eased, I'd been dumped a few more times—until I met Jinny Johnson. Somehow I've always been unable to sustain a serious relationship while pursuing my line of demanding and dangerous work. It disappointed me, wounded me, and even made me sad, but being kicked to the curb has *never* made me crazy or jealous—or even crazy jealous.

"Are you letting it go now, Bernie?"

"No, sir," he said, standing up straighter and prouder. "No, sir! I'll give it some time, that's all. Time changes everything, doesn't it? Eventually. I'll give her time to chill out and think more clearly—and then I'll approach her again." Now he looked sly and manipulative rather than just plain nuts. "If someone could help me, could talk to Alenka for me—somebody like you, Milan—to be my messenger, my Cupid, and let her know how much I love her . . ."

"Forget it!" I said. "I don't get involved in other people's love affairs—ever. Besides, I've got more pressing things to do."

"Of course," he said, snapping his fingers. "Mea culpa, I forgot. You're looking into Phil Kohn's murder, aren't you?"

I looked at my watch, and impatience grew inside me like a heartburn. "I've got a busy day ahead, Bernie."

Now he became warm and friendly; suddenly we were best buddies. "Oh, I know. How's that going? Do you have any clues? Have you figured out who killed Phil? I hope you get the right guy." Bernie Rothman could run through all of his various emotions at warp speed. If he didn't buckle his seat belt tight, he'd fall out of his spaceship.

I didn't want to get into explanations. It was none of his business anyway. "It's coming along."

"Do you think it was Tommy Wiggins after all?"

"I haven't thought about it," I said.

"There were so many people mad at Phil back in the day. It could be anybody, now—even one of the girls."

"Could be."

He cocked his head like a sparrow, listening. "Were you mad at him back then too, Milan?"

"I'm not investigating me."

He forced a laugh. "Just kidding."

I took a folder out of the drawer, sat down at the desk, and began reading it, hoping he'd get the idea and go away.

"So am I forgiven?" he said.

He'd become a whining, demanding puppy. I worried that if I didn't mollify him he'd pee on the carpet like a cocker spaniel. "Apart from your uncontrollable jealousy, Bernie, you have an anger management problem—especially over nothing. If you keep going around trying to punch people out all the time, one of them will take umbrage and slug you back."

"I know—really, I know. I'm turning over a new leaf. I'll count to ten every time. To twenty, maybe."

"Good solution."

"I—appreciate your patience with me. I know you could've killed me with one swing."

"And another thing," I said. "Give up on Alenka. She's not interested anymore. Time moves forward whether we like it or not, and it passed that relationship by a long time ago. Forget about it and get yourself a new life."

"I'll—try. I will, I swear." He leaned over my desk and stuck his hand out for me to shake. His fingers were icicles from the cold. "You're a good friend, Milan. I don't know what I would have done without you."

I listened to him clatter down the stairs and thought of all sorts of things I wished he would have done without me. I thought of a few things I wished *I* hadn't done, and one of them was accepting the job Ben Magruder offered me. My sudden invasion into the lives of people I'd once been close with and then lost track of had me feeling uncomfortable and almost voyeuristic.

They'd all changed, my high school compatriots—but I'd changed as well. Everyone changes, grows, settles. Even Cleveland has changed. The things I grew up with are gone, now—the massive old Cleveland Municipal Stadium where the Browns and Indians played. Hough Bakery with its unbeatable cakes and pastries, and Higbee's, the department store where the Cleveland elf, Mr. Jingeling, made the holidays special for every kid in town. I got my first adolescent kiss at Euclid Beach Amusement Park, but all that's left of that playland is the stone archway that used to be the entrance—and some driver recently smashed into that in the middle of the night. My parents raised me in a little house just off St. Clair Avenue in the east sixties—a neighborhood made up almost completely of Slovenians and Croatians—but few of them live there anymore. I lose more reminders of my youth every year that goes by. Working on an investigation I didn't want the best part of, I was being forced to let go of more and more of those reminders. I was alienating my classmates and losing the reminiscences of my innocent years at St. Clair High school, too.

That stunk.

"Phil Kohn was a stone druggie?" Ben Magruder said, trying not to smile as he said it. He tilted back in his desk chair and looked up at the elegant ceiling of his private office, making his handsome face look pensive. "I can't believe it. The guy was a doctor."

"Doctors take drugs too, Mr. Magruder."

"Ben," he corrected me for the twenty-fifth time—but his correction was offered absently. Trying to make me call him by his first name had by now become a habit he didn't work at too hard. "You suppose he owed money to one of the drug pushers he was buying from and they took him out?"

"Possible. But I learned from one of his acquaintances—his bookie, actually—that guys you stiff for a lot of money don't kill you before they get what they're owed."

"Kohn was a gambler, too?" He shook his head, astonished. "Jesus."

"He lived a busy life, I'd say." I shifted around in my chair. It was almost too comfortable—and too low as well, so any visitor sitting in it would be forced to look up to Magruder. "I gave all this to Lieutenant McHargue this afternoon—I had to—so the police know as much as we do."

"Excellent." Magruder rubbed his hands together like a miser. "That's wonderful news for us, because Tommy Wiggins is looking less and less like a suspect every day."

"He's still the only one who came close to blows with Kohn on the night of the murder."

"Over an old insult."

"Maybe," I said, "and maybe not. Tommy is well known for his taste in beautiful young women, and maybe the same woman was involved with both of them. Phil Kohn was a skirt chaser as well—to excess, from what I hear. There are several women who might be mad at him." I paused for a heartbeat. "Or women's husbands."

Magruder's expression didn't change, but his eyes lost their light and something curled up and died inside. "I hope that's not a personal remark."

"I'm not talking about your marriage. Back in high school your wife and Phil Kohn dated—and that's all I know."

His brave voice was miles off the mark. "Danielle has nothing to do with Kohn's death."

"Okay," I said, but I wouldn't let him tear his gaze away from mine.

"I didn't have anything to do with it, either."

"Then you won't mind if I spend a few minutes talking to Danielle."

He teetered on the brink of fury, fighting to control some inner demons. "I didn't hire you to fuck around in my own personal life," he said coldly. "Or Danielle's, either."

"I just want to go over the normal questions with her that I'm asking everyone else."

He sucked air through his nose and then expelled it from between his lips. "Is that necessary?"

"Nothing's necessary," I said. "You can pull the plug right now. But you hired me out of Wiggins's retainer. I'd have to explain to him why I'm no longer working on his behalf."

Magruder looked ready to make a negative judgment about my suit. "You think you're a pretty hard man, don't you?"

"Not so much these days. But I think I can take *you* without any trouble." I smiled so I wouldn't sound threatening—but he got the idea.

I watched the limited options play out across his face as he thought of them one by one. Should he call the building's security? Take out his desk-drawer gun and shoot me? Or fall on his knees and beg for my mercy? He finally went another way.

"Do whatever you want," he said, waving his hand languidly in the air, shooing away an imaginary mosquito. "Go ahead—talk to my wife, if it'll make you feel any better."

"Making me feel better is a good suggestion," I said. "But it's not what my job is about." I hoisted myself out of the visitor chair and the forced position of inferiority it put me in, and made my way to his office door. "Don't bother showing me out," I reminded him.

Danielle Webber Magruder lived with her husband in a stately Georgian house just one tick shy of a mansion on Edgewater Drive on the near West Side of Cleveland. The dark stone house was three sprawling stories with a large expanse of grass and shrubs in the front, and when I pulled into the driveway I could see at its edge a cliff that dropped off sharply into the waters of Lake Erie. When I called to tell her I was coming, she sounded resentful—but I was growing used to that.

In her living room I got an up-close look at her for the first time since graduation night—at the Friday reunion I only saw her from a distance with her husband. She had hardly changed at all since her adolescence. Wearing cashmere sweaters was one of her youthful habits she seemingly hadn't given up or grown out of—today her elegant top was vivid purple to complement her black wool slacks and high-heeled boots. I'd never noticed before that she had very narrow feet. She wore her inky black hair a bit shorter than when she was seventeen, but her beautiful, deep-blue eyes seemed tired and spiritless. Otherwise she still looked lovely, except she was working hard not to show she was bristling with hostility.

"This is such a goddamn invasion of privacy!" she said, moving the large coffee-table books in front of her around to form a more pleasingly esoteric pattern. The furniture inside was all modern—chosen, I was certain, exclusively by her. There wasn't a sign of Ben Magruder anywhere. Danielle hardly acted the charming hostess in her own home with me, and dealt with her annoyance by firing broadsides of sarcasm. "Do you get excited, Milan, hearing sexy stories about people you haven't seen in forty years?"

"I don't give a damn about sexy stories. I'm trying to sort things out."

She shrugged. "Tommy Wiggins? I hardly remembered him

until he begged my husband for representation—and Ben brought you into it too. What do Tommy and Phil Kohn have to do with me?"

"Phil Kohn was a major league playah—"

She laughed without mirth and shook her head. "I never heard a white man pronounce that word that way."

"And," I continued, ignoring her sarcasm, "it's possible that someone involved in his sexual escapades got angry enough to do something about it."

"One of our classmates? You've got to be kidding. Why ask me about it? I dated Phil in my junior year of high school!" she said. "Do you suppose I stayed angry at him for my entire adult life and then suddenly decided to kill him?"

"I don't suppose anything, Danielle. I'm asking."

She slumped back against her chair and sulked. The entire living room, including the chair, looked like Laura Ashley herself had spewed yellow florals and brocades onto every surface. I couldn't imagine Ben Magruder feeling comfortable, or very masculine, in this room.

"I don't call it anger anymore," she said with strange pride. "Didn't you wonder why I cried when you told me on the phone Phil was shot to death?" She sat up straighter. "He took my virginity when I was sixteen years old and then dropped me like used Kleenex six weeks after that without so much as a see-ya-later. He was a shit—and he stayed a shit—but he was my first lover and I felt empty and hollow when he got killed. Because of him I've done things since then—bad things, I suppose—to make up for my own naiveté. But I didn't kill him."

"You never slept with him after that?"

She might have been reliving bits of memory, and I thought at first she hadn't heard me. Finally she answered. "Yes, a few times. Just before our senior prom—I did it almost to get back at him. And over the past forty years there were off-and-on times, too. It was a strange sexual relationship, because I don't think either of us liked the other one a nickel's worth. I think we both used hooking up—isn't that what young people call it today, hooking up?—*I* used it as control, or an expression of my contempt. Hey, why the hell not? Anyway, it's been about eighteen months since we were—last together."

"Does your husband know?"

She closed her eyes. "He knows Phil was my first, which was long before Ben and I ever heard of one another. And yes, he knows I have affairs with other people sometimes—because he has extramarital affairs, too." She looked out the window at the winter-gray sky over the lake. "Don't get me started on him. It's our marriage and we run it the way it works for both of us. But I don't think Ben ever connected me with Phil through our years together."

"You have affairs with other people?"

"When I feel like it," she said. "Off and on." She thought about that for a second and laughed. "No pun intended. By the way, I'm not feeling like it at the moment, in case you're interested."

"I wasn't asking."

"You never know." She chuckled. "In high school, after Phil dumped me, I became very promiscuous. I can't even count the number of guys I was with during my senior year—guys, and a few grown men, too. I slept with Tommy Wiggins, too."

That jolted me. I'm not sure why, but it did. "How long did you date Tommy, Danielle?"

"If memory serves, about ten minutes or less. Whatever Phil Kohn said to him at the Holly Hop about being gay was cruel, and it wasn't true, either. Tommy was pretty inexperienced back then and didn't last very long—but I *can* back him up about being straight. At least that's how he came across." She smiled and shrugged, making a strange clicking sound at the side of her mouth. "I was what you call a wild child. I've become choosier since then."

I forced myself back to the problem at hand. "You weren't still angry with Phil Kohn at the reunion?"

"No."

"And Ben wasn't, either?"

"Not that I know of," she said.

"Were there any other women in our class who might have been?"

She stood up abruptly and walked over to the window that looked out on a lovely sculpted garden, now covered with snow, at the back of the house. “Get our whole class together again, Milan, and ask to see the raised hands of every girl who had sex with Phil when we were all young and innocent—before he grew his little pot belly and his wobbly jowls and started losing his hair. Are these girls—now becoming grandmothers—still pissed off about Phil? I wouldn’t think so.” She spun around and glared at me. “Let it alone! For God’s sake, it predates the day before yesterday. The only people I know with long-standing grudges still think the Jews killed Jesus.”

“Maybe one of them,” I said dryly, “blamed Phil Kohn for that.”

“That was very funny,” she said. “Well, have I confessed enough to satisfy you? Or do you want specific names and dates and sexual positions? Who I did it with in the backseat of a car—or on the grass in Rockefeller Park, or in somebody’s mom’s basement?”

“Okay, Danielle, I get the drift.” I got up and started for the door. “Thanks for talking to me. You’ve helped a lot.”

“I’m a regular little helper,” she said. She walked me to the door, then turned me around so we were facing each other and looked into my eyes. “I’ve upset you, haven’t I?”

“No,” I said.

“I can tell by your face, Milan—you’re all bent out of shape. What’s your problem?”

“No problem, exactly.” I struggled into my coat. “You never knew this, Danielle, because I don’t think we exchanged a handful of words during our years in high school—not even a casual hello in the hallway—but I had a hell of a crush on you back then.”

Her eyebrows lifted, although she didn’t seem amused. “You did?”

“I’m sure I wasn’t the only one who was crazy about you. You were the class beauty.”

“That’s kind of you to say after all these years. But why didn’t you ever let me know?”

“I was dating Lila Coso during our senior year. But I was also a little afraid of you, I think. I was too shy to even approach you back then.”

Danielle Magruder opened the door, hunching her shoulders against a blast of wind and lowering her chin into the folds of the purple cowl of her sweater. Her eyes met mine, though, with a kind of rueful challenge. "That's a damn shame, Milan," she said. "When you snooze, you lose. I would have fucked you, too."

CHAPTER SEVENTEEN

A case like this one doesn't just roll off my back without my feeling a thing.

Conducting investigations is my career—but it's always nicer working on an assignment when I'm not personally involved, when it's just a job that needs doing and I get paid to do it, like beefing up corporate security. But over the years I've been dragged kicking and screaming into a hell of a lot of murder cases, even if they didn't start out that way. I was shanghaied into this one, too. Dr. Philip Kohn's untimely demise was beginning to touch me where I live—and I didn't like it.

Not because I had any particular feelings about him—I hardly knew him—but because everyone from St. Clair High about whom I *do* have feelings had edged their way into the bright light shining on suspects. That made me flinch.

Suzanne Davis makes me flinch a little bit, too. She always has, because she's one of those shoot-from-the-hip people who never developed the "editor" that filters out thoughts before they escape from your mouth. We sat in the Anatolia Café, a Turkish restaurant in Cleveland Heights. We were both working on an amazing red lentil soup, accompanied by homemade pita bread that tasted better than any I've had. Suzanne looked terrific, as usual. Contrasting with a light-blue turtleneck, her black skirt ended several inches above her knees, and every guy in the room staring at her didn't even seem to consider she was in her fifties.

"Your feelings are hurt, poor baby," she said, "because you're shocked. You've rediscovered a distant and fruitless crush you had on a girl when you were both sixteen, and now she's admitting she isn't a virgin. Come on, be a big boy."

I didn't answer her because it stung.

"Besides," she said, "I did some digging on Ben Magruder and his lovely wife. He's not a likely suspect in the Kohn killing because if he gets the idea into his head of wreaking vengeance on every man who cuckolded him, he'd wipe out half the town." A nasty smile curled up one corner of her mouth. "Are you sulking because you're in the other half?"

"I'm not sulking at all," I said, sulking. "I just want to wrap this case up and never think about Phil Kohn again. Or Ben Magruder."

She scanned her notebook. "Magruder's no angel. He screws around on his wife, too—and worse than that, I hear he's got a galloping gambling jones."

"Magruder gambles?"

Suzanne nodded. "On the Browns, the Cavs, even the Indians—on out-of-town games, too. If anybody's doing something anywhere with a ball, the counselor has a bet down."

"Tell me," I said, "he doesn't owe his life to somebody like Morris Kepler."

Her eyebrows climbed higher. "Do you know Morris?"

I laughed. "I've had the pleasure."

"So have I, a few years back when I was on the ass of a deadbeat dad in Mentor who was throwing away more money on sports bets with Morris Kepler than he spent on his children. Morris was very pleasant and polite to me. He kept staring at my knees hoping I'd lose my concentration and let them slip apart, but otherwise he was a perfect gentleman. How do you know him?"

"Two of his mugs dropped by the office and tried to collect thirty-seven large from me that Phil Kohn owed him."

Suzanne whistled softly through her teeth. Now that impressed me—all my adult life I have been trying vainly to whistle through my teeth. I've never been able to make anything other than a hissing sound because of the space I have between my two front ones. "Magruder bets with him, sure. He bets with a lot of other people, too. What made Kepler think he could collect Phil Kohn's debts from you?" she said.

"I can't imagine."

She thought about it for a while. "Somebody put him on to you, Milan. Somebody's telling tales about you. Why would anyone do that?"

"Plenty of classmates have gotten cheesed off at me in the past week, but I don't know any of them who'd send Morris Kepler after me to collect Phil Kohn's gambling debt."

"Morris wouldn't believe that about you from a total stranger," Suzanne said with finality. "It's got to be somebody who's done business with him—one way or another."

"If it's not Ben Magruder, then who is it?"

"Maybe you should go back and reinterview everybody who was mad at you and find out who their bookie is."

I shook my head resolutely. "I just can't . . ." I said, and then I stopped. The answer to my question—at least one of them, anyway—had begun clanging around inside my head.

I stood up and threw an Andrew Jackson on the table. "It's been charming, as always," I said. "But I have to revisit one of my classmates after all."

She looked at her watch. It had a face the size of a silver dollar, telling you the time, weather, and temperature everywhere in the world, as well as the depth of water in which you're swimming. "It's six-thirty, Milan. Whoever it is you're ready to swoop down on probably isn't still at the office."

I put on my coat. "Drug dealers don't go home when the sun goes down."

It gets dark early in February, and the lights were on behind the door's opaque glass in Ted Lesnevich's office. I heard male voices inside, low and unintelligible as if the conversationalists were discussing something very private—or illegal.

Before putting my hand on the doorknob I patted the left side of my chest, feeling the lump beneath my parka. When I left Suzanne at Anatolia, I went home and strapped on the 9mm Glock

I always keep on the top shelf of my closet—just to make sure my trip to Lesnevich's business headquarters would be a safe one. Then I went in.

Ted Lesnevich was half bent over the desk looking at a handwritten list and talking to his visitor, an enormous African American man weighing upwards of three hundred pounds. He was handsome despite his portentous size, his face young, round, and almost childlike. He sported a neatly trimmed beard like a bad guy from a 1940s sword-and-dagger movie, a short and expensive haircut, and an attention-grabbing all-black outfit—woolen pants, fleece jacket, and a velveteen shirt. The only other color on him was gold, from a nine-inch gold cross hanging from his neck. Maybe he was the serious, pious religious type—but I didn't think so. I estimated that he was in his mid-twenties.

"I hope I'm not bothering you, Ted," I said when I walked through the door, although the venomous look Lesnevich gave me indicated I was bothering him a great deal.

"I'm busy," he said abruptly. "Come back some other time."

"I'm here now," I said.

Lesnevich glanced at the other man. "Can't you see I'm talking to somebody else?"

The heavy man stood up a little taller, the unzipped fleece jacket flapping at his broad hips.

"Somebody else can come back later, Ted—this is just between us."

"Hey, fuck you, muthafucka," the heavy man said, his basso profundo lower and more intimidating than his cherubic face indicated. I dealt with him beautifully—I ignored him.

"We've done all our talking, Jacovich," Lesnevich said. "You still think I killed Phil Kohn? Is that why you came back here again? To ask more stupid-ass questions?"

I turned to the other man and said in a very pleasing tone, "Sir, will you excuse us for a bit?"

That surprised him. "What?"

"Take a walk around the block. It's cold and invigorating out there—and maybe you'll run into some twelve-year-old kid you can turn on to whatever kind of shit you and Lesnevich are moving."

"You talk to me like that," he rumbled, "and I'll rip off your fuckin' head."

"Maybe you can," I said. "I'm older than you. But I'm not hauling around three hundred pounds, either—so you do the math."

"I'll cut your balls off, muthafucka," he said, his voice higher and less intimidating as he became agitated, his massive chest heaving. He took a six-inch-long gravity knife from his jacket pocket and expertly flipped it open with his wrist.

"Nice move," I said, "but I have a gun." I pulled my parka aside a little bit to let him see the handle sticking out of the holster. "Bullets travel faster than your knife."

Ted Lesnevich sucked in a lungful of air and blew it noisily out of his mouth. "All right, Tyrone," he said. I doubt if Tyrone had even vaguely heard of the 1940s actor with whom he shared a name, Tyrone Power—but that wasn't so terrible, I guess, because Tyrone Power had never been a very good actor. "Take a walk. Come back in ten minutes."

"Lemme stay," Tyrone pleaded, his voice rising even higher—like a teen who's just been grounded for something he didn't do. "I'll take this muthafucka down right here."

"Stop whining, Tyrone," I admonished him. "Get some fresh air. The sooner you leave, the sooner you can come back."

"Man . . ." he said. He treated Lesnevich to one last imploring look and then turned around, went out, and slammed the door behind him.

Lesnevich opened the top drawer of his desk and casually shoved his list inside it so I couldn't read it upside down. He was a little too casual, because before he slid the drawer shut I saw there was a handgun inside. Then he sat back behind his desk to take the weight off his feet. "If you're going to shoot more bullshit," he said easily, "get it over with, because I have things to do."

"You told Morris Kepler a lie about me."

"So?"

"So why?"

"Whatever I do, Jacovich, I do because I don't like you."

"Why don't you like me, Ted?"

"Because you're a jack-off," he said.

"There are lots of people I don't like either," I said, "and you're one of them. But why did you send two tough guys to my door wanting to rearrange my face for thirty-seven large I had nothing to do with?"

"I told you once."

"Because I wasn't friends with you in high school?"

"Live with it."

I sighed. "No, I don't think I'm going to."

"You'll just have to."

I stood up and walked around to his side of the desk. "And you'll have to live with a really pronounced limp," I said, removing my Glock and pointing it at his knee, "because if you don't come clean with me I'm going to blow off your kneecap."

His ruddy face got several shades whiter. "I'm not afraid of you," he said. The quiver in his voice belied his show of fearlessness.

"You should be very afraid," I said. "I'm not a good bluffer. And you're going to sing for me like a caged nightingale."

"The police'll put you away for a hell of a long time."

"For shooting a drug dealer? I doubt it. They'll be glad you're off the street. If I kill you they might ask too many questions about it—but taking out your knees will make me look like a hell of a good guy."

He stared at the door. "Tyrone . . ." he began.

"If Tyrone walks back in, I'll blow him away without a second thought—because he has a knife. He's already showed it to me."

I moved the muzzle of the weapon to within an inch of his left kneecap, a little off center so the bullet would enter on an angle and do the most damage. "I'm a busy man, Ted—so I'm just going to count to ten."

"You can't threaten me, Jacovich . . ."

"Sure I can. One-Mississippi . . ."

His eyelids batted rapidly, out of his control. "Don't point fucking guns in here," he said, almost begging.

"Two-Mississippi . . ."

I got all the way up to six-Mississippi before he told me what I wanted to know.

He reiterated how much he disliked me—but I knew that going in. He'd thought for years I was a goody two-shoes, so he got a big kick out of sending Morris Kepler's muscle guys after me, but that wasn't the real reason, he said. He wanted to distract me. It had to do, peripherally, with the murder of Phil Kohn—drug dealings, because Kohn was a user. But the last thing Lesnevich wanted was the police to find out how he made his living, and he was afraid I'd run to McHargue or someone else in the Third and rat him out. That would mean trouble from the cops and the district attorney's office—and a lot of money would be spent on his own lawyers trying to keep him out of prison and his name out of the first ring of murder suspects.

So he called Morris Kepler and suggested I was the logical guy to pay off Kohn's debts. They never did business together because Lesnevich didn't gamble and Kepler didn't mess with drugs—but Ted figured if Morris was chasing me for money I didn't have and didn't know about, I'd be too busy covering my own ass to push any further into the job of getting Tommy Wiggins off the hook—and of involving him.

And if it worked out that I got a beating from Leonard Shaffran, well, that would be an extra bonus for Ted Lesnevich's entertainment and enjoyment.

When he was finished spilling his guts, I took the muzzle of the gun away from Ted Lesnevich's knee and replaced it in my holster. A relieved blast of terrified breath whooshed out of his lungs, and color came back into his face.

"You're not as smart as I thought you were, Ted. Did you really think I was going to write Kepler a check?"

He shook his head. "I just thought it'd keep you busy—and out of my face." His lips smacked, sounding like he desperately needed a drink of water. "Listen, I'll phone Morris Kepler and call him off you, okay?"

"Don't bother; I took care of it myself." I zipped up my parka. "I'm not your hobby, Ted, so find another one. The next time I have to come back here, I'll shoot your kneecap off first and *then* ask my questions."

Now that he was feeling better, some of his cockiness returned, too. "Maybe the next time you come back up here, I'll shoot you first."

"I don't think you're good enough, Ted—and I don't think you have the balls."

He twisted his face into a grimace, thinking about it. Then he opened his desk drawer and put his hand inside.

I took two steps around his desk and kicked the drawer shut with my foot, hard, his hand still inside. I didn't actually hear bones cracking, but he sucked in his breath, moaned, and his face turned chalk white again.

"I'm impressed," I said. "You have the balls after all. But you still aren't good enough."

He yanked his hand from the drawer and put it between his thighs, making a quiet humming sound inside his chest. I took his automatic out of the drawer, ejected the magazine, and put it in my pocket. Then I tossed the weapon back on the desk, empty.

"Pretend you haven't seen me for forty years, Ted." I smiled my warmest smile. "You might live longer."

When I got downstairs, the street was already as dark as three o'clock in the morning. The February air was cold, as usual, and patches beneath my feet were slippery. I started toward my car, but I wasn't really surprised when Tyrone jumped out of the shadows of a doorway and confronted me, his chest and shoulders generously wide, taking up most of the narrow sidewalk.

"You and me ain't finished, muthafucka," he said.

"Let it go, Tyrone. We have no problems."

"*I* got problems. How you come off dissing me?"

I didn't answer him; I was busy taking off my gloves and putting them in my pockets.

"Where you get the stones talkin' to me like I'm some kinda fuckin' field hand?"

"I have too much respect for field hands. I talked to you like you're a drug pusher."

"Shit, man," he said, and he drew his gravity knife again, flipping it around to show off. He also knew my piece was under my parka—too difficult for me to get to quickly enough.

"Don' fret, man—I ain' gonna kill you," Tyrone said. "I just gonna cut you up some, so's you remember me." He bent his legs, bouncing on his feet and then moving quickly around, flourishing his blade, making feints at my midsection. I turned sideways, presenting the smallest possible target for him, and danced along with his footwork.

The blade of the gravity knife flashed in the glow of the streetlight half a block away.

I never learned how to box. I've always been pretty effective in a fight but I didn't know any fancy moves—I'm a heavyweight, not a welterweight. I did, however, understand that when a man has a knife he plans to use on another person, he's concentrating on where he's going to slash—and Tyrone, while making moves at my stomach with his evil-looking blade, was checking out my face instead. Each time he offered the knife toward me, he'd grunt aloud, so it sounded like "Ha!" or "Hey!" His ego was obviously on overdrive. He wanted to cut me where it would show—where I'd have to look at it every morning for the rest of my life, so I could never forget him.

I was inspecting his face, too. He was having a good time with me. The street was dark and gloomy but I could see his eyes almost twinkling. I watched them closely, waiting for the split second when they changed.

"Ha!" he said again, poking toward my ribs as I sucked in my breath and backed up a step, but he wasn't coming anywhere close. He moved pretty quickly for such a large man—and he had an advantage of more than twenty years on me. I had to play this well or he would indeed cut my face.

He circled around me so my back was to the brick wall, leaving me little room to evade him. Then I saw his eyes change—narrow and get mean.

The blade—Tyrone had been pointing it at my midsection since our little gavotte began—suddenly slashed upward toward the left side of my face.

I timed it perfectly, pulling my head back so the knife missed me by inches. The thrust upward left his whole body turned away from me, in profile, his right arm high across him and exposed. I grabbed his wrist with one hand and with the other pushed violently on his elbow, forcing the joint in the direction it was never intended to bend. He howled in pain, dropping his gravity knife, and I used my own weight to force him down on his knees and then flat on his face on the frozen sidewalk. I kicked the knife out of reach, and then landed in the middle of his back with both knees, ramming the breath out of his lungs.

I still had his right arm with both my hands, pulling it up behind him. He groaned, or the sound he made would have been a groan if he had any breath left. I know a lot about leverage, and it would have been no trouble at all to twist his arm up farther, to keep pushing his elbow the wrong way until I heard it snap. It was quick, reliable, efficient, and it would keep him from peddling heroin to kids for some time to come.

It would be so easy . . .

"Of course I didn't bust his arm," I said. "That's my trouble—I think too damn much."

Jinny Johnson was in my apartment when I got home. For some years now we've had duplicate keys to each other's apartments, even though neither of us drops in on the other one uninvited.

When she'd arrived and I wasn't home yet, she'd crossed the street to Giant Eagle and bought herself a salad to bring back to the apartment, then poured a glass of white wine, turned to the classical music that always plays on WCLV, and picked up one of my books to read until I got there. Now she was curled up on one end of the couch, wearing the robe with black, yellow, green, and white stripes that my son Milan Junior bought me for Christmas when he was still in high school. It was cut for my size, not hers, and she looked totally adorable wearing it.

She was still working at the white wine. A while back, she'd bought several bottles to store in one of my kitchen cabinets. She had pronounced it as dry and peppy, with a pleasing taste of fresh grass.

"You'd have put him out of business for a while," she said. We were discussing my activities earlier that evening, and my breaking or not breaking Tyrone's arm—as matter-of-factly as if we had been chatting about whether or not I should have my office redecorated.

"Tyrone would have sold drugs with one arm," I said. I'd opened a bag of pretzels, since I hadn't taken the time to get myself a real dinner and didn't feel like cooking one now. In keeping with my health-conscious attitude, they were whole wheat pretzels. "Or somebody else would have taken his place. I can't go breaking the arms of all the people I don't like. It's a horrible feeling, Jinny. You hear the crack—and you hear the scream, too."

"Yuck," she said.

"Besides—shutting down drug peddling on the East Side isn't my case."

"Not exactly," Jinny said. "Except that since you *have* been on this case—your quixotic search to pin a murder on somebody else besides Tommy Wiggins—on two separate occasions two different guys who were twice your size tried to kill you. And you messed over both of them."

"They weren't trying to kill me."

"Certainly not," she said.

"They just wanted to hurt me."

"The big tall bookie's muscle and the big wide drug peddler's muscle."

"Yes."

"What wonderful human beings," she said.

"Great Americans."

"Patriots."

I took another handful of pretzels. "I think the one guy, from the other day, was singing 'The Star-Spangled Banner' soprano after I kicked him in the nuts."

"I bet they'll hire him to sing it at next year's Super Bowl," Jinny said.

It was warm in the apartment, and the radiator clanked and banged, like all radiators do in the older structures of Cleveland. Mine was noisier than most, sounding like Tommy Lee wailing on the drums when he was working with Mötley Crüe.

Not that I know a damn thing about Mötley Crüe—my musical tastes dried up and died somewhere between Frankie Laine and Rosemary Clooney. The Mozart playing on the radio didn't count.

"Jinny," I said, "a big guy like me can find it too easy to inflict physical pain, and if you aren't careful, that translates into a bully. I don't like bullies. I hate being one, and I feel lousy about it for weeks after it happens. Most of the time, I wind up never forgetting it. You've known me a long time now—so you should understand that."

She put down her white wine. "I do understand it," she said. "The night of our first date when you ran off to find a murderer, I knew then that you were one of the good guys. That's why I went out with you a second time."

"And I didn't leave you sitting alone the second time."

She shook her head. "Not that night."

"Not since."

"No—but if it happens again, I think I can handle it like I did the first time."

"After five years?"

She scooted closer to me on the sofa. "After five years," she said, "it's different."

"How?"

"The parameters of the relationship change from the first or second date to the 750th or so date. You're like an old shoe," she said, putting an arm around my neck.

"I'm not sure I like that."

"The longer you wear old shoes, the more comfortable they get on your feet. No pinching, like brand-new ones."

The bathrobe had ridden up so that most of one leg was showing. I reached over and pinched her on the outside of her thigh, as high up as I could.

"Ow."

"Old shoes still pinch," I said.

"And old cats scratch," she said, and dug her short fingernails into the back of my neck, pulling me toward her. It didn't hurt.

Her tongue tasted of white wine—a dry, peppy Chardonnay with the slightest hint of fresh grass.

CHAPTER EIGHTEEN

Neither Jinny nor I wanted the next morning to end. We set an early alarm and got the day started in fine fashion, but then all we had time for was a quick breakfast together, consisting of a whole wheat bagel split between us—she always spread peanut butter on hers—and coffee for her and tea for me. Jinny had to report to her job at City Hall at 8 A.M., and I had plenty of work to do on my own, including dealing with pressure from the police, personified by Lieutenant Florence McHargue, and not one but *two* criminals—one a drug dealer I'd gone to high school with and one a bookie I'd never met before in my life—who seemed anxious to have me badly injured even when I'd done nothing to either of them.

What was throwing me for a loop was that nearly everyone hated Phil—a sleazy womanizer, a stone junkie, an animal abuser, and an inveterate gambler—and the list of suspects was growing.

Was it one of my former St. Clair classmates, or was the killer a total stranger to all of us? Either was possible, and the police were doing their job, stirring up everyone who ever knew him—every nurse, aide, volunteer, and doctor who worked with him at the hospital, as well as some of the patients. Lieutenant McHargue had stayed up all night trying to reach an obscenely wealthy Saudi sheik on the telephone. He had left Cleveland five months earlier after a long hospital stay singing the praises of his cardiologist, Dr. Kohn.

Strange, I thought, considering Phil Kohn was Jewish. Arabs and Jews don't get along very well in the Middle East nowadays—and that gave me another idea. As soon as I got to my office, I put in a call to the United Jewish Appeal, and the woman I finally tracked down in what they call the "development department" said that she was certainly aware of Phil Kohn and she had read the newspaper story of his death. To her knowledge, Dr. Philip Kohn had never written a check to them, generous or otherwise, to further the health and safety of Jewish people living in Israel—or to any other Jewish charity she knew about. So much for Kohn having been part of Gary Mishlove's "tribe."

Let the police chase down the outsiders, I thought. Suzanne Davis was clearing up loose ends for me—but otherwise I was a one-man band, as I've been for almost all my work since I opened my own agency. I would stick to searching among my former classmates—poking at the embers of my adolescent memories—to find out if any of them appeared even more guilty than Tommy Wiggins.

That's all I had to do, of course—get Wiggins off the hook. I'm not a card-carrying police officer anymore; finding murderers isn't my job. At least that's what the rules say—and Florence McHargue has been reminding me of that for almost ten years. Before she did it, my best friend Marko Meglich had hammered away at me, too.

"When you turned in your badge, Milan," he used to scold me, "you gave up the job of solving capital crimes like murder. It's not your table anymore, okay? You keep doing your corporate security gigs, nailing employees who steal ballpoint pens and paper clips from the supply room, or tattling on what some cheating spouse is getting away with—and leave the *important* work to us."

It just hasn't happened that way.

I'd steered clear of what I call "domestic" cases, even when I needed the money. When a wife or husband wants proof of their spouse's infidelity, I draw the line. I won't hang around outside a motel room with a camera and a high-tech recorder to catch someone with their pants down. Perhaps it was because my own marriage had rocked and then self-destructed over Lila's infidelity, but that was one road I didn't want to travel.

Yet in my current employment—trying to clear the name of Tommy Wiggins—I was stumbling over infidelity all over the place whether I liked it or not, and each new revelation about the St. Clair senior class shocked me a little more. For a guy who's spent his life in the profession I've chosen, I was so damn naive about certain things.

I wondered whether Tommy Wiggins was naive, too.

When I'd previously visited him in his hotel suite, he'd been drinking a martini—that seemed to be one of his favorite habits—and he was annoyed that I was even bothering him. Cleveland was enjoying one of its worst February snowfalls in years, and it took me three times as long to get anywhere because the plow trucks and the salt sprayers weren't working fast enough to clear our streets for driving. Tommy Wiggins was more relaxed, and seemingly in a better mood—probably because he had no reason to leave the hotel and brave the elements. When I walked into his suite, a laptop computer was open and booted up at one end of the huge conference table where he sat, along with a room service coffeepot with cups. He told me he was working on his new play.

"The police suggested I shouldn't leave town," he said, "and I can't just sit here like a bump on a log. I'd go bonkers. Besides, I try to write a little bit, no matter what, every day of my life. Christmas, my birthday, Rosh Hashanah, Ash Wednesday—I have to write *something,* or the top of my head would explode." He took a sip of his black coffee. "You want some of this, Milan? There's another cup."

"No, I'm fine, Tommy—thanks. I can come back later if you prefer. I don't want to interrupt your writing."

He waved that away. "Hell, no. Every writer alive prays that most days something or someone will come along to distract him. This career ain't as easy as it looks, except for those times when the writing fever gets to you—and then you can't and won't stop working for anything."

"Is this one of those writing fever mornings?"

He laughed. "Hardly. It's one of those bang-your-head-against-the-bricks-and-wish-you'd-become-a-proctologist-instead kind of writing mornings. So sit down and talk to me."

I took a chair. I was still cold, and the hot coffee looked and smelled wonderful to me, but I was determined to continue ignoring my coffee jones. I wanted a cigarette, too.

"You have more questions for me, Milan?"

"Not the where-were-you-on-April-sixth type of questions," I said. "But I'm trying to put together a fuller picture of the people who graduated with us, and I'm hoping you can help me."

"You were at the reunion, too," Tommy said.

"Yes, but you and I are different people," I said, even while my mind was reviewing what had now become a list of possible murder suspects. "I understand that writers look at things differently than the rest of us do. So I was hoping for your pearls of wisdom."

"Pearls before swine, eh?" He laughed at his own joke. "Well, I do have what I like to call the Writer's Eye—I'm always studying people and situations, just in case I want to include them in my next play. So let me think about it for a minute." He pushed his coffee cup six inches farther away from him and drummed the tabletop with his fingers. "One of the major reasons I was at the reunion, after a decades-long bellyache inside me that never really went away, was to walk up to Phil Kohn and tell him publicly to go piss up a rope."

"You had to have some observations about some of the others at the reunion—whether you were angry at Phil or not."

He opened his eyes wide, soulful. "Do you really want to hear them?"

"Very much."

"You might not like this."

"Part of the job," I said.

"Okay." He put down the lid on the laptop, and the monitor disappeared. Then he relaxed in his chair and took a breath as if he were readying to make a speech. "The first thing I realized Friday night—and I'd never really considered it before—was that I'm different from most of the people I knew at St. Clair High."

"Different?"

He paused before giving me an affirmative nod. "I was the

writer. I was the only artistic type. Nobody else at St. Clair was back then—except maybe Maurice Paich, and he was more ridiculous than creative."

"He walked around quoting Shakespeare all the time," I said.

"That's *why* he was so ridiculous." He pointed an index finger at me with his thumb cocked, and "shot" me, apparently to indicate approval. Glitzy show business types call that a Las Vegas gun. "I wasn't loud or pushy about my artistic longings. When everyone else played a sport or hung out on the street corner or got a job flipping burgers at McDonald's, I went home and wrote every day. I wasn't trying to sell plays or stories back then, because frankly I didn't know what I was doing. But the best way to learn to write is to do it—and do it again—and keep doing it until you get it right."

"And I won't like what I'm hearing because . . . ?" I left the question hanging.

"Because," he said, "it's hard for any of us to avoid the fact that I'm rich—probably richer than anyone who ever passed through St. Clair High School since they opened it in the mid-forties. I don't want to rub anyone's face in it, but it's true."

He got up and wandered over to the window, watching the snow fall. "And the fact that I'm famous now, too—well . . ."

"You're tripping over your own ego."

That made him laugh. "Give me a break, Milan," he said, turning to face me. I couldn't shake the idea that he was actually posing in the window. "I'm being honest. I didn't start out wanting to be famous—I just wanted to make a living doing what I love. The fame just came along with the career, and I'm stuck with it."

"If you say so."

"So, after wandering around for a while and talking to old acquaintances, I considered everyone else at the reunion as—well, different from me."

"In what way?"

He took a moment, struggling with the words he wanted to use. Finally he said, "To tell you the truth, they all come off as pretty much identical to each other. Like—well, like sheep."

"Ouch."

"I don't mean it in an insulting way," he said, and sat back down at the table. "But just about everybody stayed right here in Northeast Ohio. They live within twenty minutes of where they were born, they all grew up the same way, and they all do the same things."

"What things?"

"I don't know—Cleveland things that we all did while we were growing up. The Browns, for one thing."

"I've always been a Browns fan, Tommy."

"Clevelanders love rock and roll, and the better-educated ones support the Cleveland Orchestra. They eat sausages and perch, and drink the same alcohol they grew up on, whatever it is—Bourbon and soda, vodka and tonic, domestic beer or sweet white Riesling. They all vacation in Naples or Hilton Head every winter, if they can afford it—and if they can't, they go to Detroit and cross the bridge into Windsor and play Canadian quarter slots at the casino, because the tight-asses in Ohio won't approve casinos in their own state. Being a Clevelander makes you all proud of your city and embarrassed at the same time. There's no—individuality. Unfortunately."

I tried not to appear annoyed, but I didn't succeed. "Is that how you see us?"

"I suppose I do," he said, not even within hailing distance of making an apology. "The people who still live in this town, people of all ages—the ones with some money live slightly better than the ones without, but to me they're just two sides of the same coin. They're Clevelanders. It's not necessarily a bad thing, but that's just the way it is." He sighed. "You asked me a question, Milan—for whatever reason—and I tried being truthful. I guess it hurt."

"Tommy, since I've been working on your behalf, one guy tried to beat me senseless, and another guy wanted to slice me with a knife. So don't worry, because nothing you could say would hurt my feelings."

"I didn't mean to," he said. "You kind of caught me off guard."

"Not at all," I said. "I just learned something from you. Several somethings, actually."

He pulled the cup and saucer back closer to him and poured some more coffee. The pot had been sitting there too long, and the coffee wasn't steaming any longer.

"Several somethings—well, that should be fascinating. How did *you* see all the people we went to high school with?"

"I've been thinking about that while you were talking. I see them differently from you."

"Tell me," he said. "I may take notes."

"Knock yourself out." I took a deep breath. "The way I see our old classmates—well, everybody's changed, naturally. Some of them are heavier than when I saw them last, some are thinner, some men lost their hair or took on pot bellies, and a few of them developed double chins or fat asses. All of them, male and female, are fighting gravity with the passing of time, Tommy, you and me included. Time does a number on you—and I don't mean just the sags and the wrinkles, either. Stress and pain and experience write their own story on your face. But the funny thing is . . ."

"What?"

"Those classmates haven't all turned into carbon copies of one another. They're all different from each other, and not the way you see them. They're all unique—even though they stayed close to home and remained true to their roots."

"How is that?"

"Everyone I've talked to since Friday night," I said, "has changed their appearance and acquired maturity—even, sometimes, despite their social stuffiness. Their lifelong experiences have marked them and guided them, but down deep they're the same as they were in high school."

"You're kidding!"

"Not at all," I said. "The funny ones back then, the class clowns, are still funny. The flirty girls still flirt, the serious ones are still serious, and jocks like me still care about the Browns and the Indians. Nobody has transmogrified into a clone."

"That's hard for me to believe," Tommy Wiggins said, shaking his head. "Seeing the middle-aged people today as the kids they used to be."

"You're right about one thing. They're all different from you, but no one I talked to or observed changed from what they used to be." I corrected myself. "Almost no one."

"Oh? Who changed, then?"

"You did."

"I see. Is it because now I'm rich and famous?" he said, smiling disarmingly, almost teasing me.

"No," I said. "It's because now you're an asshole."

CHAPTER NINETEEN

There's not much you can do while driving during a whiteout, when snow falls so fast and heavy that you can't see five feet ahead of you through the white curtain. If you happen to be on the highway when landmarks and traffic signs are obliterated by the storm, when you can't even see an exit ramp to find your way to safety, it's like taking your life in your hands.

After the blizzard subsides, four-foot-high piles of drifted snow block your driveway, weigh down your roof, and make it impossible to walk on the sidewalk. You're always forced into the street itself, which also gets snowed under in quiet residential neighborhoods.

I was lucky to live in an apartment, because the maintenance guy who works for my landlord had efficiently shoveled the steps and walkways, anointing them with hardware store salt so none of our tenants would slip on the ice and institute lawsuits. I hadn't been a homeowner since my divorce, and one of the better fringe benefits is that I never have to shovel snow anymore.

I'd had a hell of a time getting around town.

First downtown to visit with Tommy Wiggins and then, in the afternoon, Suzanne Davis, who appeared in the doorway of Milan Security dressed warmly but elegantly—as if she were heading for a Junior League benefit instead of having just made the trek from Lake County through the weather.

"Who's going to plow and salt down your parking lot?" she

said, stamping her feet to shake off the snow that had collected on her fancy fur-trimmed boots. "It's like running a gauntlet."

"The company that's supposed to do that called this morning," I said. "They got snowed in."

She rolled her eyes heavenward, sat down opposite me in one of my visitor chairs, and got right down to business. "I have everything here, Milan." She took a thick folder from her briefcase and put it on my desk. "These reports are as detailed as I could make them—my interviews with nearly all of the classmates, based on the list you gave me."

I thumbed through the sheaf of papers, not looking forward to reading them. "Was anyone not forthcoming?"

"Some were annoyed at me bothering them, but no one struck me as the type to hide anything."

"Off the top of your head, is there anyone in here we should look at more closely? Anyone connected in any way with Phil Kohn or Tommy Wiggins?"

"No one who admitted to it," Suzanne said. "Some of them remembered their high school days better than others, but virtually none of them had dealt with either of our two guys as an adult. At least if they did, they didn't share it with me."

"No one seemed like they were lying?" I said. "No one who looked away, fiddled with something, played with their hair? Nobody who struck you as even remotely suspicious?"

She seemed amused. "They were all pussycats, Milan." She reached out and put her hand on the folder, fingers drumming. Then she said, "There was a name on your list that I didn't interview. Lila Jacovich."

My sigh spoke volumes.

"I know you don't think Lila had anything to do with Kohn's killing . . ."

"God, no!" I said. "I don't think Lila's ever fired a handgun."

Suzanne said carefully, "How about her—her boyfriend, Joe Bradac?"

Now it was my turn to roll my eyes. "Joe Bradac couldn't shoot anybody. He can't find his own ass with either hand."

Suzanne cleared her throat. "It's not my business, but . . ."

I waited.

"I think you ought to talk to them anyway. You might learn something that either of them saw or heard."

"Why don't you interview them?"

She shook her head. "Your ex-wife and her current boy-toy?"

I tried not to cringe.

"That's not my job," Suzanne said. "Not this time." She looked out the window at the thick sheets of ice floating placidly on the Cuyahoga. "I've probably done all the damage I can on this case, Milan. I've put a fat file of interrogations together for you—along with my own thoughts and instincts. Some of your classmates seemed very nice and some—well, not so nice. Either way, I can't go any further with it. Now I think I should move on."

"Are you running out on me?"

"Not if you really want me to stay."

I pondered that for a moment. "You're right. But I'd like you to be available, if you can. I never know when something might jump out to bite me."

"Done," she said. "But I don't see anywhere else we have to go. We weren't looking for a murderer, were we? Just trying to take the pressure off Tommy Wiggins." She changed her tone slightly. "*You* need to talk to your ex and her friend about the reunion. Just get it over with. Then you can go back to your client and his attorney—what a jerk Ben Magruder is, by the way—and to Lieutenant McHargue. Turn over the reports, and walk away clean."

"That sounds easy," I said.

It wasn't going to be easy and I knew it. When I called and asked Lila if I could drop over that night, and made a point of suggesting Joe Bradac be there too, it took her by surprise—and not pleasantly. The wintry chill in her voice could have frozen a margarita.

"Are you going to get shitty?" she demanded. "After all this time?"

"I quit being shitty years ago, Lila. I just want to talk with both of you about—business. *My* business."

"Neither one of us killed anybody."

"Until I get there tonight," I said, "let me have my dreams."

• • •

I got there at about six-thirty that evening. The house, which had been painted a bright red with white shutters ever since my parents lived there, looked pretty and cozy surrounded by the pristine new snow which, as yet, hadn't turned to slush. Lila had been fixing dinner, wearing a fluffy light-blue apron in the style of 1952. Joe Bradac had apparently just arrived home from work and was still in the greasy blue jumpsuit he lived in all day long. A little oval patch on the chest, white with red cursive writing, said JOE. He'd opened the door when I rang the bell, and as always I was keenly aware that once it had been *my* door, *my* doorbell, *my* house.

That was a long time ago.

"Hey, Milan," he said. I don't think he's capable of any other greeting. We did not shake hands.

"Joe," I murmured—always *my* way of saying hello to Joe Bradac.

The TV was playing in the living room. It's always playing except when Lila and Joe are away or asleep. At the moment it was spooling out a cartoon show. Joe Bradac wouldn't recognize a news program if it jumped out of the TV set and bit him in the ass.

I sat on the sofa, a new one purchased years after I'd moved out, a Value City special with a peculiar southwestern pattern in bright reds and yellows that was too colorful for the rest of the room. The pictures hanging on the wall were all different, too. There was little left in that house that I'd chosen or had anything to do with, and I felt how quickly time had tumbled away from me since this was my home and Lila was my wife.

She came in from the kitchen, drying her hands on her apron. "You can't stay for dinner, Milan. I only cooked two chicken breasts."

I would choke if I had dinner at their table. Lila'd never been a great chef anyway. Her modus operandi was cooking the meat until it was hot and brown, and then serving it. "That's all right," I said. "I'll only be a few minutes."

Lila sat down in one of the uncomfortable-looking leather chairs to one side of the TV. Joe lowered himself carefully into the other one as if he had hemorrhoids. He was always careful dealing with me, fearing that any unusual movement of his might get me angry.

"So, uh, what's up, Milan?" he said.

I explained to them why I was working this case, linking it both to Danielle Webber's lawyer husband and to Tommy Wiggins.

"Remember when I pointed Danielle out to you at the reunion?" Lila said to Joe as if I weren't in the room. "Back in high school Milan had quite a hard-on for her." Then she turned and looked at me with her now-patented sneer of contempt. "He had a hard-on for lots of our female classmates, Joe. Remember Rayneen Tisovic? Milan chased after her for a whole semester, but he never got anywhere with her—that's why he wound up with me."

It didn't irritate me as much as I imagined it would. "All sixteen-year-old boys have a hard-on for every girl they see. I never even talked to Danielle Webber in school." I looked right at Joe. "Joe, did you have a hard-on for Danielle, too?"

Joe was so embarrassed, he looked like he wouldn't even complain if the earth opened up a huge hole and swallowed him. Then again, Joe Bradac never complains about anything—which makes him Lila's perfect soul mate.

"The only one that I know was intimately involved with Danielle in high school was Phil Kohn," I continued, steeling my insides. "But Phil was involved with loads of women, including a lot from our graduating class." And then I looked at Lila.

She glared back at me. "If you're insinuating something, have the balls to come right out and say it."

"I'm not insinuating, Lila—I'm just wondering."

"Damn! That is so insulting."

"Hey," Joe Bradac said, attempting to cool down any environment in which Lila might get hot under the collar. "He's just asking a question, Lila. Be nice."

"Shut up, Joe," she said, and she obviously meant it, too, because he shut up as told—but her eyes didn't leave me. "So exactly what is it you want me to say, Milan?"

This was getting easier by the minute for me. All during our marriage, I'd tried not to make her angry—but we'd been apart for so many years now, ticking Lila off secretly amused me. "Just tell me your history with Phil Kohn—if you have one." I cleared my throat, putting my hand up to my mouth to cover an incipient smile. "I'm sure it won't upset Joe."

She pursed her mouth. That was her favorite facial expression for indicating disapproval—on the few occasions when she didn't blow up and yell. "I hardly knew Phil Kohn in school," she said. "But he did walk up to me by surprise at my locker one day and ask me out."

I fought to keep my eyebrows from raising up to meet my receding hairline.

"You and I had dated," she reminded me, "but we were seeing other people, too, back then."

"Did you go out with Phil?"

"I didn't want to," Lila said. "I didn't really like him. He was such a sawed-off, chunky little shrimp, and pretty arrogant to boot. But he promised me he'd get the use of his dad's car for Saturday night—a brand-new Buick, as I recall—and he tried to snow me with how much money his family had and how important he thought *he* was. So even though he turned me off, I thought what the hell—and I went out with him."

"How did that turn out? The date, I mean."

"A quiet disaster," Lila said. "We went to the Silver Grille downtown for dinner—very fancy, I must say—and then he made a move on me as soon as we got out of there and back into his car."

I waited. Joe Bradac looked miserable, shifting around on his chair like fire ants living in the cushion were attacking his ass.

"I told him where to get off—in no uncertain terms," Lila continued. "He was so gross."

"Gross?"

She shrugged. "No kiss, no hand-holding—nothing. He just asked me right out if I'd—"

"Yes?" I said.

Lila's cheeks flamed. I'd known her since we were children and this was the first time I'd ever seen her blush. She lowered her voice to a whisper. "He wanted me to give him head—to pay him back for the dinner."

Joe almost moaned, but Lila didn't deign to look at him. I

wasn't upset, though. I'd been married to her for a long time, and I knew better than anyone she was never a fan of oral sex.

"When you said no, he didn't argue with you?" I said.

Her blue eyes narrowed even further. "*Nobody* argues with me, Milan—they never have." She allowed herself a chilly smile. "Not since you've gone, anyway." She straightened her back, a position that told me she was going to get really tough. "He didn't argue, he didn't plead—he didn't say anything. He got very quiet, switched off the radio in the car so it was as silent as a tomb, and drove me right home. I don't think we ever spoke again."

"You haven't seen him since then?"

"Not until the reunion Friday."

I turned and looked at Joe Bradac. As much as I disliked him, I couldn't help feeling sorry for him. He looked as wretched as a pole-vaulter with a bellyache. "Did you know about this story before?"

He shook his head almost violently. "I swear to God, Milan, I never ever heard about this until right now. I swear to God . . ."

"Okay," I said. "Did you ever see him after high school?"

"Um—no," he said. "But my father did."

"Your father?"

He nodded. "My dad had a heart murmur, you know? This was about six years ago. So his regular doctor there at the hospital sent him to Phil Kohn because he was a big-shot cardiologist. So he goes—once—and then he switched to another heart doctor. I guess he didn't like Phil Kohn too much. And he couldn't understand the stuff Phil was saying to him."

"Your dad didn't like Phil's attitude?"

Joe shrugged.

"Was that it, Joe?"

"Well," he said. Then he stopped. "Well" had comprised an entire sentence.

"Well?" I said.

He swallowed hard. "My dad wasn't so crazy about Jews. Like Phil. You know what I mean?"

I knew what he meant. I also remembered the two or three times I ever met Joe's father when we were still in school. I hadn't liked him then, either, and now I understood why.

We talked about Friday night some more but they swore they didn't notice anyone arguing with Phil besides Tommy Wiggins. I thanked them, and before I left I climbed the stairs and knocked on my son Stephen's bedroom door, just to say hello.

When he opened it, he took my breath away—as he always has. He's nineteen now, all grown up from the lovable blond, blue-eyed, flower-faced little boy I'd adored, but with his inquiring, heartbreakingly innocent blue eyes, he still looked adorable to me. I'd never tell him that, but I'd bet my feelings for him show in my eyes.

"Dad!" he said. "Neat surprise." He hugged me, the closeness reminding me once again that he was taller than I am. My older son, Milan Junior, resembled his Serbian mother and more or less had her temperament, too—so he'd never been big on smiling, and I couldn't even remember the last time he hugged me affectionately. But Stephen had the Slovenian complexion and the happy, almost jolly Slovenian personality to boot, and his face—as it was when he was five—filled me with joy unimaginable.

"I'm glad you were here when I dropped by," I said. "It's always great to see you."

"Me too," he said. "But that doesn't mean I don't have to do homework. That's why I'm up here working instead of out having a good time."

I wondered why Lila wasn't cooking a chicken breast for him, too, except that he had lived on pizza most of his life. "I hope we can hang out some," I said.

"Maybe lunch Saturday afternoon? I'll tell you all about school, and you can fill me in on what you're risking your neck on."

"I don't risk my neck unless I have to," I said. "What I'm doing right now is only paperwork."

"I remember when I was a little kid and you got shot in the butt. Was that paperwork?"

"You were supposed to be too young to know about that."

"There's a lot of things I'm still too young to know about—but I do, Dad. Hey, I'm in college now."

"Why don't we make it Saturday night instead," I said. "We can go out for dinner and then maybe see a show together."

He grinned widely and looked over his shoulder. On his desk

next to his computer was a framed eight-by-ten of him, wearing a Hawaiian shirt, with his arm around a beautiful young woman with light-brown hair and periwinkle blue eyes. "Dad—not Saturday night, okay?"

I took a few steps toward the desk and looked more carefully at the photograph. "That must be Anne," I said.

"Must be."

"You have excellent taste—she's very pretty. I hope you treat her well."

He smiled again, his eyes twinkling. "That's why we're going out Saturday night. But Saturday afternoon—that's all yours, Dad."

I hugged him again before I left. Stephen would blossom and be special. He'd yet to choose a major, vacillating between business or economics and political science. Whatever he ended up doing, he'd be good at it.

The visit with Lila and Joe had been a waste of time—especially because I believed them. For all Lila's faults, she never lied—except, of course, while she was sleeping with Joe Bradac when she and I were still married. But on this night, talking about her brief encounter with the late Phil Kohn, I thought she was telling the truth.

I was only about six blocks from Vuk's. I really wanted a beer—or several. But I'm too old to tie one on anymore, so a long evening at Vuk's didn't seem like a good idea. I went straight home.

It's not that I miss drinking more, because I don't. What I really miss is the drinking life—sharing one or more beers with friends and strangers, all of us relaxing, ignoring our troubles, and calling the evening pleasant, even though, in hindsight, it's rarely anything of the sort.

Drinking would have depressed me anyway. I swore the next client I signed with would be a complete stranger to me. No mutual acquaintances, no shared history, not even someone who lived in the same neighborhood as I did.

Life would be easier that way.

CHAPTER TWENTY

Except for my brief moment with Stephen the night before—the smile and the hug—my trip to Lila's house was uncomfortable at best. There was a winter whiteout inside her living room, too. When we'd first split up, I saw her frequently because of the boys, arguing with her about one minute more of my togetherness with them than the court had mandated. Now that both boys were over eighteen and could do whatever they wanted, I rarely had occasion to talk to Lila about anything anymore.

And that's the way I prefer it.

The day after the whiteout was bright and sunny; the sun beating down on the snow from the blue sky was hurtful to the eyes, and if you didn't look down at the collected winter storm deposited on the ground you'd think you were in Florida for the winter. I sat at my desk in the office, reading the lists of my fellow graduates—the ones I had put together myself and the ones Suzanne Davis had compiled for me. I separated their names into two new groups—those who'd been at the hotel the night Phil Kohn had died, and those who hadn't shown up at all.

Had I wasted my time and Tommy Wiggins's money? The police were investigating in other areas, searching other alleyways, but they wouldn't tell me which ones, because when I called Lieutenant McHargue that morning to check in, she told me that what the police do is none of my business.

"It's every bit of my business," I explained to her gently. "I'm under orders to report to you as well as to my client."

"But I'm not under any orders to report to *you*."

"Wouldn't it be easier if we actually shared information with each other?"

"It isn't even easy for me talking to you on the phone."

"Sorry," I said, trying not to sound as insincere as I felt. "It just makes sense that we help each other out."

"Well, as my grandma always said to me, you just take care of *you*. We'll handle the rest of it."

I stared up at the sheet of pressed tin covering my ceiling and frowned. It looked like a stage designer's version of a haunted house up there. The crew I pay to come in once a week to clean the office had obviously been neglecting the cobwebs in the high corners.

"I *will* tell you," McHargue went on, "that at the moment nobody looks better for the murder than Wiggins. He picked a fight with Kohn, and he tossed a drink in his face an hour before Kohn was killed. Other than him, we haven't found a goddamn thing."

When she broke the connection I felt more foolish than ever. McHargue sounded out of patience, given her snarky temper at the best of times. Within days, she was going to take the situation out of my hands and arrest Tommy Wiggins for murder.

I called Tommy's hotel room and told him I was coming by later in the afternoon. He didn't sound thrilled. He didn't want to be bothered because he was on a writing roll. I ached to point out that spending the rest of his life behind bars would give him plenty of time to write—when he wasn't working for fifty cents an hour stamping out license plates or doing prison laundry. I restrained myself, however, and told him I was coming whether he liked it or not. I didn't tell him why.

I didn't tell Ben Magruder why, either, when he called me half an hour later to raise hell. Obviously Wiggins had ordered him to cut me off at the pass. "You're dealing with a very famous, hardworking man," he snarled at me. "Your job—the reason I'm paying you—is to get him off the hook, not hang him on it. You should be out scarfing up information making *other* people look suspicious to the cops, not fucking up Tommy's day—or his life.

I'm warning you—stay away from him today, Milan. I don't want you near him."

"First of all," I said, anger welling up and burning my gut, "*you* aren't paying me—Tommy is. Secondly, if you didn't have your head halfway up your own ass, you'd realize the more I'm able to clear *him,* the better he's going to look to the police. I'm not trying to put somebody else on death row, just to make sure Tommy doesn't end up there. And thirdly—if you ever choose to 'warn' me again, I'm going to come down there and play racquetball off your office wall with your head. Have I made myself clear, Mr. Magruder?"

He was very quiet, thinking about it. When I heard his voice again, he'd ratcheted it down to a whine.

"Hey, don't get mad," he said. "I'm just trying to make this easier on Tommy, and you should be, too. He's an artist! We have to treat him carefully and not upset him. He's a celebrity. Celebrities get handled differently—more gently than everybody else."

"Not in Cleveland they don't," I said.

I was getting ready to head over to Wiggins's hotel room, but the ringing phone caught me as I was heading for the door.

Victor Gaimari.

"I mentioned to my uncle last night that I'd seen you, Milan," he said. "He got all excited. He wants to spend some time with you. You know how much he likes you."

"I'd like to see him, too," I said.

"Can you come over this evening? About seven? We won't have to stay too long—he goes to bed early these days."

I looked at my watch. It was an automatic gesture. A stupid thing to do, I thought—what did checking my watch at noon have to do with visiting an old man at seven o'clock in the evening? "Can I bring anything for him?" I said. "Something he'll enjoy?"

"He's not fond of his new enforced diet," Victor said, "and any of his old favorites we smuggle in will be taken away from him. His personal nurse sleeps in the spare bedroom to make sure he behaves himself. And he can't drink anymore, either—so don't even think about a bottle of wine."

"He always drank homemade stuff anyway, didn't he? A good glass of dago red and he was happy."

"Do I need to tell you that cigarettes or cigars are verboten, too?"

"He's living a rough life."

"He's always had a hard life," Victor said with a tinge of regret. "It took a lot out of him getting to where he was, and by the time he got there his health was pretty well shot to hell. That's why I've looked after him ever since I was old enough to do it."

"That's kind," I said.

"It's not so kind. It's just what we do when it's family. So—seven o'clock works for you?"

"Sure," I said, and jotted down the address of the Don's apartment.

"Maybe you and I can grab some dinner afterwards, if that's okay."

"If I get to pick up the check."

He attempted a laugh over the phone—one of those famous phony-sounding Victor Gaimari ha-ha's. "You *don't* get to pick up the check. Let's be serious. I carry more in my pocket than you have in the bank. It's all surplus, anyway—so let me indulge myself and buy you dinner."

Victor reminds me of my ex-wife Lila sometimes. Nobody ever argues with him, either.

Tommy Wiggins was so mad at me when I walked into his suite, this time he didn't even offer me a cup of coffee.

"You told Ben Magruder to shoot me down, didn't you?" I said.

He gave me one of his better-than-thou looks and pursed his lips prissily. "I'm getting more and more irritated talking to you. I'm writing today. Why don't you, for once, leave me the hell alone."

"I'm working to get you cleared," I said, "so I don't give a rat's ass how irritated you are." He opened his mouth to say something and I cut him off. "And if you're getting ready to fire me, take your best shot—but I'm still not backing off this case. Not any more. I'm too invested in it."

"You're *invested*?"

I nodded. "I'm not going to walk away now—so fire me or don't fire me, it's not going to make any difference."

He sighed.

"However," I said, "keeping me on your payroll might—just *might*—keep you out of jail for the next fifty years. It's your call."

He gave me one of those put-upon-pie sighs and flopped down onto the sofa. "Fine. Just get it over with so I can get back to work."

I sat in one of the chairs at the big lonesome conference table and turned toward him. "Forget Phil Kohn for a minute. Tell me about your relationships with some of our other classmates."

"I didn't have relationships with any of them. I told you—I didn't belong, and I wasn't part of any crowd. Few of them ever let me forget that. *You* didn't."

"Me?"

"We were hardly good buddies, were we?"

"I was a jock, you weren't. I never held your not playing football against you. I can remember pretty vividly we were friendly, all right."

"I suppose," he said.

"What about some of the others?"

He almost laughed. "I wasn't God's gift to women back then. I don't think any of them ever looked twice at me—except Danielle, and that was a one-night stand. That was okay—I didn't give a damn about any of them, either."

"Why not?"

"The girls whose parents had a little money were so stuck up, they only bothered with guys who were as rich and popular as they were. Besides, the Jewish girls hung out with other Jews, the Slovenian girls all had other Slovenian friends . . . I was—artsy. I never fit in with any of them."

"Not Maurice Paich?"

Wiggins smiled a little. "He was okay, I guess. He never made it as an actor—not in Hollywood or New York—but I suppose he pulls in a decent living on the radio locally, so that's something."

"You were good friends with him?"

Wiggins squirmed. "We were kindred spirits, in a way."

"What way?"

He looked confused for a second. "I thought he was silly, sure, but we were both—intellectuals, I guess."

"Was that the only way?" I said.

His eyes narrowed. "I don't know what you mean."

"I know why you were pissed off at Phil Kohn, why you started a ruckus with him at the reunion. You told me that, and you've told the police, too."

"Because he accused me of being a fag?"

"You're right, he did—two weeks before Christmas, forty years ago."

Wiggins wiped the back of his hand across his mouth. "It's been eating away at my guts every day of my life since."

"Because he lied?"

"Yes, because he lied. Look, I have no problem with gays—I work in the theater, half my New York friends are gay. Mostly they're great people—creative, stylish, classy, and fun. But when I was a senior in high school and Phil Kohn called me that in front of the entire class at the Holly Hop, it hurt more than you can imagine."

I just looked at him.

"Don't get the idea," he said, his voice and posture defensive, "that I was bisexual in high school, because you're wrong. I've dated a lot of beautiful women and married and divorced two of them, so I'm not keeping secrets about my love life. I'm not gay, never was gay, never will be gay. It happens to be the truth."

"You were the only friend Maurice had," I said. "And vice versa. You were both sensitive and intellectual, and neither of you fit in with the rest of the school. Maurice admitted to me that before he even knew what to do about his sexual urges, he had an affair with somebody in high school. Maybe that was you, Tommy—and maybe Phil Kohn knew, or suspected, anyway. That's why he said what he said to you when you were chosen King of the Holly Hop."

Tommy Wiggins stood up. His arms dangled at his sides but I could see his fists knotted. He tried getting himself under control. "Phil Kohn was a goddamn liar," he said. "I'm tired of having that repeatedly thrown in my face since somebody killed him. I want it over!" He started pacing in front of the sofa. "I knew Maurice was gay when he was seventeen years old. He told me he was."

"He told you?"

"Like I said, we were friends. I was over at his house—we were talking about theater, reading plays and stuff. I noticed his bookshelf in his room had a lot of different kinds of books than the rest of us had. I noticed one—it was a book of short stories by Tennessee Williams. Not plays like *A Streetcar Named Desire*—but short stories. I took it down and started browsing through it. The title of the book was *One Arm*, and that was the name of the longest story—about a young, gay, one-armed hustler in New Orleans. We all knew Tennessee Williams was gay—or those of us who bothered with theater and plays knew, anyhow. So when I asked about the book, he got all flushed and embarrassed. He was feeling insecure about himself, and he said he hoped I wouldn't hold what he was about to say against him."

"What did he say, Tommy?"

Wiggins chose his words carefully. "He confessed to me that he had homosexual leanings."

"That must have been difficult for a young kid to admit," I said, wondering how I would have reacted to hearing that kind of disclosure when I was seventeen years old.

"We were all aware of homosexuality. But we never thought about anyone we knew being gay, or even leaning that way."

"He didn't make any sexual advances toward you?"

"He was just looking for someone—a friend—to talk to," he said. "Besides, when I told him that sometimes everyone growing up has fantasies, he admitted to me that he'd actually committed—uh—he referred to it as homosexual acts. With a classmate."

"How do you know that for sure?"

"He told me, straight out. He cried when he told me." Tommy Wiggins shook his head as if to clear away the cobwebs. "I—I cried, too, Milan."

Neither of us said anything for nearly a minute. I was staring at the wall and Tommy Wiggins was busy staring out the window, as he frequently did.

Finally, he told me the name of Maurice Paich's high school lover.

CHAPTER TWENTY-ONE

Don Giancarlo D'Allessandro's two-bedroom apartment, just behind the expansive Beachwood Place shopping center, was even more elegant and a lot newer than the house on Murray Hill in which he'd lived for more than fifty years. The living room was bigger than the entire main floor of that old house, and off-white walls looked freshly painted. The furnishings were conservatively traditional, new, and very comfortable. The carpet was champagne-colored—that's what the old man told me, but it looked tan to me. The living room windows, on the seventh floor, opened to a view of a parklike setting, now covered with snow and looking like a Christmas card, and you would have to crane your neck to the left to see that the building was only a block from the busy I-271 freeway.

The Don, Victor told me, had been living there for a little more than a year. When I arrived for my visit, he was in an electric wheelchair, inhabiting it the way a king would his throne of gold. A hand-crocheted shawl was spread over his legs, and two pillows behind his head and shoulders supported his upper body. He wore a white shirt that was now too big for him around the neck, a muted brown-and-white knit tie that must have been forty years old, wrinkled khaki pants, and a sports jacket the color of whole wheat.

Victor had let him know I was coming, and it showed in his attire. His freshly shaved cheek, when I kissed it, smelled of men's cologne that most sophisticated people stopped wearing in the late 1970s. He'd always had relatively thick hair, especially for a man his age, but it had thinned perceptibly, and his pink scalp showed through. He was wearing half-spectacles low on his nose, but I never caught him looking at anything through the lenses.

He was almost ninety years old.

Victor hovered by the picture window. He was affected in many ways, but his love for his uncle had always been genuine. When he had opened the door for me, he'd squeezed my shoulder and told me how glad he was that I'd come to visit.

The Don's nurse, Sandra, a middle-aged woman with a nurturing smile, offered to bring me something to drink, but I declined. "I'll be in the kitchen if you need me, Don Giancarlo," she said pleasantly. Then she winked conspiratorially at Victor, and left the room.

When I'd bent down to kiss the old man, he'd grasped my hand at the same time. He still hadn't let go of it, so I sat down on the sofa as close as I could get to his chair. His handshake, in years past, had always been robust and masculine, but now his fingers looked bony and fragile, as if they might easily break from even a mild squeeze.

"Milan Jacovich," he said. Ever since I met him, he'd called me by both names, always difficult for his Italian tongue to pronounce, even though he seemed to enjoy saying them. Now he spoke them more slowly than ever. "I don't see you for a while."

"I apologize, Don Giancarlo. But I've thought of you often."

He beamed. "When you make a friend, that is always so. You always think good thoughts of a friend—even when time passes. I think about you too sometimes. You are well?"

"I'm hanging in there, sir."

It took him a few seconds to parse the sentence. Then: "Victor tells me some old friend from your high school got iced, no?"

"He wasn't really a friend," I told him. "But a lot of people I've had to question are my friends. Or they used to be, anyway."

"It's hard—finding things out about your friends you never knew before. Bad things, some of them."

"Some," I said. "Not all."

"I spent lots of years finding lousy things out about people.

People I trusted—people who turned their back on me." He gently put his own hand over his heart. "It hurts, don't it? You find out lousy things, and sometimes you got to do something about it—even when you don't want to." A frown darkened his face as his eyes filled with wetness, and his grasp of my hand grew tighter and stronger, the way his grip was back in his prime. But he seemed to be in pain. It wasn't the kind of physical ache that elderly men sometimes suffer, but the deep, hidden pain that doctors can't treat.

"Never mind about that," he corrected himself. "What could they do to me at my age? Throw me in prison for the rest of my life?" He laughed a little, but it was genuine. "Don't *you* do anything that you'll regret when you get old like me."

"You never get old," I said. "You get mellow."

"What's mellow?" he said. "Like crappy French wine or something you can't taste?" He brushed a hand in front of his face as if he were erasing a blackboard. "Your boys? They're good?"

"Excellent," I said. "One's going to Cleveland State and one—the older one, all grown up—he's living in Chicago."

That piqued his interest. "Chicago? Why you don't tell me Chicago? I have good friends in Chicago—Victor will give you the names. You tell your boy call them up, introduce himself as my friend, or the son of my friend, and they'll take excellent care of him." He smiled quietly to himself. "Chicago's a good town—good restaurants. You ever been to the Como Inn? Best Italian meal in Chicago. Southern Italian, naturally—not northern." He bunched all the fingers of his right hand together and kissed the tips. "Very fine food."

"You took me there to eat," Victor said, "when I was eight years old, Uncle. I've always remembered it—how good it was."

I said, "You always loved good food, sir."

The old man crinkled his nose in distaste. "Not no more, Milan Jacovich. Every year I get older, I feel lousier, and every year they take more good food away from me—foods I love. Foods I lived for. Now—" He snorted disdainfully. "I eat like a goddamn cow."

"Uncle Gianni," Victor said soothingly, "you don't eat like a cow. You had chicken for dinner tonight. Remember?"

"How you know what cows eat? You never even seen a cow in your life."

"I've seen them," Victor said. "I've even seen them eat. They eat grass."

"You don't see them all the time," Don Giancarlo said. "What do you know? Maybe when they go in the barn at night where nobody can see them, they eat a chicken." He smiled at his own joke, but I could tell he was tiring from the argument. Ten years ago he would have kept at it all night.

"But the cows don't get to eat pork," Victor said, "and they can't eat beef either, because they *are* beef. You can't eat pork, either. So that's why you think you eat like a cow, Uncle Gianni, but you eat pretty good." He looked at me. "He has orange juice every morning, and some oatmeal."

"Sure. But they don't let me put no sugar on it. Or honey. They give me that powder supposed to taste sweet. What they call it, Victor? Stevie-o?"

"Stevia," Victor said. "It's like those other sweeteners—except this one is good for you."

"Ah, ah, ah," the Don sighed, and slumped back against the pillows. "If I had a good doctor I wouldn't be eating that shit."

"You have a good doctor now."

"Yeah—now! A few years back I went to that lousy doctor, he didn't do a goddamn thing for me." He squinted one eye at me. "That was your friend—from your school days. Dr. Kohn. That's the one who got iced, no?"

"Yes, sir."

"A junkie pig, that doctor."

"I didn't find that out until after he died."

"He was lucky *I* didn't find out till later, either."

I took one of those breaths that prepared me for just about anything, because I was afraid of what Don Giancarlo was going to say next.

"I was paying him big money, and he feeds me crap pills and doesn't even bother with me. So Victor moves me to a good doctor—and when I find out that Kohn was a junkie, I was going to . . ."

He stopped, coughed heavily until his eyes teared. I leaned forward and put my hand on the back of his shoulder; his entire body shook and vibrated beneath my touch. Finally he stopped coughing, and took about a minute to catch his breath.

"I'm not good for shit now," Don Giancarlo said, not trying to shock me but being realistic. "Back then, though, I had people, men in the family. I *have* people. I wanted to send them to this fucking Kohn for being such a shitty doctor. Ah, never mind, you know? There's lousy workers in every job. You always hear about lousy lawyers—but I have a good one. An Italian lawyer—you know him, right?"

I nodded.

"Accountants?" he said, his voice becoming weak and soft so that I had to lean forward to hear what he was saying. "Some of them guys, they can't even hit the water when they piss off the end of a boat. But I have a great accountant, now—a Jewish guy. He's a magician with the numbers. Now I have a great doctor, too—Victor moved me over there, and he started treating me right—not that *strunz*, Kohn. Six years ago when I find out Kohn was a junkie all the time he was taking care of me—and not taking good care of me . . ."

Victor Gaimari cleared his throat loudly, and it sounded like a staccato rim shot. The old man looked at him, then looked back at me, and cocked his head to one side, looking resigned. "Never mind," he croaked, and put his hand to his throat for a minute, frowning at the way he sounded. "It's over with, now. And he's dead—the doctor friend of yours. So what's the difference?"

"Uncle Gianni," Victor said, "take a sip of water or juice, okay?"

"Water," D'Allessandro said, and Victor passed him a tall glass. The Don's hand didn't shake very much when he held it, but he only took two small sips. "They make me drink water all the time," he said to me. "Victor, the nurse, everybody—when I cough or something, or have trouble catching my breath, they make me drink water. No wonder I gotta get up and take a leak three, four times a night."

"Some nights I do, too," I said.

The Don chuckled. "When you get right down to it, Slovenians and Italians are a hell of a lot alike, no?"

"I've heard that."

"They both love to sing, right?" he said. "They love to eat—except you Slovenians eat fattening crap and we eat the good stuff. And marriage?" He spread his arms wide. "Did you know in the old days a lot of Italians and Slovenians who lived in Collinwood married each other?" He pointed his two index fingers toward each other and touched the ends of his fingertips together. Then he thought of another word. "Intermarried—is that how they call it? Now, when a Slovenian woman from Collinwood marries an Italian man, she winds up thinking all the Italian women in the family—the mothers and the aunts and the sisters—are crazy, because they yell a lot, even when they say they love you." He shrugged. "Maybe they are, I don't know. I only been with Italian women my whole life—first my late wife, and then later on with Mrs. Sordetto—so I can only give you my point of view. But you know anyway, Milan Jacovich. You know a lot of things."

"Even if I spent my life at your knee, listening to you and taking notes, I wouldn't learn half of what you've already forgotten."

The old man nodded, like a king granting a boon to a peasant. "You and Victor, you're two smart guys. That's why you get along together so good. That's why you're friends. That's why you're friends with me, too."

"I'm glad we are friends, Don Giancarlo," I said, using the honorary title normally applied when addressing a mob don—and then I softened it. "Good friends—Uncle Gianni, if I can call you that, sir."

He looked at me and his eyes got damp again—even though he wasn't coughing. "You gonna come back and see me again?"

"I promise I will."

His head nodded ever so slightly and his eyes began to close. I was afraid he was going to fall asleep right there, but he was thinking, and finally spoke aloud. "So that's a promise. You gotta keep a promise."

"Relax now, Uncle Gianni," I said. "Wake up in the morning feeling good."

"Yeah, yeah," he said. "In a pig's ass." He raised a hand slightly, one finger pointing at me. "Your doctor who died. I was too old to do anything to him when he screwed me over. Somebody else might not be so easy on him. Maybe somebody you know. Look for that, okay?"

"Okay," I said. I stood up and leaned down to kiss his cheek—and he turned his head and kissed me on the mouth. His lips were chapped and dry.

"Good friends, Milan Jacovich," he said, and pinched my cheek like a loving Jewish grandmother. His fingers were too weak to inflict any pain—it felt like a caress. "Like family, no?"

Victor and I drove our separate cars over to Giovanni's Ristorante in Beachwood—the most elegant restaurant in town, but Victor was paying for it, so I was delighted. When we settled in and ordered our dinner, he said, "I hope you keep that promise—about coming back to see him."

"I will."

"Soon. You understand what I'm saying to you, Milan? Soon."

Something crunched inside my chest and I tried not to grimace.

"He cares a lot about you," Victor said. "I've never known him to care so much about anyone who's not Italian. To him, you're part of his family, he says."

"I know," I said, and took a too-big swallow of my drink—and then what I was feeling came out of my mouth.

"I love him too, Victor."

The little coffee joint calls itself Talkies Film and Coffee Bar. It's on Market Street, just across the street from the Great Lakes Brewing Company, right next door to the chic Flying Fig restaurant, and half a block west of the West Side Market. I guess they show old movies all day in one of the back rooms—hence the name. I chose the place for my appointment with Stupan Godic at ten o'clock the next morning. It was only a few blocks from his apartment, where I'd offered to meet him, but he sounded far too embarrassed to have company.

I'd called Suzanne Davis before I left, telling her where I was going to be, though I hoped I wouldn't be needing backup. Stupan Godic was a poor soul, and I had no desire to cause him more pain. Still, my health was pretty good and I intended to keep it. He came in twenty minutes late, wearing the same clothes in which he'd visited my office. His outfit must have come from a church-related distribution of old clothes to the needy—I don't think Stupan had purchased any new duds out of his own pocket except socks and underwear in a long time. He was already well stoked for the meeting; the smell of recently smoked Mary Jane hung over him like a rain cloud.

The temperature that morning had zoomed into the high twenties—practically tropical for an Ohio February, and it was warm and toasty inside the coffee shop, but Stupan wouldn't take off his parka. He sat hunch-shouldered at our table by the window, shivering in misery as I got him a cup of coffee with lots of cream and sugar, and a plate of pastries from the counter. He made it all disappear within ninety seconds, and I ordered him some more. I guess for him, that was breakfast.

The thing that struck me the most about Stupan—and not just this morning—was his desperate loneliness, from a life lived on the outer limits of polite society. What I asked him about hardly made it any easier. What little color he had in his cheeks—more from the cold than anything else—disappeared.

"You got a hell of a lot of nerve asking me something like that," he said. "It's none of your business."

"Stupan," I explained, keeping my voice soft and leaning in close to him, "the police think Tommy Wiggins killed Phil Kohn because of something Kohn said to him at the senior-year Holly Hop dance about him being gay. He wasn't—as you know—but Maurice Paich is. And when I talked to Maurice, he said he'd known he was gay since high school—and that he'd had his first experience with a classmate." I gulped down the remainder of my tea. "With you."

Stupan looked around, worried someone in Talkies would overhear us, but they were all either ordering coffee to go or deeply involved in the newspaper. He looked as though he might cry. "What do you care, Milan? Am I right?"

"I don't care about anybody's private life—I care about Phil

Kohn getting killed. If you're gay, you're gay—I don't have a problem with that."

He put away another cheese Danish, chewing thoughtfully. "I'm not gay," he said. "When I was a kid—scrawny, ugly, kind of stupid—no girl'd have anything to do with me. Not even a kiss." He indulged in a one-bark laugh. "Not that things have changed so much since then."

I very much wanted another cup of tea, but I just listened.

"Maurice and me—well, we were friends because we're both Slovenian." Stupan allowed himself the tiniest smile. "Like you, Milan. So anyways, I guess him and me were working on a science project in our senior year. He came over to my house—it was always quiet over there. My parents both worked so they weren't ever home." He sighed. "It was a rainy day, sometime before Thanksgiving. I was feeling lousy because I couldn't even get up to bat with any of the girls in class, and Maurice was down because he wanted to be a real actor and nobody ever took him seriously."

Stupan stopped talking for a moment. Then he said, "We were cleaning up the science project and talking and whining about our pathetic adolescent lives, and then Maurice just threw his arms around me and kind of hugged me—to make me feel better, I guess. Which was okay—it felt good to be hugged, I swear to God. I can't remember my parents *ever* hugging me—not in that house." There were crumbs on his plate from his stash of pastries and he quietly pushed them around with his finger. "Then he kissed me."

I was starting to regret this breakfast meeting.

"Nobody ever kissed me on the lips before," he said, nearly lost in a sad reminiscence. "No girl, no relative, nobody. It scared me, I'll tell you that—but it was amazing, too." He said it with wonder. "So I kissed him back."

He stared out the window. Market Street, just off West 25th, is a side street, but it's very busy, even at ten o'clock in the morning, and people were walking by Talkies involved in their own agendas and not paying attention to anyone else. I released a store of air from my lungs and nodded to let him know I understood.

"There was a couch down in the basement, Milan. There was

stuff piled on it—old camping stuff and things like that. But we moved it all onto the floor—"

I raised a hand to stop him. "Too much information," I said.

"We did it a couple more times after that," he said wistfully, "but I wasn't really into it, y'know? So we stopped—an' we kind of drifted apart until graduation . . ." His sudden grin was lopsided, self-deprecating. " . . . after we finished the science project."

"Did Phil Kohn know anything about it?"

Stupan shook his head almost angrily. "He was too busy with his head up his own ass—rich punk. None of the other kids knew about it, either."

"You and Phil had a fight about drugs at the reunion—and about your father. Did you argue about anything else?"

"No," Stupan said. Then: "Well—no, not really, I guess."

"You must have hated Phil for that."

He seemed tired, wrung out—maybe from two plates full of pastries and two cups of sugar-laced coffee. "Milan, I knew some pretty interesting guys in the army over there—and they didn't give a hoot for their military duty! They ran their own private drug stores out of their hooches and made millions of dollars—*millions!*—off of dumb, naive guys like me, and by the time I came home, I was hooked to the eyeteeth. There was no way in hell I'd quit doping. I've swallowed, snorted, smoked, or injected more shit into my body than anybody ever dreamt about—and I'm still takin' whatever I can afford. So there's nothin' left in me to hate anybody anymore."

"Your father . . ."

" . . . lived for another seven years after we switched doctors," Stupan finished for me. "I took it a hell of a lot better—my dad's dying from heart problems, I mean—than people whose parents kicked off while they were still in Phil's medical care. Those are the ones that probably stayed pissed off."

"I see," I said.

"Like whatsisname? Bernie Rothman? His mom died, probably because she couldn't seem to get appointments with Phil and there was nobody to take care of her. Bernie was off in Florida somewheres."

I had to catch my breath. Stupan chattered unawares, but he'd taken me completely by surprise. I had to clear my throat. "Are you saying that Bernie hated Phil Kohn?"

Stupan bobbed his head in agreement. "Hated him like bees. Phil Kohn wasn't paying a damn bit of attention to Bernie's mom. You know the way he was about her, don't you? It was because of his mom back in high school that he had to break up with Alenka Tavcar, which broke his heart. I remember when that happened."

"He loved Alenka so much," I said. "He still does."

"I guess he does—but he loved his mom even more. That's why he chose her over Alenka. Bernie Rothman's hang-up about his mother was—you know, Milan. It wasn't normal."

CHAPTER TWENTY-TWO

Bernie Rothman wasn't home when I rang the doorbell of what used to be his mother's house in Beachwood. He didn't have a local job, so I couldn't help fantasizing he was out and about, doing something crazy, like spying outside Alenka Tavcar's house.

Bernie had always been strange. In a biology class, he'd shown up once without a pencil and the teacher chided him for being unprepared. When he'd attacked me outside my apartment building in the snow, he hadn't really been prepared either. What could I expect from Bernie this time?

I drove around for a while until I found a decent-looking restaurant in which to have lunch and kill some time. It disturbed me that my hand trembled nervously as I lifted the cup of tea. I was sick unto death of this case, of Tommy Wiggins, of anything to do with Phil Kohn, and especially of old classmates I'd nearly forgotten.

There are countless articles written about how successful in the workplace the louse or the snake in the grass really is, and that you get ahead better and faster by being a bully than by sticking to nice-guy principles. That's why I'm a one-man corporation, a lowly private eye who works my butt off and never seems to get a few bucks ahead—while Phil Kohn, who had lived with the moral compass of a sewer rat, wound up rich and powerful.

Of course, Phil Kohn is dead, and I'm still here.

After a Denver omelet that I didn't even finish, I found my way back to Bernie Rothman's house.

This time he was home.

"Milan," he said when he opened the door. His cheeks were still flushed from the cold. "I was out doing some shopping. Come on in."

He led me back to his kitchen, and we sat together on stools at the tall counter. Two shopping bags were sitting on the corner, one from Trader Joe's and another from Macy's. For a century Macy's was strictly a New York City tradition, with its Thanksgiving Day parade every year, complete with high school marching bands from all over the country, Manhattan celebrities, giant helium balloons looming over the gawking crowds, and a big finish with Santa Claus on a huge sleigh. Now there are Macy's stores everywhere, including Cleveland.

"Look what I got," Bernie said, fishing his purchases out of the Macy's store bag. "I bought a couple of sweaters. I didn't have many warm clothes in Florida, but now that I'm going to be staying here I'll have to get a whole new wardrobe." He shook one of the sweaters out so I could see it—mostly white with splashes of beautiful sea blue, and a small patch of sunny red-orange. I've never been to Florida, but the colors, even on an all-wool sweater, seemed to remind me of the Sunshine State. "Besides, I want to look my best when I see Alenka again." He held the sweater up in front of him. "What do you think? Sharp-looking, huh?"

"It's a nice sweater," I said. "But I thought you were going to give up on starting the Alenka romance all over again."

His smile was wide and proud—Lewis Carroll's Cheshire Cat lived somewhere inside that grin. "I was going to give up, I really was. But I thought about it some more—true love is like a chronic cold, it just never goes away—and I changed my mind."

"When we were at St. Clair," he continued, "we were all dopey adolescents just beginning to learn which way is up. Now we've absorbed some lessons over the years—like when you really want something, you do whatever it takes to get it and not worry what other people think. So here I am, and I want Alenka, for the rest of my life—and I'm not going to walk away."

"All right," I said.

"All right? That's your take on it? All right?"

"Bernie, it has nothing to do with me."

"But you kissed her," he said, the accusing tone creeping back into his voice. "I saw you do that."

"I don't know about Florida, where you've been living, but in Cleveland it's common to kiss or hug good friends, especially when you haven't seen them in a long time. It wasn't a passionate kiss, and if you have a problem with the friendly kind then you'll have to learn to deal with it."

He made an effort to relax his face until it seemed benign, scrubbed of all anger. "I have no problem," he said cheerily, "I was just wondering." He took a small box out of the shopping bag and opened it. Inside was a bottle of men's cologne. "You ever wear this stuff?"

"No," I said.

"The lady at Macy's talked me into it—she was wandering around the cosmetics department and she stopped me to talk. She sprayed a little on me—she says it'll make me smell sexy to women."

"Good for you."

He pulled off the lid and squeezed the spritzer, wetting his palms and rubbing them together, then patting his face. "Does it smell good?"

"I can't tell."

"Here, try some on yourself." Bernie proceeded to engulf me in a cloud of olfactory overload. I pulled away, but a few droplets hit my neck—the rest soaked into my collar. "Put it on the next time you have a date with your special lady," he said. "You'll love it, and I bet she will, too."

I'd probably stink for days now. "I never wear cologne."

He put the cologne back in the sack. "How about some tea?"

"No, thanks. I want to talk to you about something."

"Talk away." He moved to the cupboard, where he took down a mug and a box of his Egyptian tea. I envisioned him drinking that bright pink brew while wearing his new white sweater—one drip of it on the sleeve and he'd have to throw it into the trash.

"When we spoke at the reunion—you were telling me about your mother passing away."

He set the tea kettle on the stove, then dropped the tea bag into the mug. "Just last year. It was the saddest thing . . ."

"She got substandard cardiac care—I remember your telling me that."

His lips narrowed to a straight, angry line. "Fucking bastards," he said.

"The doctors?"

He nodded bitterly. "They don't give a damn about patients unless they come from overseas and are worth billions."

"You're talking about Phil Kohn, aren't you?"

He hesitated for a nanosecond. "Yes, I am. But you know that, don't you? Stupan told you this morning."

"He called and told you?"

"Stupan Godic is a total dumbshit," Bernie said, "but as loyal as an old dog. Sure he called me. I asked him to tell me whenever he talked to you, Milan. Because you're so involved in the Tommy Wiggins–Phil Kohn thing." He smiled. "He told me you spent about fifteen dollars on his pastries, too. Stupan loves pastries and sweet things. Most junkies do, don't they?"

The whistle of the tea kettle interrupted him, and he jumped a little—but *just* a little. He carefully poured the water into the mug; the pink tea fairly glowed.

"Phil loved sweet things too," he said. "Crazy, isn't it? A cardiologist with a sweet tooth? But that's because he was an addict." Then he laughed. "Dr. Phil Kohn—Dr. Phil. I'll bet he wished he was the other Dr. Phil, making millions of dollars on TV. You think?"

"How did you know Phil was a drug addict?"

"I didn't at first. If I'd known, I wouldn't have allowed him anywhere near my mother. Naturally."

"How did you find out?"

Bernie looked sad. "After she died—I was suspicious. Before I returned to Florida after her funeral, I—paid somebody to find out about him for me."

"You hired a private investigator?" I said.

"Not exactly. I paid somebody who had direct knowledge about Phil Kohn, and he did all the snooping around that I needed."

"Stupan."

"Yes. I didn't know him well in our school days, and of course living in Florida I wasn't in touch with him at all, but when my mother's obituary appeared in the *Plain Dealer,* he called with his sympathies. He's a kind person, don't you think?" He cocked his head. "*You* never called me that time, Milan. That wasn't nice of you."

"I don't read the obituaries."

"Too bad," he said. "Stupan told me that Phil Kohn had treated his father for a heart condition years ago, and he didn't like Kohn much, either. So I did him a favor—gave him money—so he could learn something about our famous doctor. He asked around, including a lot of our fellow graduates, and found out about Phil's womanizing. That took him several phone calls. About his drug use? That just took him one."

"To Maurice Paich," I said.

He raised an eyebrow. "That's very good, Milan."

"Maurice and Stupan have somewhat of a history," I said. "So when Stupan called him, Maurice opened up to him and admitted Kohn was blackmailing him to score drugs."

"That's what I hear," Bernie said.

"From Ted Lesnevich."

He nodded. "I never knew a damn thing about Ted in the old days—I just remembered him skulking around. But when Stupan mentioned his name, I dug out my old yearbook and looked up his graduation photo." He shrugged. "Even then he looked like a seventeen-year-old drug pusher."

"We have a similar memory," I said, but I wasn't smiling.

"We have lots of things to remember together," Bernie said. He sipped his rose-hip tea, and it reddened his top lip. "Nice," he said, "very bracing. But it needs some sugar today. I want to be sweet, Milan."

He opened a drawer, and I realized too late that he didn't keep his sugar in there. There was a sound like a kid firing a cap gun, and a tremendous spasm of pain erupted all through my body. I fell backwards off the stool. I didn't know until later that I'd cracked my head on the marble counter on the way down. That's why I wasn't conscious anymore.

CHAPTER TWENTY-THREE

It wasn't a nightmare, but it wasn't a pleasant dream, either, because I didn't go to sleep naturally, nor do I remember the specifics of the dream. There were a lot of women involved, though—Sonja Kokol, Danielle Webber Magruder, Alenka Tavcar, Maurice Paich's wife Meredith, Shareeka Washington, my ex-wife Lila, and Gerry Gabrosek with the Grand Canyon–deep cleavage. Perhaps there were others I couldn't remember. Even Jinny Johnson was in the dream as well, and I couldn't figure out why, because she didn't belong there.

All these women were slowly advancing on Phil Kohn—still alive for some reason—with their arms outstretched, wanting to touch him and connect with him. But Phil kept backing off as though he were afraid of them, shaking his head, fading away. Pretty soon he was gone and then I woke up with a painful start, groggy and trying to figure out where I was.

I was lying on a cement floor without my shoes. I was in an enclosed cell of some kind, probably sixteen feet square, its walls made of heavy white-painted bricks. The room wasn't cold, exactly—on the other side of the door I could hear a boiler humming and clanking its February song. I was in a basement someplace. When I tried the thick, heavy door, I found it was securely locked from the outside. Double-locked, as it turned out. I wasn't surprised.

There was a fish-eye peephole in the door, about five feet high, and I scrunched down to check what was on the other side. When I closed one eye and looked out with the other, I could see that old boiler, and beyond it a corner of the basement stacked high with what looked like empty TV, sound system, and computer cartons.

I straightened up, pondering, and shoved my hands in my pockets as I often do when I'm thinking. That's when I noticed that my watch, belt, and wallet had been taken from me while I was out cold. I didn't even have small change in my pants anymore.

I turned around and surveyed the room again. There was a light fixture overhead with a pull chain, the forty-watt bulb glowing. High on one wall there once was a window or opening but it had been closed and bricked over many years before. I got the idea that in the early days of the house, which was close to a century old, this used to be a coal storage room, and the delivery of coal probably took place through that long-ago window.

The floor was relatively clean. Over in one corner was a twin-size mattress with a clean sheet thrown sloppily over it, a folded-up Amish-style quilt, and a pillow. Against the far wall a worn but serviceable upholstered chair was next to a small table containing a stack of eight nutritional bars, supposedly for me to eat when I got hungry.

I was hurting in several different places. I put my hand to my head, where it hurt the most, my fingertips caressing a sore lump the size of a golf ball on the back of my skull. Waves of dizziness flowed and ebbed, and pain throbbed from my crown to behind my eyes. I ascertained that I had whacked my head when I fell and was probably struggling through a concussion, which is why I was asleep in the first place. My chest and abdomen were sore, too—but it was a different kind of pain, and as I carefully probed around my body I jumped when I pushed on a stinging spot on my left side. I pulled up my sweater and shirt to see the two matching rattlesnake-style wounds. That's when I realized that in his warm and cozy kitchen while he was drinking his tea, Bernie Rothman had shot me with his Taser gun—in the general vicinity of my heart.

My feet and ankles were sore, too. I leaned down—with care,

not wanting to black out again—and rolled down one of my socks. My ankle was red and bruised, and a bit swollen. The other ankle seemed the same.

Why?

Woozy, I eased myself into the chair and was surprised there wasn't much beneath the cushion to support my weight. I sank down into it so that my knees were almost as high as my shoulders. My parka, now dusty, had been tossed onto the mattress. My sweater over a dress shirt and black turtleneck afforded me all the warmth I needed at the moment. I struggled to rerun in my mind my kitchen conversation with Bernie. I realized I had marched right into the home of a murderer and practically accused him of the crime.

Shooting pain across my eyes nearly rendered me unconscious once more. I wanted more than anything to close my eyes again and snooze—but I knew from past experience that going to sleep after a concussion could be damaging. So I fought to stay awake, battling just to keep my eyes open. Without my wristwatch I didn't even know what time it was—or what day, either.

A hell of a long time passed. It felt like three hours or so. Finally my head stopped hurting so much, the egg at the back of my skull had partially diminished, and my stomach was rumbling. I opened one of the bars—peanut butter and granola, it said on the front. It tasted like faux-chocolate-covered library paste and two-day-old hay.

It then occurred to me that there wasn't a bathroom in here. It didn't matter to me—yet. But not too far in the future I would need one.

I wondered why Bernie Rothman had stashed me in the cellar. As far as I knew, it might be in another house altogether, halfway across town. I didn't even have a window to gaze from. I had survived the crack on the head, but I feared I might die too soon—of sheer boredom.

More time passed, and I was close to falling asleep, concussion or no, when someone knocked on the door.

Actually knocked.

How very polite, I thought, considering I couldn't get the door open if I wanted to.

"Milan?" the voice said, and I recognized it at once. "Are you okay?"

I got up and moved to the peephole. It was Bernie Rothman's face looking back at me, all right, and he was smiling. "Are you decent in there?" he said through the door.

"Let me out of here, Bernie," I said.

"I don't think so, Milan." Each of us was staring at the other's eye through the peephole. "Sit down in the chair," he said, "and don't move. I'm coming in."

I didn't move.

He said, "If you're not sitting in that chair, I'm going to shoot you with the Taser again, and there isn't a damn thing you can do about it."

I still didn't move.

"If you don't sit down, I won't come in there again, no matter what. When you run out of water and the rest of those granola bars, tough shitsky for you because you won't get any more to eat or drink—ever. Do you want that?" He waited for about ten seconds, growing impatient. "Answer me, okay?"

"No, I don't want that," I said.

"Then go sit down and don't get up until I tell you."

Chastened like a second grader, I slouched over to the chair and sat down. After a moment tumblers clicked on a lock, and then the door swung open and Bernie Rothman was standing there with the Taser gun in his hand.

"Stay still, Milan," he said. He came in, closed the door, and leaned against it.

"This is nuts," I said.

"It can't be helped."

"Why am I locked up here anyway?"

He sighed. "It's a long story."

"I'd like to hear it. I don't have anywhere else to go."

"To put it simply—you get in my way."

"How?"

"As I said, it's a long story. It started with you making a clumsy pass at Alenka."

"I didn't—"

"Shush!" he ordered. "That's not the important part."

I shushed—but he just stared at me, readying his thoughts. "I was unhappy you were dealt into this business," he said finally. "The police weren't going to harass me because I haven't lived anywhere near Cleveland for years. They seem to have locked in on Tommy Wiggins and weren't bothering with the rest of us." He shook his head sadly. "Then *you* started putting your two cents in. You wanted to find some classmate more logical as the killer than Tommy. Is that why you wound up here? Because idiot Stupan told you that Dr. Phil Kohn let my mother die?"

"Something like that," I said.

"This is his fault, then—Stupan's."

"It's nobody's fault. Things happen . . ."

He shook his head. "Certain people make them happen. Sometimes it's foolishness, like Stupan's. I can forgive foolishness, because we're all cursed with it in one way or another. *You* are foolish, too—you should never have kissed Alenka." The skin on his face grew taut and angry. "Evil is another thing altogether. Phil Kohn was evil. He had a gift from God, the gift of healing. But he was so consumed with drugs and gambling and womanizing, he didn't even bother with healing much anymore. That's why my mother passed away—from his neglect." There were beads of perspiration on his forehead and his upper lip, and for a moment he almost looked like a hounded Richard Nixon—but he stood up a little taller, which didn't help him very much, and threw his shoulders back with what might have been hubris. "That's why Phil Kohn is dead."

I felt a wave of sadness and pity—because Bernie Rothman was very close to insanity.

"Did you use that stun gun on Phil, too?"

"I didn't have to," he said. "I had a real gun. I just walked up to his car—he saw me but he didn't even know I was mad at him—and shot him twice."

"Do you still have the gun?"

"I'm not stupid. Of course I don't have it anymore. On my way home that night I threw it off the Detroit-Superior Bridge into the river. I wiped off my prints, too, just in case somebody found it before the water washed it away."

"Go to the authorities, Bernie," I said. "Tell them what you've told me. They'll understand. They can help you."

His expression changed back to friendly again. "I don't need help. Everything's just fine now."

"But . . ." I said.

"No more, Milan. I've said what I had to say. Let's just drop it." He became pleasant, helpful. "You want to use the john before I go? No problem, there's one down here."

"Down here? Are we still in your house?"

"Naturally."

"How did you get me down the stairs from the kitchen?" I said. "I'm too big for you to lift."

"It wasn't easy," he admitted. "I had to grab you under the arms and drag you down the steps. I'm afraid your feet and ankles got banged up a little in the process. Sorry about that."

"What about my shoes—and my belt, wallet, and wristwatch?"

"I had to take everything away that you might use as a weapon," he said. "By the way, you had seventy-three dollars in your wallet. But you don't need to buy anything down here." He waved the stun gun at me. "Stand up—slowly." I managed to haul myself out of that ridiculously low chair and onto my feet. I couldn't stand up any faster if I'd wanted to. I didn't have to use the bathroom that minute, but I wasn't sure when my next opportunity would come along—and I remembered the late Katharine Hepburn airily observing that one should always take advantage of the opportunity to use the facilities.

"I'll back out first and stand away from you while you come out," Bernie said. "Turn left, go past the stairs—I'll follow—and there's a little enclosed potty. There's no weapon in there. I even took the wooden roller off the toilet-paper holder—the roll is on the back of the john. There isn't a sink where you can wash your hands, but there's a bottle of Purell hand sanitizer in there. You'll want them clean for the next time you eat." He smiled. "It's a tiny plastic bottle, so don't get happy thinking of throwing it at me, because it won't hurt."

He backed out of my little room, standing with his back to the boiler. The Taser was leveled right at me. "I don't want to hurt you again, but I will if I have to. You know that. So just take it easy."

When I emerged from the room into the full basement, Bernie was approximately seven feet away from me. That's as close in proximity as we'd been together since I woke up.

"Move along," he said.

I shuffled across the basement to where a toilet had been installed, enclosed by wooden walls that didn't go all the way to the floor. "Take your time," Bernie said. "Nobody's going to peek."

I went in, pulled the chain at the overhead light so another forty-watt bulb glowed, and looped the little hook inside the door into the eye. That hook was indeed the only thing in there not made of paper or secured to the pipes, but it was so small it wouldn't land a largemouth bass, much less stand in as a weapon. I stood there peeing, feeling four years old again, with Bernie hovering outside ready to mow me down if I did anything wrong.

What I hadn't yet discerned was why I was here in the first place. He obviously knew I'd figured him for the Kohn killing. Why hadn't he simply shot me, too? Whatever the reason, I was grateful. As long as I was alive and walking around, I still had a chance.

To do what, exactly, I had no idea.

I flushed, squirted Purell on my hands, pulled the chain to extinguish the bulb, and went out into the basement again. Bernie was waiting, pointing.

"Go back into your room," he said.

My room.

I moved slowly. He was behind me. "I know you're bored silly down here. Next time, I'll bring something to read. The newspaper, maybe."

"That will be nice," I said.

"I won't bring the whole paper at once, though. You can wrap that up tight and use it like a club. I'll bring you one section. When you finish it, give it back to me and I'll give you another one. What do you want to read first? The sports pages? In February there isn't much in the way of sports going on in Cleveland except basketball. I know that's not your sport, is it? You played football."

My mind started working. "Did you ever see me play, Bernie?"

We got to the other side of the basement. Bernie leaned against the back of the boiler and motioned me to go inside. "Sure, I watched a lot of games."

"I loved playing," I said, turning around slightly. Bernie still had the stun gun, but he looked more relaxed at the moment. "But I was only a nose tackle. My best friend Marko Meglich—remember him? He was the one that had all the fun. He was a wide receiver."

"I remember," Bernie said.

"One of the glamour positions," I said, turning even more and grinning at Bernie Rothman. "That's how he used to get all the girls."

I laughed. Bernie laughed, too. While he was laughing I lunged for him.

He was surprised. I managed to get my arms wrapped around his neck and started wrestling him to the floor. Then he fired the Taser gun again.

That time it got me in the neck.

CHAPTER TWENTY-FOUR

This time I didn't knock myself silly hitting my head on a counter. But the pain from that was nothing compared to the experience of being Tasered. This time, staying conscious, I didn't miss a second of it. I wound up on the floor in the doorway to the little room, rolling around while my head, face, and extremities jerked and twitched wildly, and sustained a long spasm during which I lost control of my entire body from the assault on my nervous system. Since the Taser prongs hit me in the neck, very close to my throat, it was impossible for me to breathe or swallow during the attack.

I thought I was dying.

When the spasms finally ceased, Bernie ordered me to crawl back into my room and lie on the mattress until I felt better. Then he left, double-locking the door again. I was shaking, and still convulsing slightly. My throat was scratchy and sore, and the tormented muscles in my neck screamed with sharp, prickly tension.

It didn't matter that I was currently unable to talk—because there was no one to talk to.

So I sweated it out in silence, and eventually my spasms and twitches subsided and then, blessedly, stopped completely. My mind began to work again, and I went back to figuring out why I was here. What was the point? Bernie Rothman killed Phil Kohn. I knew it, and he knew I knew. When he zapped me the first time, why didn't he just kill me, too?

I must have spent more than an hour lying on my mattress, thinking about it. Finally I was too wiped out even to use my mind anymore. I was tired, and my shoeless feet were cold. I pulled the quilt up around me, but it wasn't doing the job, so I spread my parka over the top of it. Then I fell asleep.

At some point I imagined I heard voices—speaking softly. I could tell one of the voices belonged to a woman and the other to a man, but I couldn't make out what they were saying. Maybe I was dreaming again.

I woke up, still sore and stiff, feeling even more tired than when I'd gone to sleep. Had I snoozed through the night, or had I just catnapped for twenty minutes or so? I had no way of knowing, and it was driving me crazy.

I levered myself up off the mattress, padded over to the door, and started rapping on it with the side of my fist. I yelled "Hey!" and "Bernie!"

After a few minutes I heard him on the other side of the door. "Are you all right, Milan?" he said.

"I need to use the bathroom again." In my own ears, my voice was raspy and raw—my throat muscles hurt like hell.

He ate up half a minute thinking about it. "Go sit in the chair," he said.

I did as I was told. "I'm in the chair," I called out to him. He fumbled with the key in the lock, finally opening the door. He had the Taser gun again.

"Feel better?" he said. Part of the newspaper was folded up under his arm, and he carried a small carton of orange juice. His freshly shaved face was a healthy ruddy color, as if he'd been out in the cold, and he was wearing a different outfit than the last time I saw him—a deep purple sweatshirt and washed-out designer jeans. I deduced that I'd slept through the night.

"I brought you some O.J.," he said, "and the sports section. I'll set everything on the floor and you can get it when I leave." His smile was almost kindly. "I don't want to zap you again—it's not good for your health or your nervous system. Please don't make me, all right?"

I raised both my hands in a gesture of surrender. "I've learned my lesson."

"Excellent! I don't want to injure you, Milan. I really like you. But I can't have you attacking me every time I come down here. As long as you're my guest, I want to treat you as well as I possibly can, all right?"

I didn't answer him, but my curt nod was sufficient.

"Are you going to eat any of those granola nutrition bars for breakfast? Or should I bring you some toast and cereal?"

"That'd be better," I said.

"All I have are Cheerios and Froot Loops."

I suppressed a shudder. Froot Loops for breakfast are one step away from eating the carpet. "Cheerios will be fine."

"I have whole wheat bread—made with spelt. Butter and jelly on the toast? I have grape or strawberry jelly today."

"Just butter."

"Excellent. You want to use the potty?"

We repeated last night's strange expedition across the basement, him a few steps behind me, but this time I didn't give him any reason to zap me. Twice was enough.

When we'd returned to my little prison and I'd sat in my low-slung chair, he said, "When I come back, I'll trade you for the front part of the paper. Okay?"

Whoopee.

I heard Bernie climbing the basement steps. He was gone for approximately fifteen minutes—and that's a guess. Without a watch or even a window to know whether it was light or dark, time had lost its meaning for me. When he came back he was actually balancing a tray with all my goodies in one hand—the one not holding his little weapon. There were two buttered slices of whole wheat toast, a bowl of Cheerios—served in a cardboard bowl, the kind you take to picnics—and a half-pint carton of low-fat milk beside it. The front page section of the *Plain Dealer* was folded neatly next to the Cheerios. There was even a spoon—a cheap white plastic one I couldn't file down into a shiv even if I wanted to. Oh, yes—a neatly folded paper napkin was on the tray.

"Throw your sports section over here," he said. "Fold it neatly first, okay? Don't throw it so it comes apart and I have to bend down too long to get it."

I folded up the sports section and skittered it across the floor to his feet. He bent from the knees like a Playboy Bunny, not taking his eyes from me, put the tray on the floor, and retrieved the paper.

"Enjoy," he said. "By the way, you had company last night."

"I did?"

"Your friend and sometime partner, Suzanne Davis. She came by at about ten o'clock, looking for you. You were probably asleep down here, though, and I didn't want to disturb you. So I told her the truth—that you'd been here earlier, we talked in the kitchen for a while, and then you had someplace to go."

"Someplace to go?" I chuckled. "That was inventive of you." It wasn't inventive at all—I'd left Suzanne's machine a message telling her of my planned whereabouts, just in case something went wrong. Something exactly like this.

But Suzanne had come and gone—my only outside help—and I was stuck.

"Did you let her go, Bernie?"

He looked offended. "Naturally. She seems nice—attractive, too, in a tough old broad kind of way. I wouldn't hurt her. I had no reason to."

I toyed with the idea of not believing him, but it was a bad idea for me to make a fuss. "Did Suzanne happen to notice my car parked right outside your house?"

"Oh, I moved that out of sight last night. It's about six blocks away, parked in a neighbor's driveway, around behind their house. They aren't home—they went to Hilton Head for two months. They even sent me a postcard. I'll move your car within the next few days and park it in a long-term garage somewhere." He shook his head in a begrudging sort of admiration. "You surprised me showing up here, but I've been improvising since you knocked on the door. I handled it very well, don't you think?"

"I don't know about surprise," I said. "For instance, if you weren't planning on keeping a long-term prisoner, who bricked up the window and put a thick door with a double lock and a peephole on the entrance to an old coal room?"

"I did that for my mother about two years ago. In this neighborhood, punk kid gangs break in and rob elderly people all the time, and Mom was scared to death. So I had this little room rebuilt for her." He knocked cheerily on the open door. "She could hide, and peek out through the little fisheye to make sure no one knew where she was."

"You have all the answers, Bernie."

"Most of them."

"I'd still like to know why you're keeping me here—and what you're going to do with me. Do you plan to keep me locked up forever?"

"No, Milan—not forever."

Bernie Rothman's eyes were wide and wild, and he barely blinked them. It was the same look you see on the faces of fanatics, terrorists, and low-budget movie monsters. That was the moment I knew his plans—that he was eventually going to kill me.

"I have to keep you out of the way so nobody notices you," he said, trying to save the moment and assuage my fears. He didn't even come close to it. "After the police make up their minds it was Tommy Wiggins who killed Phil, they'll forget about you altogether—they might think you chickened out and left town for a while. So they'll nail Wiggins for murder. Then I'll quietly collect Alenka and we'll go away somewhere—far away where no one will ever bother looking for us." He frowned again. "No one will ever disturb her again the way Phil Kohn did."

"Phil Kohn never even hit on her," I said. "He hit on her daughter."

"That's a lie!" He leveled the Taser gun at me. "Don't lie to me, or I'll hurt you again. It wasn't Alenka's daughter; it was *her*. I know that. He—forced himself on her."

"Who told you this?"

He looked vague. "I just *knew*! The two most important people in my entire life—my mother and the woman I love—and he injured both of them. That's why I came back to Cleveland to kill him. I didn't give a goddamn about the reunion, because I didn't care about seeing most of those people again. But I wanted to see Alenka—and to kill Phil Kohn. I wanted him to die where everyone would see it." Bernie was breathing raggedly. He was just about over the top—but he wasn't so enraged that he couldn't pull that trigger again, so I stayed in my chair.

"And that's why you and she are going away together?"

He nodded. "We're going someplace quiet—and lovely." He smiled blissfully. "We'll be so happy there."

He wasn't thinking clearly, even in the moment. "Bernie," I said, "have you and Alenka agreed to this?"

"Uh—not yet, no. But she'll come around to my way of thinking. In time." Bernie Rothman was growing more bent with every moment.

"What about me?"

He let his eyes wander. "When the time comes I'll arrange for someone close by to come and let you out. You'll be pissed off at me by that time—but you'll be free."

I just stared at him. He had no intention of keeping me alive to tell everyone where he and Alenka had gone.

"I was out shopping," Bernie said matter-of-factly. "I picked up sandwiches from Subway—they're very healthy for you, or at least that's what that guy Jared says on television. I guess he's lost over a hundred pounds." He shook his head. "I wish to hell Gary Mishlove would lose that weight—he'll add a decade to his life. Anyway, I have roast beef, ham and cheese, or all-veggie Subways for you, Milan—along with chips. Think about which flavor you want for lunch." He looked earnest again. "You can have one of each if you prefer."

"You're very kind," I said, not meaning it. "Is there any way I can get something down here to read besides the newspaper? I'm going loony tunes sitting here by myself, staring at the walls."

"Hmm. I have some paperbacks upstairs," he said. "I'll rip them into sections and bring you the first one. I can't let you have lots of books at one time—you can stuff them in your sock and use it as a blackjack on me."

He had my shoes somewhere—probably upstairs—and my socks were already very dirty. "How about a small TV set?" I said.

Bernie laughed. "Don't be silly. You could throw a television set at me. Enjoy your breakfast."

He left me alone again, the front page of the morning paper my only company. I checked the weather report first—today was going to be warmer, temps in the high thirties, and no more snow for a while. The international stories were depressing, as usual—five more military heroes, including one from southwest Ohio, had died in Iraq from booby traps or suicide bombs for no reason whatsoever. It was a lousy headline over extremely tragic news, but one that had been recycled and repeated every morning for the past five years. I should have stopped reading the front page back in 2003.

I ate the toast first and then emptied the small milk carton over the big bowl of Cheerios. Bernie had left me no sugar, though, which usually camouflages the cereal taste. Ah well—skipping sugar was good for my weight.

I was screwed. Even lifers in prison, without possibility of parole and locked down in solitary, are at least allowed one hour a day to get out of the cell, walk around, exercise, perhaps inhale some fresh air, and pretend to themselves—just for that hour—they're really the same kind of human being as everyone else.

There was little for me to do but exercise, to fill up *some* of my enforced alone time, however long that might be. I sat on the floor—it was cold as hell on the cement, the kind of chill that creeps into your bones when you're not looking—and performed thirty sit-ups. The last ten were difficult, and I regretted not having done them *before* breakfast. Then I knocked out thirty push-ups. I've never been what one might call an exercise fanatic—I haven't done that religiously since my college football days—and the modest number of repetitions was just about all I could come up with.

The active endorphins didn't make me feel happy or heroic. I was seven inches taller than Bernie Rothman, and I outweighed him by at least sixty pounds. I could easily tear him to pieces once I got my hands on him—but he'd more than evened things out between us, because the Taser never left his hand. If I could get it away from him, I could be free—but he was at least six feet away from me at all times, and would zap me the moment I looked like I was going to attack. The last stun I'd suffered must have been like a grand mal seizure, and I didn't want to go through that again. I had no idea what one or two more seizures like that might do to my heart—or to my nervous system.

I didn't know what it might do to my brain, either. I was terrified by the mere idea of spending the rest of my life in one of those nightmare joints they used to call an "old folks' home," a glorified warehouse where unfeeling people store their aged and disabled parents to stare like vegetables at a blank wall and drip their Cream of Wheat all over their pajamas.

I paced around my cell for what seemed like an hour—if indeed one can pace in such a small space. Pretty soon my head was jammed with useless fantasies about escape. I flopped down on the mattress, feeling the hard cement floor through the padding, and pretended I had a Stroh's, enjoying the next half hour or so feeling sorry for myself.

CHAPTER TWENTY-FIVE

Sitting quietly in my rump-sprung throne, I stared up at the ceiling. It was covered with thick insulation of some kind, colored a dull shade of pink. I knew I'd have little trouble tearing it down if I had something solid to stand on besides the old chair or the spindly table next to it, either of which would probably crash under my weight. If I removed the insulation, there would be no way I could rip out the boards to create a hole big enough for me to fit into and emerge someplace on the main floor. I had nothing to use but my fingers—and I'd make so much noise doing it that my jailer would show up with his Taser at the ready.

I had to hand it to Bernie Rothman—it appeared he had just about everything covered so that it was impossible for me to escape. The prospect was grim. There was a john on the other side of the basement, but no place I could wash, shower, shave—and I was stuck in the clothes I was wearing. I would grow dirtier, shaggier, and more rank with every day that passed—like Edmond Dantès, the once and future Count of Monte Cristo, locked in a rat-infested dungeon in the Château d'If.

Why not? Otherwise, Bernie would either have to shoot me or poison me. Either way, that's messy. It's hard to dispose of a body, too, especially one as big as mine. If the police discovered my decomposing remains before Bernie wanted them to, they might put two and two together. That would reflect badly on Bernie.

But if he waited to finish me off until just before he flew the coop, he'd be living it up in some obscure country with Alenka Tavcar before I attracted any attention—and that would be against Alenka's will, which bothered me almost as much as my anticipated demise. Bernie yearned to live in the warm tropics, so I assumed he'd head for some hidden beach town in Costa Rica—one of the few places American criminals can run to and hide in plain sight where no U.S. extradition can touch them.

I was damned if I'd allow that to happen. But I needed some sort of weapon with which to fight back, or else I was plumb out of options.

I was thinking about turning something handy into an effective counterattack weapon when Bernie Rothman knocked briskly, told me to sit in my chair while he watched through the fisheye peephole, unlocked the door, and came in with a cheery smile, a lunch tray in one hand and the ever-present zapper in the other.

As promised, he'd brought three sandwiches from Subway, along with two small bags of potato chips and a large drink—he told me it was Diet Sprite—poured into a flimsy plastic cup. He was also offering the first half of a paperback book, without a cover and obviously torn away from the second half. He put everything down on the floor, and I could see from across the room that the half-book was the beginning of *The Last Coyote*, one of Michael Connelly's earlier mystery novels. It was a great detective story—but I'd read it before.

"I hope these Subways are okay," Bernie said. "If not, you have the granola bars. I'll bring something else for you to eat tonight. You like pizza? I can send out for Pizza Hut or Papa John's. What toppings do you like on it? I'll bet you're a pepperoni guy."

I gritted my teeth, trying to be as cheery as he was. I can lie with the best of them. "I prefer sausage," I said, "with mushrooms and black olives."

"Good choice." He looked almost sad for a moment. "Listen—I feel bad about all this." He waved a vague hand at the little room. "I hate it for you to be uncomfortable, Milan. So tonight, with the pizza, I'll even bring you down a beer. How does that sound?"

"Peachy," I said.

My tone evidently gave me away, and he took it as crankiness. "Don't be like that. Don't be sarcastic, because it hurts my feelings." He looked at the Taser in his hand, pointed directly at me, and then his eyes met mine. "People get older and one day they look at the past and realize they've lived their whole lives having things taken away from them. Things. So they want to take those things back—and get even with the people who screwed them. That's all I'm doing here." He bent his knees slightly—what the Playboy Clubs used to refer to as the Bunny Dip—and collected the detritus of my breakfast. "Be on my side, Milan."

He waited for me to offer my sympathetic support—but I would have spontaneously combusted before I'd give him the satisfaction. Not hearing what he wanted to hear, he just shrugged. "I'll see you later this evening," he said, quietly letting himself out of the room. The door locks clicking into place sounded like a rolling clap of thunder inside my head. I damn well had to get out of there.

Munching on the subs, I started remembering the reunion, and the regret and chagrin that had followed. Not only was Phil Kohn killed—and that really didn't touch me much because I'd never liked him in the first place—but I was dragooned by Tommy Wiggins, by way of Ben Magruder, into invading the lives of people with whom I'd shared my beginnings and forced to look too closely at their secret truths. Many of them lived in quiet desperation, more likely to bottle up and ignore their pain than to deal with it. That depressed me worse than anything else.

Sonja Kokol had admitted openly that race relations in the twenty-first century hadn't improved much on the east side of Cleveland, and had not wanted any of her African American classmates coming to the reunion. In talking to Shareeka Washington I discovered to my surprise that she didn't like Sonja and her type any better than they liked her. Booker Bratton was living in the discreet hell of a veterans hospital with nothing to which he could look forward besides more of the same. Even if the lack of a reunion invitation didn't bother him—he was far too fragile to attend whether he wanted to or not—it bothered the bejesus out of me.

I know some people are more small-minded than others, but Sonja really surprised me. She'd remained one of my best friends my entire adult life, and now I knew our lifelong friendship would never be the same again. Alex Cerne wasn't going to be my buddy anymore, either, and he probably wouldn't like it when I came in for an oral checkup every six months or so. Now I'd have to find a new dentist.

Ted Lesnevich had moved from unpleasant teenager to drug dealer. Stupan Godic had taken his now-faded memories of a brief high school homosexual affair with Maurice Paich to war, and returned from Vietnam without much of a backbone—a burnt-out, pathetic junkie. Maurice himself had lived as a closeted gay for most of his life and wound up losing his pretty young wife.

There were so many of them now—Gary Mishlove now lived a depressing existence in a drab little apartment, terribly lonely and morbidly obese, a massive heart attack waiting to happen. Matt Baznik, a close friend through much of our adulthood, hardly spoke to me anymore, and his wife Rita Marie had lied, saying that in time he'd come around. I doubted that.

Almost all my other married classmates were having relationship difficulties, including Danielle Webber, who'd given up her virginity to Phil Kohn forty years earlier and was now married to the lawyer who hired me in the first place—good old Ben Magruder.

Tommy Wiggins was our most successful St. Clair High student, but his silly longtime anger simmering against Dr. Phil Kohn had landed him squarely on the hook, and I was employed to unhook him by laying the blame on someone else. Wiggins, talented as hell when it came to writing Broadway comedies turned into popular Hollywood films, turned out to be the biggest jerk at the entire reunion.

Except Bernie Rothman. Let's not forget him, because he was not only the murderer everyone was looking for, but he was as mad as a hatter—and I'm not even sure what a hatter is.

The old boiler outside my door clanked, but it wasn't throwing off much heat—at least not into my closed-up room. I wiggled my shoeless toes around to get the circulation pumping, then got myself out of the chair and picked up my parka, throwing it over my shoulders to help warm me up, at least until Bernie returned with the pizza—hopefully hot. But that would be hours from now.

Could I survive down here much longer, mentally, without anyone to talk to, without anything to do, without anything to read except half a novel I'd read before? The boredom would destroy me before Bernie Rothman ever got around to it. My wheels, I feared, were going to come off the track.

I played idly with the zipper on my parka as I grew more morose. What was the difference if I broke the zipper? I'd never live long enough to wear it again.

Then it hit me.

A way out.

A long shot, I admit, but it was something.

Something.

I hoped I could do what I had to before my sausage pizza came through the door with Bernie, a plastic cup of beer, and his Taser.

I put the parka across my lap and began working on the bottom end of the zipper with my fingers, trying to rip out the strip of fabric on which it was attached. It was difficult—my fingers and thumbs were too big to do much with such a small strip of fabric. I split open one of my fingernails in the process, which was painful. It was harder work than I had imagined.

I raised the hem of my parka to my mouth, nibbling carefully on the fabric, trying to separate the zipper from the parka. Every so often I'd bite down on the metal zipper teeth and gasp with the pain, but I tried to be quiet about it—especially when I bit too hard and broke off the tip of my eyetooth, leaving the nerve exposed.

Damn, that hurt! I spat the partial tooth into my hand and put it in my pocket. I don't remember why. Maybe I was fearful of losing any part of myself, even a tooth. The pain was sharp and never really went away—it sent little jolts of agony from my upper jaw into my head with every heartbeat. It wasn't bleeding too profusely, but I had nowhere to spit the blood. I had to swallow it.

A bit of advice, just in case you might need it someday—never try to bite anything metal if you have filled cavities in your mouth. If you do, and the metal hits your fillings, you'll remember it for the rest of your life.

I heard him coming down the stairs. I could tell from the sound of his steps how small and insignificant he was. He was walking carefully, and I knew he was carrying things, especially his Taser. I was breathing heavily, my chest thumping like Thor's hammer. If Bernie took it into his head to zap me while my heart was going overtime, it might kill me on the spot. I sat back in my chair, looking over my knees, and tried to appear as relaxed as I could. Maybe he'd think he had frightened me into placid innocence.

"Milan, are you sitting down?" he called through the door. "Good boy. I'm coming in now, okay?"

The tumblers clicked, the door swung outward as it always did, and Bernie entered. A pizza box was tucked under his left arm, and he carried another plastic cup. I could tell there was beer in it. Wasn't that sweet of him?

It would have been sweeter had he not held the Taser in his other hand.

"I got you the pizza," he announced. "You can eat an entire medium, can't you?"

I nodded, trying to keep my lips close together so Bernie wouldn't notice my broken tooth. "Thanks, Bernie, this was very nice of you."

"Tomorrow I'll get you some hamburgers. Or cheeseburgers—you probably like them better."

"Bacon cheeseburgers," I said. "And fries."

"Yikes! That's a lot of cholesterol."

"And not from a fast-food joint, okay, Bernie? Get them at some decent restaurant around here."

"Whatever you order, Milan. I want you to be comfortable."

"Uh-huh," I said, wanting to wring his neck. "Listen, I want to go to the john again before I eat dinner. Is that all right?"

"Sure." He put my dinner down on the floor and backed out

the door, standing as far from me as he could while keeping the zapper pointed at my chest. I came out slowly, arms dangling at my sides, and headed across the basement again toward the little enclosure that surrounded his downstairs toilet, with him several steps behind me.

"Don't rush," he said, "but the pizza's nice and hot."

"I'll hurry." I stepped into the little room, shutting the door. I counted to fifteen. "Do you worry about cholesterol, Bernie?"

"I used to," he said through the door. "But the doctors told me my numbers were too high, so I went on a serious diet to get it down to normal. I wound up losing eighteen pounds in the bargain, too."

I counted: Beat. Beat. Beat. "Is that what Phil Kohn told you?"

He sounded appalled. "I'm talking about my doctor in Florida."

"Well, now you look a lot slimmer—for Alenka."

"I know." There was pride in his voice.

"But what if she still won't go away with you?" I took the only weapon I had from my pants pocket. "She might be hard to convince."

"I can convince people," Bernie said. "Once you and I got things straight, look how nice we're being to each other."

It cost me my broken tooth, but I'd ripped both sides of the zipper out of my parka and tied them together into one long strand almost six feet in length. I started rolling it up loosely. "You won't use that stun gun on Alenka, will you, Bernie?"

"God, I hope not." He actually sounded sincere. "That'd be my last resort."

I tucked the folded-up zipper into my right hand, holding one end between my thumb and forefinger. "I want you to be happy too, Bernie—because we're such good friends." I flushed the toilet and opened the door, looking right at him. "Under the circumstances, I'd like to be best man at your wedding. When the rabbi asks for it, I can hand you the ring. How does that sound?"

He looked too shocked to answer. Then he said, "We'll talk about it." He gestured with the Taser. "Let's go eat your pizza before it gets cold."

I moved past him, walking slightly slower. I heard his steps behind me—he was wearing shoes and I wasn't. "What's to talk about?" I said. "Or aren't you planning to let me go at all?" I glanced back at him; he was about six feet away. "Are you going to kill me? You'll keep me alive until the cops arrest Tommy Wiggins and then you'll kill me?"

His face was twisted, more in sorrow. "Milan," he whined, "don't get like that again."

That's when I spun around, relaxed my hand, and swung my arm. The zipper swished through the air like a whip, catching him full in the face.

He howled, stumbling backwards and almost falling, but he held on to the stun gun. The teeth of my zipper had opened small cuts in his cheek, but the pain seemed to give him some inner manic energy, because he was raising the Taser into firing position. I refused to go into another epileptic fit. I flailed at his face with the zipper again. This time it got him across the eyes.

"Oh fuck!" he screamed, shutting his eyes and dropping the Taser. We both dived for it, but Bernie had one hand over his injured eyes, and I was bigger and stronger, and knew all about tackling from my football days.

"Give it to me!" he growled, his voice raspy and hysterical like the voice of the demon inside Linda Blair's head in *The Exorcist*. I wrenched the Taser away from him, pushed him over on his side, and clambered to my feet. I was exhilarated; I wasn't afraid of Bernie and his zapper anymore.

"Calm down, Bernie." I took five steps backward. "It's all over now."

He got to his feet, too, his eyes crazed, white flecks of spittle on his lips. "I'll kill you," he screamed—and launched himself at me, both his feet leaving the ground.

He was as crazed as someone on angel dust, imbued with strength he'd never realized he had. If I punched him hard enough to put him out of commission, I might injure him seriously. But I had to stop him, and under the circumstances, I had no other choice.

The prongs of the Taser hit him in the stomach, almost in the center of his body. I watched him writhe and jerk on the floor for a few seconds, arms and legs flailing and face distorted as his head bounced around on the cold cement. Then I wrapped my zipper around his wrists several times, twisting his arms up and back and tying his hands behind him.

I waited until the spasms stopped. When I tried to talk to him he couldn't—or wouldn't—respond. So I picked him up like a heavy bag of cement and carried him up the stairs, depositing him on his mother's old flowered sofa. Then I called the Third District police precinct and asked for Lieutenant McHargue.

CHAPTER TWENTY-SIX

"Tommy Wiggins was so relieved to get out of this town," I said, "that when he thanked me profusely and told me goodbye, he actually kissed me on the mouth."

We were at a corner table in the dining room of Nighttown. They serve dinner late in there, and Jinny Johnson, Suzanne Davis, and I had dropped in for a nightcap. Jinny was sitting on my left, her foot rubbing softly against my calf as we ate our dinner. On my right was Suzanne Davis. From her angle, she could see what Jinny was doing. It made her smile.

"Tommy said I should call him whenever I get to New York," I continued. "He'll have great seats for whichever of his plays is on Broadway—and if there isn't one, he said he can pull strings to get me into any other show I want to see."

"Wow!" Jinny said, "I'm dating somebody who can actually get free Broadway tickets." She rolled her eyes. "It's Christmas in February."

"He can put his free tickets in his ass," I said.

"Wiggins is a born-and-bred Clevelander," Suzanne said. "I'm surprised he doesn't think of our town as home."

"Most people do," Jinny said. "But the ones who are rich and famous, where people line up around the block waiting for a chance to kiss their lily-white butt, tend to forget where they came from."

"He also forgot it's not the best idea to start fights with somebody in public." Suzanne laughed aloud. "Besides, tossing his drink in Kohn's face in front of everybody he ever knew was a big waste of gin and vermouth."

"The one I feel sorry for," Jinny said, "is Bernie Rothman—that poor, demented soul."

"That poor demented soul killed Phil Kohn," I said.

"Because Kohn let his mother die?"

"Yes—and because he thought Kohn seduced his long-lost love, Alenka. He was hoping like hell Tommy Wiggins would get arrested and put away forever, so he'd be free to kidnap Alenka and drag her away with him to some equatorial hideaway against her will—and if she complained too much he might have gone off the rails again and killed her, too." I cleared my throat. "Let's not even talk about what he was going to do to me when the time came."

Jinny Johnson lovingly covered my hand with her own. Her hand was small and delicate—next to mine it looked like the hand of a doll.

"What are they going to do with Bernie anyway?" Suzanne asked, looking around for a waitress to bring her another drink.

"They've got him in a lockdown mental hospital for testing. If they discover he's a nutcase, they'll store him somewhere until, if, and when he gets cured. If they find him sane, he'll have to stand trial for murder."

"You think he should?" Jinny said. "Be tried for first-degree murder?"

"I'm no psychiatrist."

"If you ask me," Suzanne said, "he's as crazy as a shithouse rat." She caught the eye of the waitress and simply waved a nearly empty drink at her.

"I'm not so sure," I said.

"What would you do if you were the D.A.?"

I was nearly finished eating a medium-well-done prime rib—purists maintain that it should be eaten rare, practically raw, but I just don't like it that way. I pushed what was left of my baked potato all over the plate. "If I were the D.A.," I said, "I'd prosecute."

"Ask for the death penalty?"

It took me too long to reply. "I guess not. First of all, he's unhinged."

"And second of all?" Suzanne smiled, but the question was probing.

"Second of all," I said, "he was a friend of mine."

"Your *friend,*" she said, leaning into the word, "told me when I came looking for you that you had someplace else you had to be." She made quote marks with her fingers. "And all that time you were locked up in his cellar eating granola bars and reading half a book. That's some friend, Milan."

Both women were considering me with pity. I suppose I looked pensive, because I sure as hell felt that way. "I don't have many friends left, Suzanne."

Suzanne said, "You have lots of friends. Me, Ed Stahl, Vuk from the old neighborhood where you still pop in for a drink now and then, and about a dozen others I could mention."

"I'm thinking of just about everyone I went to high school with. Too many of them told me secrets in the last couple of weeks, and now those bridges have finally been burned."

"Build new ones," Suzanne said.

"What?"

"Make new friends—some you'll never have to question or investigate or suspect."

"Like a priest?"

"It wouldn't hurt," she said, laughing. "Just look around, for God's sake—there are lots of nice people in the world. You've been poking in the wrong area for too long. Your fellow grads haven't been your friends for the last forty years."

"Sonja?" I said. "And Alex? They were my friends right up through two weeks ago."

Jinny said coolly, "I never liked Sonja anyway. She's always been a real bitch—you just chose not to notice it."

"Hey!" Suzanne almost barked. "Don't you two start." She turned in her seat to face me. "You're a bad-news bear, Milan. Tie your shoes before you trip over them." She poked me in the shoulder. "Get a life, as they say."

"Milan, look on the bright side," Jinny said. "If you'd shot Bernie Rothman dead instead of just zapping him with a Taser, then you'd have something lousy to feel guilty about. As it is, you should feel *good*—Tommy Wiggins might have been tried and convicted for a murder he didn't commit if not for you."

"Tommy wasn't my friend either," I said.

"Because he's a jerk? Good. Now you stop being one."

I drank the rest of my beer, not enjoying it. "I'll bet he didn't mean it about free tickets anyway."

Our cars were parked behind Nighttown, and after dinner we all went outside into the cold and Suzanne waved goodbye and set off for home. The storms that had plagued me through the Phil Kohn investigation were finally over, so I didn't have to worry about her on the highway. Then Jinny and I drove back to my apartment, just two blocks or so up Cedar Road.

I parked and we strolled to the front door, stopping at the bottom of my outside steps, holding hands and not saying much. Jinny said, "I think it'd be a good idea if I went home alone tonight, don't you?"

"Why?"

She hunched her shoulders beneath her heavy coat, hands buried in her pockets. "You've been in a mood for the last few days. You're bummed out, and my guess is you're just not up for any—festivities tonight. You'll go through the motions because you're so damn polite, and it'll be mediocre for both of us. I thought maybe you needed some time to think—alone time."

"I don't need to think about us," I protested.

"I don't either. That's not on the table. But you need to think about other things, and it's better if you don't try bouncing stuff off me tonight that I don't understand."

"I don't want to put any pressure on you."

"The pressure will be on you, Milan. Just think about it, chew on it, and get through it."

We kissed goodnight, and she walked up the hill a few steps to where she'd left her own car, leaving me standing there on the sidewalk in the cold. It was nowhere near a final goodbye kiss, because we'd passed that point years before. But it did look like a romantic closing shot in a movie—big embrace with music swelling to a crescendo.

We didn't feel that way, though.

I've learned a bit about goodbye kisses over the years. About six weeks later I experienced another one. Victor Gaimari invited me to have dinner at his uncle's apartment, promising the meal would be catered.

It's awkward to show up for dinner without a host gift, but I couldn't bring wine or candy for the old man, since his doctors had forbidden both, and flowers were unseemly for Cleveland's Italian godfather—not while he was still alive to smell them. Finally I found a CD—remastered and sounding brand new—of Enrico Caruso singing tenor arias. I knew the Don always loved Italian opera.

He was in bed when I arrived—a king-sized bed in a very large bedroom. He was wearing white silk pajamas and an elegant-looking paisley robe. In all the years I'd known him, I'd never seen him wearing anything but a tie and jacket.

I kissed his cheek and gave him the CD, and he insisted that Sandra, his nurse, play it immediately. He smiled and closed his eyes while we listened to the first aria—but he held on tight to my hand, his own arm swaying to the music.

Sandra helped feed him whatever mild, innocuous food he was supposed to eat, but Victor and I dined royally, our catered meals set out on TV tables on either side of the bed, along with a superb bottle of Cabernet Sauvignon. I chatted with the Don—it had grown difficult for him to talk much, but he did ask about the Phil Kohn case, and listened intently and with a certain amusement as I explained it to him.

When the evening ended—at about nine o'clock, which was already past Don Giancarlo's bedtime—he motioned me to sit on the edge of his bed.

"I know you a long time, Milan Jacovich," he said.

"Long time, Don Giancarlo."

"You and me, we come from different places—we look at things different."

I smiled down at him. "Not so much anymore."

"I always respected you," he said. "You're honest, no bullshit—that's worth respect."

"I respect you, too. I always have."

He nodded, understanding. "Thanks for coming to see me.

Hanging out with an old Italian man like me, it must be a pain in the ass for you."

"It's an honor," I said, "and a pleasure."

"It honors me to know *you*." His voice was getting weaker—fading away. "You're a good man, Milan," he said—and when I realized he hadn't added my last name as usual, a small chill ran up my spine. "You'll stay good. Because you know what's right."

Victor Gaimari was holding his breath. Now he let it out, and I glanced over and our eyes met.

Giancarlo D'Allessandro put his hand on my cheek. His skin felt fragile, like papyrus. "*Mi famiglia,*" he said to me in little more than a whisper. "*Mi figlio.*" Then gently he pulled my head down so I could kiss him goodnight.

Victor walked me out to the elevator. When the door slid open, he said, "You'll never know how much my uncle appreciates seeing you—and how much I appreciate your being here." Then he hugged me with both arms. We were nearly the same height and the same age—except he was olive-skinned and brown-eyed, and his nearly black hair, which hadn't ever receded, was showing gray, while I was fair-skinned, had blue eyes, and had lost more hair over my lifetime than Victor ever dreamed of.

As I rode the elevator downstairs, I thought hard about what the old man said to me in Italian. I knew what *famiglia* meant in Italian—family—but I wasn't familiar with the other word.

I didn't learn what it meant until two weeks later, after Don Giancarlo D'Allessandro had passed away in his sleep. I attended the funeral mass at Holy Name Cathedral in Little Italy, and there must have been more than a thousand mourners trying to get in. More than half of them were Italian, but I also recognized the mayor, most of the city council, the sheriff, the chief of police, the Special Agent in Charge from the FBI office, and almost every major radio, TV, and newspaper personality in town. They were all there out of sadness and respect.

More than one hundred fifty cars stretched for over a mile, flying their little purple funeral flags as they drove out to the cemetery. After the elegant coffin was lowered into the ground, everyone filed past Victor Gaimari and shook his hand. Most people hugged or kissed him.

When it was my turn for the embrace, Victor put his mouth close to my ear and told me the meaning of the other word Don Giancarlo had whispered to me the last time I had kissed him goodbye.

I understood then what a goodbye kiss really meant.

That was several weeks after my misadventure in Bernie's basement and my awkward dinner with Suzanne Davis and Jinny. The morning after that dinner, Jinny and I talked on the phone and assured each other that everything was all right. We were both relieved—but I still had much to think about in terms of old friends disappearing from my life and new ones out there waiting to be made.

In the meantime, I had an appointment with Lieutenant McHargue later that day. She'd asked me to write up a report—as full and detailed as possible—about my investigation. I hate writing reports, although it's usually the last requirement of any particular job.

McHargue looked tired. Maybe she always looked tired, but this was the first time I'd noticed. As head of the homicide squad, she didn't put in her forty hours a week and then go home and forget it—she was in the office early every morning, dealing with something new and terrible. Cleveland is nowhere near the murder capital of America, but it's not Happy Valley, either.

"Thanks," she said cryptically when I put the folder on her desk.

"It's all in there."

"If it's not," she said, "I'll be on the phone to you again."

"I'm pretty close. I don't think I missed much."

She took a sip of her tea and looked at me thoughtfully. "You usually don't." She shook her head. "God damn it," she said mildly.

"What?"

She did something with her mouth the way Cary Grant used to—not quite a scowl, even though a dimple appeared in her cheek. "Jacovich, why didn't you stay on the force?"

"Too dangerous."

"You've been shot, beaten up, almost killed several times, and now you can add being a Tasered kidnap victim. If you had a badge, you'd have a partner, too—and that wouldn't have happened to you."

"Police officers never go out alone?"

"Not if I can help it," she said.

I weighed my next words before speaking. "I would have been in Marko Meglich's way on the force. He was a political guy, always on the lookout to get himself a better perch. That's not me—and I didn't want to block his rise to celebrity because he was my best friend."

"From the time I became a Cleveland police officer, I idolized Mark," she said simply. "For all his bullshit—and he was a master at it, by the way—he was still the best cop I ever knew." Coming from the all-business McHargue, this was veering into the area of personal conversation.

"He was," I said. "I guess I wanted independence—to do whatever I needed to without the rules of this department hindering me. And I didn't want Marko's celebrity star shine spilling over onto me because I was standing too close to him."

"Don't give me that crap," McHargue said. "Your name and face are in the paper all the time."

"That can't be helped."

"Because you're good buddies with Ed Stahl, and some other people at the *Plain Dealer*." She shook her head, looking around at the small, meanly furnished office that was the throne room of her kingdom—ruling a world in which she wasn't likely to endear herself to anyone. "I suppose that can't be helped either. You make your friends where you can."

"I wonder why I've never made friends with you, Lieutenant," I said. "We've known each other going on ten years, now, and never a friendly word between us. Why is that?"

She didn't scowl the way she usually did, but thought it over a while. "I've devoted my life to this department—and put my ass on the line to do it—while you walked away because you didn't like the rules. Secondly, guys your age don't usually warm up to women in powerful roles. So that's another reason."

I nodded. "Okay, I guess—if that's the complete truth."

She sat up straighter in her chair, about to say something difficult. "Then there's the race thing."

"Come on, Lieutenant," I said. "I played football and I soldiered with a lot of men, and I never even noticed what color they were. I still don't notice."

"Maybe—but you were born too early to learn to play nicely with others."

"Marko Meglich was my age and went to my school, too."

"Tell me about it. Marko never gave me a second look, never gave me a smile or a pat on the back or an 'attaboy.' No bad words were said, but we both understood it, and we kept a respectful distance."

"That's hard to hear. Marko never said anything the slightest bit bigoted to me."

"You weren't on his shit list," she said.

"Then I apologize. It makes me feel lousy—all these years after he died."

"You don't have to apologize. You're you—and you're good at your job. I've seen that whenever we cross paths."

"And butt heads," I said.

"Mine's harder than yours."

"You're right."

"You get in our way—but I can tell you're a pretty decent person."

"Think so?"

She leveled a red-painted fingernail at me. "Don't let it go to your head."

"If it makes any difference, I think you're a decent person, too."

"Gee whillikers!" she said with more than a hint of sarcasm. "Now do we hold hands and sing 'Kumbaya' together?"

"I don't sing," I said. I swallowed hard, feeling some rogue butterfly doing flip-flops inside my stomach. I'd lost so many friends in the past few weeks, the thought of making a new one scared me silly. "But maybe you'd like to have lunch some day—when you're not too busy."

Her scowl threatened to return. "Are you asking me on a fucking date?"

"No," I said. "I already have a significant other."

"So do I—a husband."

I blinked. I had no idea she was married. Suddenly I felt desperate—desperate to make Florence McHargue my friend. "Do you suppose," I said, "either of them would mind if we had lunch together? This is your precinct, so you can pick the place."

"I can't imagine why I'd want to."

"So we could—get to know one another. So maybe we can become friends."

She practically did a comic double take. "You mean, you and me?"

"Friends, colleagues on the same side—whatever name you call it."

She stared at me for a long moment. Then one side of her mouth was lifted into a reluctant, crooked grin, and her eyes crinkled fetchingly at their corners.

"Friends, huh? You want us to have lunch together and get to be friends?" She wagged her head back and forth, unbelieving and obviously amused. "Well, I'll be a son of a bitch," she said.

It was the first time I had ever seen her smile.

ACKNOWLEDGMENTS

My appreciation to Holly Albin—my friend, partner, collaborator, and lover. How did I ever write anything before you came along?

My thanks, as always, to Dr. Milan Yakovich and Diana Yakovich Montagino.

And a shout out to all my former classmates from Nicholas J. Senn High School in Chicago. I've thought about them for forty years before attempting to recapture them in this book. Remember our own Christmas-season Holly Hop—and don't be mad at me.